AFFAIR

Laura Caldwell

THE ROME
AFFAIR

ISBN 0-7783-2309-9

THE ROME AFFAIR

www.MIRABooks.com

Printed in U.S.A.

ACKNOWLEDGMENTS

Thank you to my editor, Margaret O'Neill Marbury,
my agent, Maureen Walters, and the crew at MIRA—
Donna Hayes, Dianne Moggy, Loriana Sacilotto,
Katherine Orr, Craig Swinwood, Sarah Rundle, Don Lucey,
Steph Campbell, Margie Miller, Rebecca Soukis,
Carolyn Flear, Kathy Lodge, Dave Carley, Gordy Giohl,
Erica Mohr and Andi Richman.

Thanks to everyone who read the book—
Christi Caldwell, Katie Caldwell Kuhn, Kelly Harden,
Clare Toohey, Mary Jennings Dean, Pam Carroll,
Karen Uhlman, Joan Posch, Dustin O'Regan, Beth Kaveny,
Jane Jacobi Mawicke, Ted McNabola and Kris Verdeck.

Thanks also to those who helped me with my tireless
questions about murder prosecutions, including
Detective Kevin Armbruster, criminal defense
attorney Catharine O'Daniel, former prosecutor
James Lydon and former police officer Giovanna Long.

Most of all, thank you, thank you, thank you to
Jason Billups.

Prologue

She sees lights. Lights in the sky—stars, she corrects herself—and lights from beautiful apartments with accomplished people inside. She is close to those people right now, very close, but she wonders if any of them will notice her dying.

She has never been the type to imagine her own death. In fact, she has felt immune to it, as if death was something that happened to other people. She always assumed there was time.

But there is precious little time left. It has been only an instant since it started, and she knows there are maybe one or two such moments left.

And strangely, there is relief.

1

I understand now that innocence is relative. I know that the night before I left for Rome, I felt jaded. After all we'd been through, I thought I'd aged somehow and lost my sparkle. I only wish I'd grasped then that the fall from innocence was a very long one.

"Why do you want to go to Italy with Kit?"

Nick sat on the bed and watched through the bathroom doorway as I went about my nighttime ministrations—cleanser, toner, moisturizer, eye cream. Why I used all this crap, I wasn't sure.

"I have a pitch at that architectural firm, and you can't go because of work," I answered. I leaned toward the mirror and dabbed cream around my left eye.

"You've hardly seen Kit in years," Nick said.

"You don't have to see a friend to be a friend."

Although Kit had been a bridesmaid in our wedding four years ago, she'd moved to California shortly after to try her hand at acting. We didn't talk every week, or even every month, but we never lost the bond best girlfriends have. After a few years of escalating credit-card debt and many failed auditions, Kit was back in Chicago, and I was more grateful than ever to have her near. At thirty-five, most of my friends were moms—what I thought I'd be, too—and they were no longer available for nights at wine bars, let alone trips to Rome.

"Why are you so worked up about this?" I asked Nick.

"I'm not, Rachel. I'm just curious."

But my husband, Dr. Nick Blakely, was worked up. I could tell from the way he ran his fingers through his curly, close-clipped hair and rubbed at the spot between his eyes. He was also acting overly casual. His tie was loosened after a long day seeing patients, and he leaned back with one hand on the creamy ivory sheets of our bed, but there was a stiffness to the way he held himself.

"You have to be careful in Italy," he continued. "Especially with the guys."

"Is that right?" This came out sounding a bit like a taunt, and I let it hang in the air.

How strange that after all the therapy, after all the crying and the repiecing of our relationship, it was Nick who worried about me, as if retribution lay in wait around a corner somewhere.

"Nick, I've traveled to Rome before. I *lived* in Italy."

"You were twelve when you lived there with your family, and it was for six months. And since then you've always traveled with me. Now it's just you and Kit. I mean, I'm glad you're going with someone, but you still have to be careful," Nick said. "There are all sorts of guys who love to prey on American women."

"I am *quite* sure I can handle the Italian men," I said.

I took a second's pleasure in the stricken look that flitted across his face, but even now, I hated to see him hurt.

"Nick," I said, moving to the bed and sitting on his lap. "You don't have to worry about me."

On Saturday, Nick dropped Kit and me at O'Hare airport. The arrival gates were mobbed with cars and cabs, all with doors and trunks ajar. The May air was balmy, with sudden gusts of wind that sent stray papers floating into the air.

"Golden Girl," Nick murmured, hugging me fiercely.

That nickname of mine had started with Kit. "Golden Child," she used to call me when we were growing up. It was mostly based on my last name— Goldin—but it was also because I was an only child of relatively affluent parents, and I had, quite simply, enjoyed a very nice time of it. I knew that was true, even when I was young.

When I met Nick at an art-gallery party in Chicago's Bucktown neighborhood, he immediately began calling me Golden Girl. Again there was my name, and Nick said he saw a gold light in my pale green eyes, too.

When we got married, despite changing my name to Blakely, I felt so lucky and so special I thought I would be the Golden Wife. I thought I'd have the Golden Life.

So far, it hadn't turned out exactly like that.

I hugged Nick back, thinking that it was usually he who went away on business trips, leaving me at home, saying little prayers that the paper he had to present would go smoothly, that he was sleeping okay and not drinking too much or eating too poorly. But I was ready for some girls' time with Kit. Now it was *his* turn.

Nick finally let me go but held one of my hands in his. He looked at Kit. "Have a nice time," he said formally.

Nearly everyone talked to Kit that way since she'd returned from L.A. No one knew what to do with her, I suppose. She hadn't quite found a career, she didn't have a boyfriend or husband. She'd been a struggling actress in L.A., a hard-luck existence most of us in Chicago had little in common with. And yet Kit also had a sparkly kind of mystery about her. Even now, she wore rose-colored mirrored sunglasses and a taupe chiffon scarf around her neck, her rusty red hair tousled artfully. If she took off the glasses, you could see that her blue eyes were almost purple, depending on what she was wearing, and those eyes had a sly, knowing way about them. She looked like an intriguing woman, a Hollywood starlet on the lam. As one of her closest friends, though, I knew she was hurting from her failures out West.

"Thanks, Nick." She smiled at him.

I breathed a sigh of gratitude for that grin. Those who knew about our marital problems were furious at Nick. They either refused to talk to him, or they made snide remarks when they did. I knew he was getting sick of being the whipping boy, and I didn't like it, either. Although I could taunt him and stalk away all I wanted, I didn't want anyone else treating him badly.

"Meet you at the ticket counter?" I said to Kit.

She readjusted the scarf around her neck. "Sure thing."

I turned to him when she'd left. "What are you going to do while I'm gone?"

"Work. Miss you like crazy."

I smiled. "Get some sleep, huh?"

Nick and I spent our evenings together again, but after I'd gone to bed, he would work late into the night on a new paper, hoping it would bring him a partnership. He'd gone into plastic surgery not for the glamour surgeries and the money they brought, but for the real treatments that could help people. But now that he was at the best plastic surgery office in the city, he had to perform those glam surgeries, and he had to publish to get promoted to partner.

"I doubt I'll get much sleep," Nick said. "I've got to take a couple of board members to dinner, too."

"When do they decide?"

He rolled his eyes. "A month or so."

Despite his feigned nonchalance, Nick was anxious about making it on The Chicago General Auxiliary Board—what everyone in the city called *The* board. It was a group of handpicked young and influential people who threw parties, ostensibly to raise funds for Chicago General Hospital, where Nick was on staff, but really to identify themselves as the crème de la crème of Chicago society. Nick wanted to get on the board not only to improve his chances of becoming partner, but also because he'd always been a member of the in-crowd growing up in Philadelphia. His father was a longstanding politician, and although the Blakelys had never been wealthy, they were exceptionally well connected and admired. They were invited to every soiree and function in town. When Nick took off for med school, and eventually his residency in Chicago, he said he was leaving Philly so that he wouldn't ride his family's coattails. But the limelight was a place where Nick was accustomed to being. He missed it. And although I could be just as happy in our basement painting my black-and-white photos as I could be at a grand charity ball, I supported Nick. I'd known our social life would be a busy one.

Nick kissed me on the forehead. "Good luck with your sales pitch, hon."

I closed my eyes, leaned into him and inhaled the warm scent he always carried, as if he'd just come in from the sun. "Thanks. And really, Nick, make sure you sleep enough."

"You know I only sleep with you."

We both froze for a second. It was the kind of remark that was supposed to be light, but was now only a reference to what *used* to be true.

"Seriously," Nick said, rushing in to fill the silence, to fix it. "I meant I'll be up all night because I won't know what to do without you."

I took a step back and looked away. To my right, a dad struggled to extract a stroller from the trunk of his car. *That* was the kind of problem I thought Nick and I would be having at this point—how to fit the stroller in the car, where to put the crib, what color to paint the nursery.

"Rachel," Nick said. "I'm sorry."

I knew he was sick of apologizing, and the truth was, I was getting sick of hearing it.

"C'mere," he said, pulling me to him again.

He kissed me, and despite myself, I responded. Before, we had been like everyone else. Now, we were passionate people, fighting for our relationship, and Nick was a man who couldn't get enough of me.

"Be careful, okay?" he said, holding my face in his hands.

"Nick, I'm not gone that long."

"Tell me you'll be careful."

"Of course I will be. I'll strap my purse around me tight. I'll watch out for gypsies."

He studied my face. "I'll miss you," he whispered.

"I love you," I said in response, because that was true, and it might not have been true to say I'd miss him.

2

It's been said that Rome lacks the languid, friendly allure of other Italian cities, but the Roman mornings, at least to me, are undeniably charming. The colors stun the mind—the thousand shades of gold that are impossible to capture on film or in memory. Even when I've taken black-and-white photos of the city and painted on them, I can't adequately capture a Roman morning—the way the sun gives a misty yellow glow to every corner of the city.

It was that pale yellow blush that struck me as we stepped out of our cab, just around the corner from the Piazza di Spagna.

"Wow," Kit murmured for at least the tenth time since we'd landed. She embraced me as the cabbie lugged our bags from the trunk. "You are amazing for bringing me here."

I had used most of my air miles to upgrade us

both, and I had paid a few hundred dollars of Kit's ticket, as well. Since moving back from L.A., Kit was short on cash. Not that this was anything new. I'd known Kit since first grade, and ever since her father died a few years after that, money had been tight. I used to pay her way into the movies and buy her bracelets at Claire's Boutique so she could be like the rest of the girls. Money was even scarcer now. Kit told people she worked "in the marketing department of the Goodman Theatre," which was true and sounded respectable enough, but the plainer truth was she was the department secretary. She collated, she stapled, she answered phones. She made very little money. What she had usually went toward the bills surrounding her mom's cancer treatment.

"I'm glad to do it," I told Kit, squeezing her hand. I was filled with a giddy feeling of promise, of a friendship renewed and, with the exception of my sales pitch tomorrow, a few days away from reality.

Kit and I checked into Il Palazzetto, a restored palazzo near the Spagna subway station. My mother had been to Rome the previous summer with her new husband, a real-estate mogul much older than she, and they'd stayed for two months at Il Palazzetto. She insisted Kit and I would be crazy to book anyplace else. When we stepped into the small foyer, I could see why.

The floor was a mosaic of colored stone. Sunlight flooded down the spiral marble staircase with its twisted, wrought-iron railings. On the second floor, our room had soaring ceilings, Roman columns and walls draped with gauzy, flowing fabric.

I opened the French window of our room, just in time to catch the sight of the pristine, white sun hitting the Spanish Steps.

I smiled over my shoulder at Kit.

"This is going to be good," she said. Her voice told me she was excited in a way she hadn't been in a long time. "This is going to be really good."

I turned back toward the Roman morning and nodded.

Nearly everyone loves Italy. An adult who says, "Oh, I adore Italy" is like a child who says "I love Disneyland." *Of course you do*.

The funny thing is that Italophiles believe it is they who have discovered Italy. They feel this love of all things Italian—the food, the ocher sunsets, the wine, the slow-moving life—which begins when they set foot on the dusty streets of Rome and ends when they head home. Every Italophile senses it is he who loves Italy more than the next, who understands her more deeply than the rest.

Kit and I were no exception. We had only three days to spend in Rome, so instead of sleeping the day away, we pushed past our jet lag and out into the city for a walk and some coffee.

We found a neighborhood bar in Piazza Navona, a long, U-shaped square with a tall obelisk and a Bernini sculpture and fountain in the middle. The piazza used to host chariot races, but now held cafés and strolling pedestrians.

"God, I needed this," Kit said as we took our seat in front of the bar, our cappuccinos and a basket of rolls in front of us. She flipped back the napkin and offered the basket to me. I took a crescent roll, and she did the same.

"Me, too," I said. "How's your mom?"

She shrugged, her taupe chiffon scarf lifting around her face. "She's doing everything she's supposed to, but she knows the chemo is killing her at the same time it's supposed to be curing her."

"That's horrible." I thought how lucky I was to have two healthy parents. Healthy, divorced, never-speak-to-each-other parents, but who could knock it? "I'm sorry," I said. Ineffective words.

"We'll be all right." Kit shook her hair away from her face. That wavy russet hair was one of the things that drew people to Kit. Not just men, who were staring at her even now as they passed us on their way to work, but the women, too. Her hair was glamorous, fiery—two traits most women wanted a little more of.

"God, look at her, will you?" Kit nodded toward a gaunt, striking Italian woman who was crossing the piazza. She wore a short black skirt and a pink shawl. Her black hair was swept up in a knot atop her head, and she clicked past us smartly in four-inch herringbone stilettos, despite the treacherous cobblestones.

"What do you think?" Kit said. "She's in advertising, right? Or maybe fashion?"

"She could be a secretary. Even the civil servants here are dressed to kill."

"Right, but her husband has money. She's definitely married."

We both peered at the woman's left hand, and sure enough, there was a diamond ring that looked large even from a distance. "You got it," I said.

This was a game Kit liked to play—guessing at people's lives, then inserting herself mentally into those lives as far as she could. It was what had led her to acting.

Kit turned back to me. "Speaking of being married," she said, "how's Nick?"

"Fine. I think."

"You think?" Kit's eyes narrowed in concern.

After Nick's affair last year, which took place over the span of a weeklong medical seminar in Napa, he had confessed months later. It was a Tuesday night, and I was slicing a tomato for salad. The time was 8:07 p.m. I remember this, because I held the knife in one hand and the large tomato in the other. The tomato's juice was seeping like blood, and it suddenly seemed obscene, morbid. I checked the microwave clock, wondering if I had a few minutes before Nick came home to make something else, something more benign like spinach salad.

I hadn't heard the door open, but I heard the creak of a floorboard in our house on Bloomingdale Avenue. Nick stepped into our kitchen and began crying so hard, his immaculate doctor's hands cradling his face, that I thought someone had died. He had no idea why he'd done it, he said. He could only say that he wanted—*needed*—something new. He had felt it like a constant, terrible itch. But now the only thing new was how much he hated himself. I stood silently through his confession. When I found my voice, I begged him to tell me it was only one night. I might be able to deal with only one night. Nick shook his head and cried some more.

I made him move out for three months. I walked around stripped bare, so that the most mundane things inspired tears. During that time, I realized that infidelity is about much more than the physicality of the act. Of course, the physical can't be ignored. The raw images of Nick with some other woman—their mouths clinging, bodies locked—hounded me, even made me do the clichéd run to the toilet with my hand over my mouth. Despite my mental gymnastics to avoid such thoughts, I always imagined the woman as gorgeous, maybe with gleaming, honey-colored hair and a strong, tanned body. This helped, strangely, because it gave some reason to what Nick had done. He had been lured in by someone stunning—someone tall and blond and entirely different from me, with my small frame and dark hair.

She wasn't anything special, Nick told me at least a hundred times, just someone he met at a Napa restaurant. He knew it was his fault, not hers, but he still hated her now that it was done. He hated Napa. He hated the restaurant where he'd met her.

It was at this point in these discussions I always held up my hand. "Stop. Please," I'd say. Although

I had an image of her in my mind, I didn't really want to know about this woman. I didn't want to hear about the restaurant where she waitressed or maybe that she was supporting a child or that her sister had died the previous year. I didn't want anything to overly personalize her.

I stayed with him because, unlike Nick, I did not want something new. I wanted him, and us, and a family, and everything I'd invested in. Before he'd told me, we'd been ready to get pregnant. But instead of a baby, Nick's infidelity got us a therapist, Robert Conan, whom we'd seen twice a week until recently.

Conan told me that the glorification of this woman as an Amazonian goddess was "certainly not healthy," but it was the only way I could cope. I chose to view the woman as an otherworldly, goddess-type creature who'd floated into Nick's path one day, led him astray for five nights, and then left our world, hopefully for the very hot hallways of hell.

Nick and I were officially back together, but I still had a hard time.

"One minute it's like we're back to normal," I told Kit, "then the next he'll say something or I'll say something and we'll remember."

"And then?"

I took a bite of croissant. It was flaky and buttery but suddenly hard to swallow. "And then it's awful."

Sometimes I was in love with Nick, proud of how we'd weathered the storm that had swept through our lives. Sometimes—when I picked up a wine from Napa Valley or saw a TV show about infidelity—my insecurity raged. Sometimes I hated him.

"God, now I'm sorry," Kit said. "What a sad pair we are." She put her cup down and threw an arm around my shoulders, hugging me across the table.

I hugged her back. Throughout high school, college and my early years in Chicago, my life had been refracted through the lens of my girlfriends' eyes, particularly Kit's. When I got married and she'd moved, I thought I didn't need the insights or affirmations as often. But now, to be in the company of a friend gave me an optimistic charge. A good bout of girlfriend bonding was exactly what I needed.

Over Kit's shoulder, I saw the sun moving across the piazza and beginning to warm the gray stone man in the center of the sculpture. Water splashed from the fountain, cleansing him.

Sitting back, I raised my cup. "Let's have a toast. To Italy, and to a wonderful few days of escape."

"To fabulous fucking friends!" Kit said. She let out a little holler, which drew looks from the people in the bar, and we touched our cups together.

Kit and I spent a languid first day, moving from one overpriced store on the Corso to the next, laughingly enduring the saleswomen who glanced pityingly at our American fashions and wondered out loud (they didn't know I understood) whether we could afford the skirts we were looking at.

We were giddy and goofy from lack of sleep, and this was Italy. Nothing bad could touch us. We had dinner on the Via Veneto, doted on by the rotund proprietress who was different in every way from the saleswomen we'd encountered.

"Eat! Eat!" she kept saying. "You are nothing but bones."

Food kept appearing at our table like wrapped presents under the tree—saffron risotto with gold leaves, pink salmon drizzled green with dill sauce. So, too, the men appeared. "Married," I kept murmuring, holding aloft my left hand, reveling in the attention but somehow proud again of my marital status, while Kit grinned and flirted and sent them away, even as they sent us sparkling decanters of chianti. We tripped home arm in arm, laughing with memories already made.

But the next morning I was walloped by a bout of jet lag that made the previous day's tiredness seem like child's play. I couldn't believe I had to attend a meeting, much less make a lengthy pitch on complicated architectural software.

I showered, but it failed to wake me up. I left Kit in her sumptuous bed, with plans to see her after my meeting. I headed for a neighborhood bar, where I downed two espressos, neither of which had any effect other than to make me blink more often and feel more dazed.

A twenty-minute cab ride took me over the muddy Tiber River and through Trastevere, onto a tiny, winding, cobblestone street with stone palazzi on either side. The driver stopped and pointed at an iron gate with the number thirteen etched in the stucco. When I got out of the car, I saw a small brass plaque announcing Rolan & Cavalli, the largest architectural firm in Italy. A twinge of anticipation fluttered in my belly.

I had fallen into a sales career five years out of college, after I decided I had to get the hell out of advertising, an industry I'd misguidedly battled my way into. I thought I'd use sales as a sort of break, that I'd probably return to advertising (for no one truly left, one of my bosses had once said) and find a job at a better agency, or at least one that didn't want me to specialize in the tedium that was account management. But I loved sales—the rush, the wondering, the cliff-like highs and even the lows.

The lows had been few until recently, when the economy slowed and construction slowed along with it, leaving many architects wondering if they really needed our pricey new software to help them design buildings. The U.S. offices of Rolan & Cavalli had finally come around and begun using the software after almost a year of my working on them. Now, I was here to convince the Roman architects that their Italian office needed the software as much as their American counterparts. Laurence Connelly, my boss in Chicago, was counting on me to land this account. "You'll bowl over those Italians, Blakely," he'd said in a rare attempt at encouragement. "Go get 'em."

The gate buzzed, and I walked into a large courtyard with a white cherub fountain in the middle, a few cars and scooters parked to one side. On the opposite side of the courtyard, double doors made from heavy pine swung open and a portly man in his early fifties stepped outside, extending his hand.

"You are Rachel Blakely?" he said in formal, heavily accented English.

"Yes, hello." I quickly crossed the courtyard and shook his hand.

"I am Bruno Cavalli. *Benvenuto*. Welcome to Roma."

"Thank you very much. It's a pleasure." I pumped his hand once more, surprised that the owner himself had greeted me.

I felt the exhilaration of an impending pitch, a potential sale. Sometimes being in sales was painful—particularly when you were faking your way through a cold call or getting shot down from a company you'd been working with for five years—but the anticipation and bursts of elation from my job had gotten me through Nick's revelation about his affair. It had given me back some of the confidence he'd stolen. And here in Rome was potential. Here, I might close again.

Bruno showed me through the front doors and through a sitting room decorated in shades of sienna and white. We made small talk as we walked, passing offices and drawing tables. By the time we reached the conference room, a round space with a large, mahogany table in the center, I was feeling charged up and ready to sell Bruno and his team—four men and two women—on the excellence of our software.

Bruno introduced me to the team, and I thanked him in Italian, then switched to English. "Thank you all for having me and for your time today."

One of the team members, a paunchy man in an olive green suit, turned his head and leaned an ear toward me. A few others nodded, but as I moved from a few introductory remarks into my pitch, I saw perplexed glances. I slowed my words, but I quickly realized that although Bruno had near-perfect English, his staff did not. Some knew a few words, but when it came to talking architecture, they were only used to Italian. As the confused looks around the table increased, my adrenaline faded.

Finally I halted my words. "*Capite?*" I said. Do you understand?

The man in the olive suit shook his head. A woman held up her hand and rocked it from side to side. "*Cosi, cosi.*"

I glanced at Bruno, who shrugged. "*Italiano?*" he said.

I struggled not to rub a distressed hand over my

tired face. While it was true that I'd lived here for six months as a kid and studied Italian in college, and while it was also true that I could order wine with the best of them and eavesdrop on snotty saleswomen, I didn't think I could give an entire pitch in Italian, certainly not to describe complex architectural concepts. My company, Randall Design, had sent me, knowing I was the only one in our sales team with any Italian skills, but I'd been given the impression that I would mostly rely on English, stepping in here and there with a few Italian phrases.

Still, I would give it my best shot. I launched into my pitch in my schoolgirl Italian. The first few sentences came out okay. Then I started to stumble. I had to halt frequently to think of the proper words, the proper tenses, how to form a sentence. Pitying glances came from around the table.

I shuffled along until I heard *"Scusi!"* in a high, cultured voice.

The speaker was a woman with white hair pulled back in a low knot. She had raised a delicate hand. A braided gold bracelet adorned her slender wrist.

"Si?" I said eagerly. Questions during a pitch gave me motivation; they revealed that the client might be interested.

But the white-haired woman rattled off a lengthy

question at such a rapid speed I only picked up every fifth word or so.

I took a breath and tried to respond to what I thought she might be asking—a question about our 3D capability. I mangled a few words; I forgot others. A man to my right wore a look of complete confusion and leaned closer, as if I onlyneeded to talk more loudly. The woman with the white hair shook her head dismissively.

Bruno offered to translate, and the question-and-answer session, which should have taken ten minutes, took about forty. My pitch limped.

After two hours, Bruno stood from his chair. "*Grazie,* Rachel," he said, looking at his watch. "If we might take a break."

I nearly kissed him with gratitude.

But then he continued, "Two of our members will take you for a meal. We will finish this afternoon." He spoke in Italian to the team members, all of whom nodded.

"Oh…" I said. I thought of Kit at the hotel, waiting for me. I'd promised we'd have the afternoon together, that I'd show her some of my favorite Rome sites, aside from the Gucci store. I thought of how badly I wanted a shower and a glass of wine and a nice long chat with my girlfriend.

But Bruno was giving me another chance, one I needed and appreciated.

"Thank you so much. That would be lovely," I said. "Could I please use your phone?"

I called Kit from Bruno's office and apologized. She was silent for a moment. "It's okay, Rachel," she said then. "I'll just go wander. Good luck."

"Thanks. I'll need it."

My hatchet job of the language continued its shamble at the *ristorante*, where they took me to lunch. There was no reprieve, only more questions about the software—questions that took me decades to decipher and centuries to answer. This sorry situation continued during my afternoon presentation of the product itself. I noticed every sigh from the team members who couldn't understand me. I saw them glancing at their watches.

When the meeting ended—*finally*—I buttoned my jacket and shook Bruno's hand. They'd consider the software and let me know, he said. Yet when I met his eyes, I could see the decision was already made, and the answer was no.

I walked through the office, tapped of all strength, mental, physical or otherwise. How wonderful it had sounded back at the office—

oh, I'm going to Rome for a meeting! But the reality had been as fun as the middle seat on an overnight flight.

3

Slumped in the back of the cab, I began to think of how I'd tell my boss, Laurence, the news. He wouldn't be pleased.

I paid the cabdriver and tried to cheer myself up by thinking about a night out with Kit. Professional disaster or no, there were bottles of wine around the city, just waiting for us to open them.

But when I got back to the room, there was a note.

Rach,
Met the most amazing guy! He works for the French embassy. He's taking me to some place called Ketumbar. I figured you'd be exhausted and would want to sleep. See you later tonight. (Maybe!)
Kit
P.S. I hope your pitch went great. I'm sure it did. Thanks again for bringing me to Rome. I'm in love with this city!

I tried not to be disappointed. I'd left her alone all day, after all, and she was right, I was exhausted.

I took off my clothes and slipped on the heavy, silk hotel robe. Then I made the dreaded phone call to Laurence and told him about the pitch. "The owner told me before I left that his team spoke English, but they couldn't understand the whole pitch."

"I thought you spoke Italian."

"Not well enough to get through a whole pitch."

Silence on the other end.

"This is not good timing, Blakely," he said, his voice as prim and severe as a schoolmarm's. "We lost the Ricewell account today."

"What?" Ricewell was a huge architectural firm, and one of our biggest clients. Their purchases of our software, and its yearly updates, accounted for a large portion of our profits. "What happened?"

"I can't go into it now. Randall wants to talk to me." Terry Randall was the company's not-so-pleasant owner. He made Laurence seem like an easygoing beach bum. "You're sure Cavalli isn't going to buy?" Laurence asked.

The afternoon flashed before me—the disdainful glances from the white-haired woman, sympathetic ones from Bruno. "I'm pretty sure."

"Jesus, Blakely, I didn't need this. I'll see you

when you get back. And have a great time over there." His voice was thick with sarcasm. "I'm glad somebody's getting a vacation." He hung up.

I lay back on the bed and dialed Nick's work number. It was late morning in Chicago, and it was his day to see patients at the office, but I wanted to hear his voice.

Tina, the receptionist, answered. "Hi, Rachel!" she said cheerily. "How's Rome?"

I turned my head on the pillow and looked around the room. The windows were open, the breeze making the curtains sway and billow. "Beautiful. Thanks for asking. Hey, is Nick busy?"

"He's not in today."

"What do you mean?"

"He took today off. It's super warm here, like almost eighty degrees. He said something about golf."

"Oh, all right."

But Nick didn't golf anymore, at least not unless he had to. He had played on his high school team in Philadelphia, an intense experience that diminished his love for the game, and so now he played with the other doctors at his office only when he felt forced to do so for appearance' sake.

"Did anyone else take the day off?" I asked hopefully. "Like Dr. Adler or Dr. Simons?"

"Nope," Tina said, cheerful as ever.

I got off the phone and dialed our home number, trying to hold my flaring suspicions at bay. Maybe he was just using golf as an excuse, and he was home working on his paper. Maybe he was coming down with a cold. My own voice on the machine answered after four rings, politely asking callers to leave their name and number. I hung up and dialed Nick's cell phone. It went right to voice mail, as if turned off by someone who very much did not want to be reached.

Something as heavy as lead crept into my chest.

I got up from the bed and went to the French windows. I pushed them farther open, hoping the sight of the Spanish Steps would lift my spirits, but the orange glow of the sun setting somewhere over the city only made me melancholy for company, for my husband, or at least the husband I used to have. The white marble steps seemed covered with couples taking in the coming twilight. As far as my eye could see, people were holding hands, speaking softly into each other's ears.

Where was he? Why take off work on a Monday, only two days after I'd left? Why hadn't he mentioned it?

I thought about all the talks we'd had after his affair. *Why, why, why?* I'd asked over and over. *Why did you do it?* Nick shook his head, his eyes anguished and disbelieving, as if he couldn't quite accept what he'd done. He said it was a product of his boredom, his worries about whether he'd make partner at the office, whether he'd make it onto the board. He needed something new and exciting to distract him, and when she walked into his life in Napa, he felt she would bring him that excitement, if only momentarily. He swore there was nothing wrong with our relationship. He wasn't bored with *me,* he kept saying. He wasn't harboring any kind of resentment toward me.

In some ways, I was relieved by his answers, or lack of them. Because I didn't want anything to be inherently wrong with us. I wanted Napa to be a colossal, bumbling, impulsive mistake.

But I'd never stopped to think that maybe he couldn't control such impulses. I didn't even ask if he wanted to.

I shut the windows and yanked off my robe. I started the shower, turned the heat high and stepped inside, letting the water pound my skin.

He's at it again. That was all I could think. It wasn't the goddess from Napa this time, but someone else. Unbelievable. How smug I'd been this week, thinking how much he'd miss me. How sure

I'd been of his devotion when I turned my back to him at the airport.

Nick's career couldn't handle a divorce right now. Hadn't he told me that in so many words while we were seeing the therapist? We'd sat side by side on the maroon leather couch in Conan's office, while Conan himself, a large man with a trim gray beard, sat on a wide leather recliner.

How had Nick put it? "Rach, listen, I know this is unfair, but I have to ask you something. It's…" His words drifted off, and he gave me a guilty glance.

"Go ahead, Nick," Conan prompted. "Everyone is entitled to a request here."

Nick nodded. "I would appreciate it if you wouldn't tell so many people about our…our troubles."

It was our second visit when Nick said this, and I looked at him with disgust. "You slept with another woman. *Over and over* for a week." I saw Conan studying me as my voice drove up in volume, so I took a breath and lowered it. "And now you want *me* to be quiet?"

"I am so sorry, Rachel," Nick said. He reached out and touched my leg. "Like I said, I realize this isn't fair. But you know how they are at the office."

In short, the partners at his medical practice looked favorably not only upon exceptional surgical skills and the publishing of papers, but also on charitable work and a clean, traditional private life.

I had assumed Nick wanted our marriage to work because he loved me, because he made that colossal, impulsive mistake, but now I began to wonder if he'd just been patching things up until he was a partner and a member of the board, when he could do anything he wanted with his life.

In the shower, a few frustrated tears slipped from my eyes, but after a minute, I began to hate my own confusion and self-pity.

I got out of the shower and called Nick's cell phone three more times in quick succession. I started to despise the sound of his cheerful yet soothing physician's voice—*You've reached the voice mail of Dr. Nick Blakely. Please leave me a message. If this is a medical emergency…*

I called the concierge and asked her to make a reservation at a good restaurant within walking distance. I dried my hair, recklessly directing the hair dryer any which way, never lifting the brush from the counter, so that the natural, erratic waves took over my dark hair. I put on black pants and high-heeled satin sandals. No more feeling sorry for myself. I had no idea what Nick was doing, but I was in Rome, and I was going out for the night.

As I walked to the restaurant, I filled up with the *feeling* I always got when I was in Rome—satiated though I hadn't yet eaten, overwhelmed by antiquity even though I hadn't yet waited in line to see anything. Beauty and history surround you in Rome. They're inescapable, and their presence buoyed me, if only for a few moments.

The last time I'd been in Rome, Nick and I had strolled hand in hand over cobblestone streets, me gripping his arm when we crossed particularly choppy spots, and we stopped at nearly every *osteria* for a glass of wine.

I pushed the thoughts of Nick from my mind as I spied Dal Bolognese, the restaurant where the concierge had booked me. It was tucked next to one of Piazza del Popolo's twin churches. The place had white tablecloths and umbrellas out front. Soft light and classical music spilled from the white-curtained windows.

I stepped inside and looked around, my eyes immediately landing on a man talking to the maître d'. He wore tan linen slacks and a long-sleeved maroon shirt. His hair was dark brown, his skin tanned, and faint lines ran from his eyes to his full mouth. He had one hand on the maître d's shoulder.

For some reason, the man turned to me as if expecting me. His expression when his eyes met mine said, *Ah, there you are.*

For a moment I forgot where I was. I don't know how long I met his gaze. Surely it was too long, for the maître d' stepped around him, and said, "Madame?"

I stayed mute, still looking at this man, who felt brand-new and at the same time intensely familiar. One side of his maroon shirt collar had fallen aside, and I was drawn to the sight of his tanned skin below his collarbone.

"Madame?" the maître d' said again.

I dragged my eyes away, but I could still feel him staring at me.

"*Prenotazione per uno*," I managed to say. "Blakely." I felt relieved to have spoken in coherent Italian, even if it was just a few words.

"*Si, si*," the maître d' said, glancing down at the reservation book. "Your table, here." He gestured toward an umbrellaed table in front of the restaurant. "Please."

I took a step to follow, but I couldn't help stopping and turning. The man in the linen shirt was still standing there. He was still watching me.

"Your table," I heard the maître d' say behind me.

"I should go," I said to the man. Stupidly, I realized. He was a few feet away from me, and why was I talking to him at all? He hadn't even spoken.

Feeling foolish, I turned again, followed the maître' d and gratefully took my seat, hiding my face with a tall, leather wine menu.

I ordered buffalo mozzarella and asparagus to start, then porcini risotto. While I waited for my food, I sipped from a glass of crisp white wine. But I hardly noticed the tart apple flavor as I glanced around the restaurant. Where had he gone? But then, what did it matter? I quickly finished the glass and ordered another.

I ate my mozzarella when it came. The cheese was so fresh, it must have been made that day. Yet I had to struggle to appreciate it, more focused on the fact that the restaurant was full to capacity, and everyone was having a delightful time. With their friends. With their spouses.

I ordered another glass of wine with my risotto, a creamy concoction that somehow turned my stomach. I pushed the rice around on my plate, imagining Nick in the bed of some woman. Then a thought struck me. He might have her—whoever the hell she was—in *our* bed. I was glad I wasn't in

Chicago then. I could easily become one of those people who chased their straying spouse with a semiautomatic.

The waiter had just handed me my bill when the man I'd seen earlier appeared at my side.

"*Ciao*," he said. His voice was low, smooth.

"*Ciao*," I answered.

"I will call you then."

I blinked a few times. "Pardon me?"

"I would like to call you."

"Look, you don't know me…"

He smiled. It was a kind smile, one that bore the experience of many years. I thought he must be in his mid-forties. How is it that Italians wear their age so well?

"You are alone in the city?" he said.

"No, no. I'm with a friend." I realized the ridiculousness of this statement.

"Please," he said simply. The collar of his shirt, which I could tell up close was made from a soft, and probably very expensive linen, had fallen aside again. He made a gesture to right it. His tanned hands were long and elegant and dotted with splatters of paint. Artist's hands.

"You don't know where I'm staying," I said

somewhat coquettishly. I felt a pleasing blaze in my stomach at my boldness.

"Yes," the man said. "True." There were flecks of green in his smiling brown eyes. "Where shall I call you?"

I shook my head and forced out a little laugh. I knew Italian men loved to seduce American women, the thought being that they were—sexually speaking—much easier when on the road, particularly in Europe. I wasn't one of those women, although clearly this man thought I was.

"I'm sorry," I said, "but I can't do this." I put some euros on my bill. Feeling silly, I stood. "Excuse me, I have to go."

The man bowed slightly, then stepped aside. "Of course."

I moved around him and without looking back, I headed out into the warm Rome night.

When I pushed open the door to our room, I saw that Kit was still gone. I checked for messages. There were none, not from my husband or Kit.

I called Nick's phone. That grating message again. I called home. No answer.

I slipped between the cool white sheets, and waited for sleep to envelop me. I dozed, my mind working through short bursts of dreams, all of them unintelligible but filled with the color of Rome's gold. I awoke and kept thinking about the man, although I knew this was illogical. I turned over in bed.

Just as I did, the phone rang—an unfamiliar bleat that reminded me I was far from home. I sat up and stared at the phone. I looked over at Kit's empty bed, then lifted the receiver.

"Hello?" I said. *"Pronto?"*

"Giorno." It wasn't Nick. It wasn't Kit. It was him. I just knew. *"Giorno,"* he said again when I didn't respond.

"Is it morning?" I said.

"Soon."

A pause.

"How did you get my number?" I asked.

"My friend who works at the *ristorante*. He told me where you were staying."

"Oh." More than anything, I was surprised at how flattered I felt that he'd searched me out.

"Please do not be angry. It is hard to explain, but I feel I have to see you, to know you."

"I'm not angry."

"You will meet me?"

I thought of Nick. Of course I did. And the image

of him, which should have stopped me—his round brown eyes, his curly, light brown hair, the constellation of freckles over his cheeks—instead incensed me.

I threw back the sheets and said, "Yes."

4

"*Ciao*," I called to the sleepy guy at the bell desk, as if I always left my hotel by myself in the wee hours to meet a man who was not my husband.

I stepped out into the inky night. The kiosk across from the hotel, which sold water and pizza, was closed, the apartments surrounding the hotel dark. It was not nearly morning, as the man had said, and daylight seemed far away, as if I might never see the sun again. I liked that thought.

My body felt light, made of air. I moved down the street like a patch of fog. He had told me to meet him halfway up the Spanish Steps. As I took the first white marble stair, I halted. The Spanish Steps are hundreds of feet wide and sky-high, so what exactly did "halfway" mean? The first landing? The second? Ignoring the questions, ignoring common sense, I climbed.

My shoes went *tap, tap, tap* as I padded upward, and in my chest, behind my ribs, a drumbeat of anticipation began.

I glanced up for a moment and saw the moon— a small, yellow globe—and the dark sky behind it. The steps were nearly empty of their usual crowd, but somewhere on them, young Italian men were singing. Out of the corner of my eye, I saw a few pairs of lovers. No single man in a linen shirt. My eyes climbed the huge stairway for him. Maybe he wouldn't come? Relief. Disappointment.

At the second landing, I turned and stared down toward the fountain. A few stragglers were gathered around it. Maybe he was one of them? Had I walked right past him? But he'd said "halfway." I remembered that for sure. Maybe "halfway" was some Italian lingo. The confusion nearly pulled me from my dreamlike state. I started to process what I was doing, or at least how I hadn't a clue of what I was doing.

But when I turned back to look up the steps, he was there.

"*Ciao,*" he said.

"*Ciao.*"

He came to me and took one of my hands. I felt a flutter through my belly and my limbs. "I don't know your name," he said.

"Rachel."

"And I am Roberto."

The singers broke into a slow, haunting song. The strum of their guitar wafted and lilted until it surrounded the two of us, as if the song was being played for us.

"*Rachele*, *Roberto*," he said, gesturing to me and back to himself. "This is meant to happen."

I clasped his hand tighter.

Roberto and I sat on the steps for an hour or so, talking softly, about Rome, about art. When the singers were chased away by the *polizia*, he stood and took my hand again. He led me away from the steps and began to guide me over the cobbled streets.

His apartment was only a few blocks away on Via Sistina. The short distance meant I didn't feel scared or pulled too far. Inside, his floors were pine-planked. His artwork—canvases done in red—hung from the walls.

He stood behind me as I surveyed the place.

I noticed a small canvas on an easel, and I walked over to it. The painting was a series of thick, wine-red slashes, with small remnants of black beneath them. And in the center, amid the chaotic red, was a lighter area. On closer inspection, it was the profile of a woman, her face downcast.

Roberto came to my side. "It is you."

I laughed. "Oh, you painted this tonight, after you met me?"

"No, I painted this ten, maybe eleven years ago. I did not know this woman I painted. She was here." He tapped his forehead. "Then I see you in the *ristorante* tonight, and I know. It is you."

"Come on." I laughed again. "How many women have you told that story to?"

"Only you," he said simply. He nodded at the painting. "It is you."

On closer inspection, the woman's hair was shoulder-length, like mine, her eyes small but lashes long, also like mine. And there was something about the high curve of the cheekbone that made me feel, if only for a sliver of a second, as if I was looking in a mirror.

"It is beautiful," I said. *"Bellisimo."*

He moved behind me. He put his hands on my shoulders, then lightly drew them up my neck, into my hair, lifting it. "No. You are beautiful."

He leaned down, his breath in my ear. *"Bellisima,"* he said. *"Bella."*

He repeated it over and over—*Bella. Bella.*

Bella. His hands curled in my hair. His lips, warm and so soft, touched my neck. *Bella. Bella.*

It became a mantra he spoke as he led me to an old-fashioned brocade day-bed, right below one particularly vivid canvas. Slowly, gently, he unbuttoned my shirt and pulled it from my body, unwrapping me the way he might a precious painting.

When he lowered himself over me, Nick was in that room somehow. When I felt the full weight of Roberto's body, I was punishing Nick—and myself. But I loved it. I craved it. I needed it.

In the morning, I let myself quietly into the hotel room. I had felt dreamy and languid tiptoeing through Roberto's apartment door, but now the bright light of morning—*God's flashlight*, my mother used to call it—made me feel exposed and slightly seedy.

I expected the room to be dark, Kit still with her man from the French embassy or else buried deep in her covers. Kit was a notoriously late sleeper, always the last to get up in the morning, but the room was filled with light, and there was Kit. She sat at a round table in front of the opened French windows, coffee and a basket of rolls in front of her. Outside, Rome was starting to awaken, the sun growing more gold over the domes of a thousand churches.

"Morning," Kit said. She was wearing one of the hotel robes, and her hair was wet and combed back. She looked clean and fresh.

"Hi." I stood uncertainly, then stepped inside and let the door fall closed behind me.

I wanted, suddenly, to throw my bag on the bed and rush into a telling of my night, the way I used to when we were younger. I wanted to tell her what it was like with Roberto on that daybed, how we'd moved to the floor, a couch and finally his bed. I wanted to laugh, to say, "I've had two hours of sleep!"

But I stalled. I couldn't jump into a story of my infidelity, and how I'd quickly joined Nick's ranks, when I'd been so shocked at *his* actions. Also, it felt somehow wrong to give any of the sexual details. Marriage had sealed my tongue to those kinds of conversations. And finally, I realized right then that the years of geographical distance between Kit and me had created some emotional distance, too.

"How was it?" Kit said.

I took a few steps inside. "What?" I turned my back to her, setting my purse carefully on a dresser top.

"Rachel, it's me."

I turned. Her violet-blue eyes looked concerned, and I noticed lines around those eyes that didn't used to be there years ago. But then, I had such lines, too. Somehow the fact that we were both growing older made what I had just done seem embarrassing, unseemly.

"What do you mean?" My voice sounded false to my ears.

She pushed aside a cup of espresso. "Where did you meet him? Someone from your meeting?" Her voice was full of kindness, and I felt relief at the friendship I heard there.

I shook my head.

"Someone you met at dinner?"

I hesitated once more. An overwhelming desire to sleep covered me like a wave. I was too tired to figure out a way to lie to Kit.

I nodded. I searched her face for disappointment, but there was none.

"So how was it?" she asked again.

"Unbelievable. Amazing." The words were out of my mouth before I'd had a chance to consider them.

"Well, you got back at Nick," she said quietly.

"It wasn't like that."

"I'm sorry. I don't mean to be harsh. It's just that he deserves it."

Silence trickled into the room. Outside, on the Spanish Steps, the sound of a woman's laugh rang out.

"Sorry," Kit said again.

"No, it's all right." In truth, I liked that Kit was protective of me. "It's really not about getting back at him, though."

But of course it was. Because I thought he was probably doing it again. Right now, possibly. I thought about telling Kit my suspicions, but my shame stopped me. Before I'd come to Rome, I had been sick of being the one who was right for so long, the one who sat on the moral high ground of our marriage. With regret seeping in, I now wished to return to that spot.

Kit studied me. I sat on the bed, feeling the satiny-smooth cotton sheets beneath my legs. I thought of Roberto's hands on those legs, on my thighs, parting them.

"How was *your* night?" I said.

Kit smiled. "Wonderful. I'm sorry I wasn't here when you got back."

"It's okay. I was gone all day."

"Wait until you meet this guy."

"What's he like?"

"Gorgeous. Sweet. Perfect." She chuckled. "But you'll have to judge for yourself."

"You're seeing him again?"

She gave me a beseeching look. "If it's okay with you. I mean, I told him no, but he's called three times."

"Wow. That's great."

"Yeah. He's a doll. I mean, I really feel like he could be someone special." Her eyes were bright with hope.

"Well, of course, then. You should see him." Kit was always looking for the man who could make her happy, the way her family never had.

"Join us," Kit said. "We're going to some emperor's house. Nero, I think. I guess it's really interesting. It'll be great."

"No, thanks. I'm just going to sleep."

"No, come with us!"

We went back and forth, the exhaustion crawling over me, until Kit finally relented.

We sat silently for a few moments, the sun surging through the windows and filling our room.

"Are you okay, Rachel?" Kit said at last.

I felt something trembling inside me. "It's ironic, isn't it?"

"What do you mean?"

"Well, you know. Nick with that woman and now…" I raised a hand, as if I was in a classroom, identifying myself. I felt a strange, mortifying pride at what I'd done, but more than anything I felt twisted with guilt.

"I guess so," Kit said simply.

"Did Nick call?"

Kit shook her head.

But he did.

The *bleat, bleat* of the phone startled me out of sleep like a smack to the head. It took me a few long moments—the persistent bleat still sounding—for me to remember Rome. And Roberto. I thought he was calling me again. And, in that instant, I was happy. Schoolgirl, pulse-skidding happy.

I rolled over with a little grin, and I lifted the phone.

"There she is!" Nick said, as if he'd been calling me over and over instead of the other way around.

I froze.

"You there?" he said.

I pushed myself to a sitting position, leaning against the tufted headboard. "Yeah, I'm here."

"How's Italy?"

Why did he sound so cheerful? I could only think of one reason.

"Where were you yesterday?" I asked, my voice steely.

"When?"

"Yesterday. All day. I called you at the office, and they said you were *golfing*. I called you at home and on your cell a million times."

"You left one message," Nick said.

"One message on your cell, and one at home."

"Right. And by the time I got them, it was the middle of the night over there. I just woke up, and I called you first thing."

I glanced at the nightstand clock. Two in the afternoon, which meant it was six in the morning at home. "What were you doing all day that you didn't have your phone on?"

"I...I was working."

"You weren't working. I told you I called your office."

"Yeah, well, I was working on something here."

"What?"

He sighed.

"Nick, where *were* you?"

Another silence. "I don't want to tell you."

I laughed, harsh and bitter. "I bet."

"What's that supposed to mean?"

"I think you know."

"Rach, c'mon."

"No, you c'mon. Again, Nick? *Again?* I'm gone a couple goddamned days, and you're at it again? Who was she? Why don't you just make us a grand cliché and tell me it was your nurse?"

The silence now was eerie. Do not speak first, I told myself, aware, vaguely, of how childish this was but not caring.

I heard him breathe out, hard. "Rachel," he said in his practiced, doctor's voice—composed despite disaster, "I can't tell you what I was doing. It's a surprise."

"What do you mean?" I tried to untwist my legs from the sheets.

"I took the day off work. I put my pager on in case the office called, and I turned off the other phones because I was doing something for my wife."

My wife, my wife.

There was too much sun in my room. Too damned hot. I stood, intending to close the drapes, but my brain seemed to slosh about in my head. I nearly lost my balance, as if I were standing on a boat in rough seas. And then there was my husband. Talking still, saying something, far away. He sounded calm, but angry and disappointed. I could tell. It was the way I'd sounded for much of the past year.

"Rachel?" he said. "Are you there?"

I sank onto the floor right next to the bed. I noticed the black satin sandals I'd worn the night before. They lay where they'd been kicked off. Carelessly. Wantonly.

To believe or not to believe.

"Why don't you have some faith in me?" Nick asked on the phone.

I retorted something about losing my faith in Napa. I said I thought I'd left it at a restaurant.

Neither of us said anything for a long time. I kept glancing at the sandals—glittering black on the thick cream carpet. I chucked them across the room, out of sight.

I heard the distant beep of Nick's pager. "Shit," he said. "I've got to get to the O.R. Rachel, listen. Enjoy your last day over there, and we'll talk about this when you get home. I'll show you then."

"You'll show me?"

"I'll show you my surprise." He paused. "And I'll show you how much I love you."

I took a breath. Had I been breathing since the phone rang? It didn't seem so.

"I do love you," he said.

I rolled that around in my mind. It seemed true

from my side as well, despite everything. "I love you, too," I said grudgingly.

As I hung up, there was a rap at the door. "*Uno momento*," I called, pulling on a robe.

The front desk clerk, Bettina, stood outside the door. "For you, Rachel." She held aloft a foot-tall square wrapped in brown paper. "Delivery."

"*Grazie*." I wondered if this was somehow the surprise from Nick. "And have you seen my friend? Kit?"

Bettina grinned. "She is with Frenchman, I think."

"Okay, *grazie*." If Kit was here, she could help me decide. To believe or not to believe.

I took the package to the table near one of the windows. Outside, it was another sunny Roman day, the Spanish Steps loaded with backpacking tourists holding cameras. Today was windy, though, and people held on to hats, as well, the women's hair flapping in the wind.

There were no markings on the package except for my name and *Il Palazzetto* written in black marker in a hand I didn't recognize. I turned it over. Masking tape held the paper together and it easily came undone. Inside was the small painting from Roberto's apartment. The one of the woman he'd said was me.

I couldn't pull my eyes away. Why had he sent this? I turned over the canvas and saw a note taped to the back. It was a small rectangle of heavy ivory paper, folded in half.

> *Mia Rachele,*
> *You have only a small time in Roma. I would like to spend that time with you. But if you cannot, then I want you to have this. Please take it to Chicago and remember me. I will remember you.*
> *Roberto*

If I chose to disbelieve my husband's words, I should pick up the phone now. I should call Roberto, and not only thank him for the painting but tell him to meet me.

I set the painting on the table. I opened the windows and leaned out, hoping to catch a little sun on my face, and with it, a decision about Nick. Another one. Hadn't I leaped over enough moral and mental hurdles to get to this point? Deciding to forgive him. Deciding to trust him again. Now he was asking the same. And I was no longer the innocent.

I squeezed my eyes shut and pictured the gallery where I'd met Nick during a spring art festival in Bucktown, the same gallery where we had our wedding reception three years later, when Nick's brother and our parents and our friends gathered together in that high-ceilinged room filled with jazz and champagne and sun and art.

I thought of the way Nick always looked at me, especially when I entered a room or a conversation. Nick had a way of furrowing his brows when he listened to someone speak. He was, I'd always said, one of the best listeners I'd ever met. He truly wanted to hear what someone was saying. He wanted to learn, to understand. When I spoke though, the corners of his mouth turned up in a small grin. His brown eyes softened and filled with pride.

And then I thought of Nick's eyes and the way he'd looked at me that night in our kitchen. The night he'd told me. After his confession, he'd held me lightly by the shoulders, as if I was a balloon that might float away. He'd bent down until our eyes were even. *I made a mistake,* he'd said. *The most awful, most cruel mistake. But I will never do that to you again. I promise.* I could see the anguish in his eyes, the paleness of his skin making his few freckles stand out in sharp contrast. *I promise, Rachel. I promise.*

To believe or not to believe.

I crossed the room and found Roberto's note. I

fingered it. I remembered his fingers on my body. I thought of Nick's words—*I was planning a surprise for you... My wife*.

I thought of our bungalow on Bloomingdale Avenue. I thought of the family we planned on having.

I took the note to the window. Outside the wind was still buffeting the people on the steps. I held my fist outside. I unclenched my hand. I watched the scrap of white float into the Roman air.

5

Nick was waiting for us at O'Hare when we landed, which meant he'd left the office early. I wondered if this was because he loved me, as he had said so many times over the past few months—as he'd said on the phone when I was in Rome—or because he felt guilt that he'd done it again.

"Golden Girl," Nick said, when Kit and I reached his car.

I smiled. No matter what was going on with us, I always loved when he called me that. He was wearing a suit with a silvery tie and the cuff links I'd given him on our first anniversary. He looked the part of the elegant surgeon. I felt a rush of pride.

He hugged and kissed me, then turned to greet Kit. "How was the trip?"

"Great," she said.

Kit was wearing the earrings her Frenchman,

Alain, had bought for her. They were made of little pieces of green glass, like tiny, emerald chandeliers, and they made her hair gleam a more beautiful auburn.

Looking at those earrings, I remembered how I'd felt after Nick gave me my square sapphire engagement ring. I'd shown it to Kit, who'd expressed happiness, but I knew she'd been envious, wondering why *she* wasn't the one getting married.

Now the tables had turned. Alain had told her he was being transferred back to Paris, and he would fly her there when he was apartment hunting. Kit was already envisioning herself in France and I envied her for the clean, simple beginning of it all.

"Did you have fun?" Nick asked Kit.

Her eyes shot to the ground, and she nodded. She looked guilty.

I wondered if Nick noticed, because if I was reading her right, Kit was feeling guilty because of me. She knew about Roberto. I hated myself for putting her in a position where she had to keep quiet about this. But then, wasn't that what female friendships were based on—the ability to hear the other's dirty little secrets, to sympathize with her, to tell the other the honest words she needed to hear, to build her back up, to make sure she no longer felt shame at what she'd done, and then to forget, forever, those secrets?

"Your chariot," Nick said, gesturing to the navy-blue BMW he'd bought last year. "Let me get your bags. And what's this?" He nodded at Roberto's canvas, covered again in brown paper, which I'd carried on the plane.

"A painting." My voice rang high. "A souvenir."

Nick held out his hand. "I'll put it in the trunk."

"No, no. I've got it."

Kit's eyes shot away from us.

The ride home was filled with my chatter. Nick smiled when I told him about our delicious first-night dinner in Rome; he groaned and said, "Oh, babe," when I recounted the meeting with the Rolan & Cavalli architects. It felt good to be with him, but I couldn't ignore the flashes of Roberto, nor could I forget the questions—*Nick, what were you doing while I was gone?*

The whole time, Kit was silent in the back seat. I turned every so often and tried to draw her into the conversation, but she only smiled back, a sad, resigned kind of smile, and I assumed she was embarrassed for me. Or maybe she was thinking about her mother, about the fact that the vacation was over and it was time, again, to face the hard realities of her illness. When we dropped her off at her mom's place—an old apartment building in River Forest that looked more like a roadside motel—I couldn't help but remember the house they used to live in, before Kit's dad died. It was only a few miles away, just down the street from where I grew up, but it was a well-tended Georgian, with a huge oak in the center of the front lawn.

"Thanks, Rachel," Kit said to me. "It was a great trip." She hugged me, avoided Nick's eyes and headed quickly for the door.

I glanced at Nick, but if he saw something strange in Kit's behavior, he didn't comment. "Ready?" he said, putting the car in gear. "I've got something to show you."

We exited at Armitage and wound our way to Bloomingdale Avenue, a tiny, brick street west of the city. On one side of the avenue stood the stone wall of an old rail line, the top of which now served as a planter for trees and bushes and, quite often, an impressively charming display of weeds. On the other side, a few turn-of-the-century bungalows, like ours, mixed with large, single-family homes built in the past five years.

Many Chicago residents knew nothing of Bloomingdale Avenue. After living in the city for years myself, I'd never seen it. But Nick and I took a walk one day during our engagement. We were tired and nervous about getting everything done before the wedding, and we wanted to simply be outside. It was chilly but sunny that autumn day, and we ambled this way and that, talking about the wedding and our jobs and our family and who to seat next to whom. At some point, we stumbled onto Bloomingdale, and with the sun striking orange through the trees, it seemed an enchanted avenue.

There was a For Sale sign in front of a white bungalow that had a wide front porch and a cedarshake roof. The street and the house were like nothing we'd ever seen before, but we looked at each other and we nodded. It was as if we knew. We called a real estate agent as soon as we got home. We closed on the house a month later, just in time for our wedding.

Nick turned into the alley and parked in the garage behind our house.

He took my hand, and I followed him through our tiny back garden, just starting to bloom with daffodils, and up the wooden back stairs into the house. Nick switched on lights as he led me through the kitchen with its wood-and-glass cupboards, original to the house, and down into the basement.

It was dark on the stairs. "Nick?" I said, almost faltering as I followed him halfway down.

"Okay, stay here." His hand slipped from mine, and I was gripped with sudden fear.

Then light flooded the basement. I blinked. This was not our dank basement with boxes of discarded clothes and books and my painting table set up into one tiny corner. This was an entirely new room.

I hurried down the steps and ran my hands over the walls—once gray cement but now papered a pleasing sage-green. I stared at the floors, which were now covered with straw matting, on top of which sat an Oriental carpet in tones of orange and green. A bookshelf rested against the left wall, filled with my art books. The fluorescent strips no longer hung from the ceiling. Instead, a globe pendent provided a warm glow. Against the far wall was an old mahogany artists' table with a slanted top. Two of the photo paintings I'd been working on had been clipped there.

"Nick?" I said.

"Do you like it?" He put a hand on the table and beamed at me. "It's your painting room. It's all yours."

"You did this for me?"

"Yeah, yeah. I took a few days away from the office. I've been working like crazy." He looked around the room with a grin. "I was thinking it needed some artwork, though. Let's see that painting."

I glanced down and realized I was still holding Roberto's canvas in my left hand. "Oh, I don't think…"

But Nick was already taking it from me and peeling off the paper. "It's great. God, it looks like you. Who's the artist?"

I froze. "Um…"

Nick held it against the wall, right over the mahogany table. "It's perfect. What do you think?"

I watched my husband smiling broadly, holding the canvas painted by Roberto. Why had I been so quick to judge? Why had I assumed he was cheating again? Panic and dread surged up my throat and pushed a tear from my eye.

Nick's grin started to falter. "Rach?"

"This is the most beautiful room I've ever seen."

He looked relieved, happy. He placed the painting on the table and held open his arms.

I brushed away the tear and rushed into them.

6

One Sunday a few months after Rome, Nick and I were in my new basement room. The globe fixture infused the place with cozy light, while a beam of hot August sun pushed its way through the sole window into the cool. Nick lounged in the plush chenille chair we'd put in the corner, and he had the Sunday papers fanned out around him. He liked to read the business section of one, then the book section of another. He felt that Sundays were the one day he could be unorganized, capricious. I stood at my artists' table, swiping a solvent on a black-and-white photo to prime it for painting. It was a shot of Lake Michigan, and the Chicago skyline beyond that, taken from Diversey Beach. I had already printed and painted this photo twice before, but the blues I mixed kept making the sky too cartoonlike, the teal of the lake too austere, the city too gray.

"Are you ready for that benefit coming up?" I asked Nick.

I loved afternoons like this, conversations like this. They made me forget what I'd done in Rome and how I'd never been able to confess.

Nick gave a rueful laugh. "The printers haven't done the programs yet, and of course that's my department."

"Well, you're on the board now," I said in a teasing tone. "You'll have to handle it."

Nick had finally made it onto the board, but he was essentially a pledge in a grown-up fraternity. As low man on the totem pole and someone trying to make it as an official member, he'd been given much of the unglamorous work that went into planning the board's benefits and charity balls.

"Why did you ever let me join?" he said.

I turned, a wet cotton ball in my hand, and smirked. We both knew he loved being on the board. He loved the kudos it brought him from the docs at his office and the new friends it brought into our lives. The limelight he'd grown up in was back—albeit a tiny, probationary light. The truth was we were both on trial for the board. As a result, we were busier than ever with dinners and cocktail parties and lavish benefits. It tired me more easily than it did Nick, who preferred to gripe grudgingly and enjoy every second. And ultimately, seeing him pleased made me more happy than anything else.

As I turned back toward the photo, my eyes landed on the wall, on Roberto's painting, still hung where Nick had insisted, right above my table. My stomach swooped and sank, as it did every time I saw it.

I'd told Nick the painting was a souvenir. He took that to mean it was a symbol of a memorable Roman trip, and he wanted such a thing in the new room he'd created. But to me, it was mostly symbolic of a grave mistake. The fact that my husband had put it there tortured me.

Every once in a great while, though, when I was able to push past the guilt, the painting was a symbol of sex and confidence and desire, all of which I'd lacked for a while before Rome. But now Nick and I had those things again. The sex was passionate and the ghosts were gone. It was as if my night with Roberto had driven away the woman Nick slept with in Napa. I knew that such a thought was somehow sick and wrong—what kind of person needed a matching bout of infidelity to cancel out the other?—but the effect couldn't be denied. I no longer thought of the woman as a goddess. I no longer felt insecure or bruised. I realized how much I loved this man, my husband, and because of that, we'd grown assured again in our relationship.

"Nick," I said impulsively.

"Yeah, hon?"

"I want to take down this painting."

"Your Rome painting?"

I nodded.

"It looks great in here. Why?"

I stared at its slashes of red and gazed at the girl, who seemed to be me, in the middle of it. My throat threatened to close. "I just don't like it anymore. I don't need it."

When Kit and I had returned from Rome, I agonized over whether to tell Nick about Roberto. Nick hadn't told me about his affair until a few months after Napa, but the point was he *had* eventually. He'd had enough respect for me, and for us, to come clean with his sins. In those weeks after Rome, I understood how impossibly difficult that must have been for him, and I cherished him all the more for it. But I found I couldn't do the same. Not because I didn't respect him as much, or our marriage. On the contrary, I adored him; I adored us, the way we were now, again. It was simply that we'd already been through too much. Another transgression would splinter us irrevocably.

It sounded like a cop-out to my own ears, yet in my gut I believed it to be true. And so I kept my mouth shut, and a little piece of my heart grew black from the secret, the lack of fresh air. But it was my fault, I reckoned, my cross, and I was bearing it willingly. I didn't need the painting to remind me.

"What will we put there?" Nick asked.

"My photo paintings. I'll be done with this one by the end of the week, and I know I'll get it right this time."

"Out with the old, in with the new?"

"Exactly." If the painting was gone, maybe I could forget. Maybe I could forgive myself.

Nick stood from the chair, the newspapers crinkling. "Let me help you, then."

Together, we leaned over the high table and each took a bottom corner of the canvas. Carefully, we lifted it higher, then together we pulled it away from the wall.

"There," Nick said.

"Yeah." I grinned. The wall looked clean now, ready for the future. I stowed the canvas in the closet.

Nick crossed the room and hugged me. I pressed

myself into him, my arms around his back and felt myself stir. "Want to go upstairs?"

He groaned softly. "Absolutely."

The phone rang. "Don't answer it." I ran my tongue up the side of his neck.

"Let me make sure it's not the service." Nick grabbed the phone off the arm of the big chair and looked at the display. "Kit," he said.

I took his hand and began leading him up the stairs. "Definitely don't answer it."

I hadn't spoken to Kit very often since we returned. She spent much of her time with her mom or on the phone with Alain. But the truth also was that Kit made me think of Rome, and I wanted to forget it. In the same way I'd wanted the painting out of sight, I was inadvertently avoiding Kit.

Nick and I climbed the basement stairs, passed through our living room which was overly warm with late-afternoon sun, and went up the stairs to our bedroom.

At the foot of the bed, we kissed hard, our hands clawing at our clothes.

The phone rang again. "Sorry," Nick mumbled. He twisted away and glanced at the bedroom phone on the nightstand. "Kit again."

I lightly bit his collarbone. "Ignore it."

But a minute later, the phone rang again.

"You better get it," Nick said, slightly panting, his shirt off, his pants halfway down.

I groaned but grabbed the phone and answered it, holding my discarded T-shirt over my breasts.

"Rachel?" Kit said.

"Yeah, hi. What's up?"

She broke into sobs.

"Kit, what's wrong?"

"It's my mom," she said, still crying. "It's everything."

"Where are you?"

"I'm at the hospital."

In the parking lot of Chicago General Hospital, the sun beat on new asphalt, making my shoes stick as I hurried from my car. Inside the doors, the arctic blast of air-conditioning made me shiver.

I wrapped my arms around myself, realizing I had no idea where I was supposed to go.

"Cancer center," said the woman at the information desk, handing me a map of the hospital campus. Chicago General was a vast complex, only a block from Lake Michigan, and although my husband was on staff, I rarely had occasion to visit.

I headed back outside, into the stifling afternoon.

Using the map, I tracked down the cancer center and the chemotherapy unit, where Kit's mom, Leslie Kernaghan, was supposed to be. And there was Kit, standing outside a glass-walled room, small tears skimming her features.

She smiled bleakly when she saw me. Her face was splotchy and her eyes were pink and raw, making their purplish hue sharper. Her red hair was flattened on one side, as if she'd just been roused from sleep.

I hugged her, then brushed her tears away with my knuckles. "What's going on?" I looked inside the glass wall and saw Mrs. Kernaghan, or at least a withered, gray version of her, sleeping on a hospital gurney, tubes in her nose, IVs in her arm.

Kit took a deep breath, which caught in her lungs. "She needs this procedure tomorrow. It's a new radiation treatment combined with chemo. It's experimental, but it's her best chance to survive. The thing is, the insurance isn't covering anything anymore." Kit stopped and her shoulders shuddered. More tears streamed from her eyes. "But Alain told me he'd pay for it."

"Oh, how sweet," I said.

"He said he'd wire the money right away. We didn't get it. Then he told me yesterday he was getting on a plane. He was going to come here for the procedure, and he was going to pay for it."

"Wow."

"Yeah, it sounded great," Kit said bitterly.

I could guess the rest. Situations like this, where men disappointed on grand scales, were always happening to Kit. "He didn't come."

She shook her head. "He said he had an embassy function he couldn't miss, and there were problems transferring money overseas. When my mom found out, she started panicking. You should have seen her, Rach. She couldn't breathe. Her eyes were bulging."

I put my arm around her.

"She's stabilized now," Kit continued. "I talked the doctor into doing the radiation tomorrow, but they'll never let us do chemo without payment. It might be the only thing that can save her."

Kit started to sob—quietly and desperately—with her hand against the glass wall, as if to touch her mom.

I tightened my arm around her shoulders and pulled her close. "Honey, I'm sorry. Doesn't the Chicago General Board have a fund to help cancer patients?"

Kit gave a curt shake of her head. "They helped

us a year ago, when mom was having surgery, but they cut us off."

"Why?"

She shrugged. "There's a cap on how much they'll give one person, I guess. We don't qualify anymore." She turned to face me. "What am I going to do?"

"Could you get a second mortgage on her condo?"

"It's an apartment. She rents."

"I could get Nick to talk to the board. He's a member now, you know."

"I didn't know."

"Well, he's what they call an associate member. He hasn't officially made it yet. But I'll talk to him, and maybe the board can help you out again."

"That'll take too long. We need help now."

"Then we'll give you the money."

"You'd do that?"

"Of course. I should have thought of it sooner. How much is it?"

"Three grand."

"Okay. Sure."

"I know it's a lot, but…" She looked at her mom again, and her face twisted in agony.

"It's fine. I'll talk to Nick, and I'll come back—"

"No, don't," Kit said. "Please don't tell Nick."

"Why?"

"I'm embarrassed. And my mother is, too. She hates being a charity case. Please."

I thought about our finances. We had joint checking and saving accounts, as well as joint investments. If I took money from any of those, Nick would notice. But I also had my own savings, started long before Nick and I were together.

Kit sank her face into her hands, her shoulders trembling. "I just don't know how much more I can take."

I kissed her on the head. "It's going to be okay. I'll get you the money. I'll go talk to your mom now, and then I'll meet you here tomorrow morning, okay?"

She raised her head and gave me a fierce hug. "You *are* a good friend." She said it in a way that implied she hadn't been so sure about that a moment before.

On Monday morning, I went to work at seven. With the office cool and still empty, I checked my e-mail, returned calls from Friday and made appointments to call on an architectural firm the next day. As other employees trickled in, I checked my watch, waiting for nine o'clock, when my bank would open its doors and I could get Kit the money she needed. Because I was getting the funds from a savings account, I couldn't write a check.

At five minutes to nine, my boss, Laurence Connelly, stepped into my office. His suit coat was already off, and he wore his usual suspenders, a too-shiny pink tie and a smirk. "How's it going, Blakely?"

"Just fine." I tried a smile, but since I'd gotten back from Rome without the Rolan & Cavalli account, things had been icy between Laurence and me. Every time Laurence tossed it in my face, which was often, I was reminded not only of my failure at the meeting but how I'd failed my marriage, as well.

"How was your weekend?" I asked.

He ignored the pleasantry. "Are you seeing the Baxter Company soon?"

"Tomorrow."

"Get them to up their service agreement. We need that cash. Got it?" I knew what he was saying behind the obvious words—salespeople who didn't bring in that cash could be fired. He'd already let four people go this year.

I stood, signaling the end of the conversation. "I know that, Laurence. That's why I'm going to see them."

"And what about Thompson & Sons?"

"I'm calling on them today." I tossed my purse over my shoulder and reached for my sunglasses at the edge of my desk.

"Where are you going?"

"To the bank."

He crossed his arms. "You can do your banking at lunch."

I thought of Kit's mom, tubes extending from her arms, like a battered boat tethered to a dock. "It's important personal business. I'll be back soon."

"*This* is the business you need to be concerned about." He pointed to the floor with a stubby, manicured finger.

I moved toward the doorway, hoping he'd step back. "I made my numbers last month." Translation: *Back off, blowhard.*

"Doesn't sound like you're doing too well this month."

"And that's why I'm seeing the Thompson people today and Baxter tomorrow."

He wasn't moving. I knew Kit was at Chicago General, pacing, waiting for me, while her mother waited, too.

I angled a shoulder and pushed past him, trying to ignore the heavy, musky cologne he apparently thought was sexy. "See you later, Laurence."

Outside on Monroe Street, the August air lay like steam over the Loop. People rushed for the doors of buildings—and for the air-conditioning—the same way we all rushed for warm shelter in the winter. I got in a cab and directed the driver north to Lincoln Park Savings & Loan, the small community bank where I'd done my banking since college and where Nick and I had opened accounts after we got engaged. We no longer lived in the neighborhood, and it was rare that either of us actually had to visit the branch.

I stepped inside the chilly confines of the bank and waited in line for one of the three tellers who appeared unruffled by the fifteen or so people already waiting for their services.

Ten minutes later, I finally made it to a teller.

"How can I help you?" asked a young man wearing a white shirt and blue tie.

"I need a money order for three thousand made out to Katherine Kernaghan."

I thought of Nick then. I should tell him—I should come clean about *something*—but this was merely aid for a friend who desperately needed it, with money that was truly mine, which I'd earned. And Kit had asked me not to mention it.

The rationalizations didn't help much. It only reminded me of the other, larger, secret I'd kept from him.

Two minutes later, I was in another stuffy, airless cab, speeding toward Chicago General.

Kit had changed clothes from the day before, but she was standing in the same place, her hand on the glass window.

I stood next to her and looked inside. Her mom was being tended to by a thermometer-wielding nurse in pink scrubs.

"How's she doing?" I said.

"Same." Kit's voice was devoid of emotion.

"Are you working this week?"

"Goodman gave me the week off."

"That's nice."

"Yeah." Neither of us moved. "Were you able to get the money?"

"Of course." I handed her a white envelope with the money order inside. I felt like I was doing something illicit.

Kit took it and put it in her purse. "It's unfair, isn't it?" she said, still looking at her mom. The nurse had finished up, and signaled Kit that she could come in. Kit barely nodded in return.

"Yes," I said. "It's entirely unfair."

"Some people get nothing in life. They never get a goddamned thing. And then other people get it all, no matter what they do."

"Yeah," I said, not exactly sure what she meant.

She turned to me. Her eyes were clear again, not red like last night. "Like you, Golden Child. Everything is perfect for you."

I opened my mouth. I was about to remind her of Nick's affair, of my own, of my parents' divorce and my sliding status at work, of how I'd thought I'd be a mother by this time in my life but how my marital problems had derailed that plan. But the fact was, despite it all, I knew those were not the world's worst problems. I knew how fortunate I was. So I just nodded.

"Yep," Kit said, with bitterness in her tone. She turned back to the window. "Everything works out for you."

I felt stung by her words, but I knew she was hurting and scared, so I said nothing. I went inside the glass door and said hello to her mother. And then I left. In the cab, heading toward the Loop, I realized that Kit hadn't thanked me.

7

Oftentimes, when I think back about Kit, I try to put my finger on the exact minute it all began to crumble and slide. When an earthquake happens, there's always a quiet rumble that starts the disastrous movement. Sometimes I think that rumble might have gone as far back as our childhood together. Other times I think maybe it was the moment at the hospital, outside her mother's room. But no matter where it started or why, I can always pinpoint the moment I knew with certainty the slide had begun—the night of the Weatherbys' dinner party.

We'd been told it was "a get-together with just a few board members," and being a Monday night I'd envisioned pizza and beer. I should have known better. The members of the board always lived large.

"A toast to one more month of summer," said

Joanne Weatherby that night. "And to Nick and Rachel." She raised a glittering champagne glass.

The dinner crowd of twelve responded with clinking glasses and inquiring smiles sent our way.

"Eat, eat," Joanne said, taking her seat. She was a tiny, blond woman and had been the executive director of the board for twenty-five years. This impressed me as much as her gargantuan, two-story, candlelit Michigan Avenue apartment, her designer clothes and the fact that, from what I'd heard, neither Joanne nor her husband had ever held a job.

"If I could just say a word," Nick said, standing and holding up his glass. "Rachel and I are very glad to have met you all. We feel fortunate to call you friends." He paused to take in the nods from the group, then raised his glass a little higher. "To the success of the board."

The group raised their glasses once again. "To the board!"

When Nick had taken his seat once more—on one of the white, silk-covered chairs I was terrified of spilling on—and appetizer dishes of caviar had been served, all eyes fell on us. Again.

"So, Rachel, where do you two live in the city?" asked Valerie Renworth, a thin, raven-haired woman with round green eyes.

I should have anticipated such a question. After all, this was what it had been like since Nick made the board—dinners and charity balls and lots and lots of questions for the new couple. It was as if Nick and I were getting our fifteen minutes of fame in a certain, tony Chicago crowd. But we both knew this was a trial. We hadn't been truly accepted yet.

Unfortunately, I was in mid-bite when Valerie asked her question, and the saltiness of the caviar caught in my throat. I coughed it down, tried for a discreet sip from my water glass and answered as fast as I could. "Bloomingdale Avenue. Do you know it?"

Valerie shook her head.

"Well, not many people do know it," I said, warming to my topic. "It's this tiny street south of Armitage. It runs only for a few blocks alongside an old train line. We've got a little bungalow there."

"It sounds charming." Coming from someone else, this could have been a backhanded slight, but Valerie had an easy, open way about her, and I smiled in return. I suppose she was used to people liking her. She was married to Charles Renworth, a man I had yet to meet since he was often out of town on business, but whom everyone knew owned half the commercial real estate in the Midwest.

"It is charming," I said, glancing at Nick. "My lovely husband built me an artist's studio in our basement. It's the perfect house now."

"Except for the cab situation," Nick said. "In terms of taxi availability, we might as well live in Gurnee."

Everyone laughed. I shot a confused look at Nick. Like me, he rarely said anything bad about our adopted street. Bloomingdale was like a member of the family, whose faults would never be discussed in public.

"And you work, is that right, Rachel?" Joanne asked. She sounded bemused, as if she found the concept of employment as cute as a kitten.

But there was nothing cute about my employment situation right now. Baxter Company hadn't renewed their service with us, and Thompson & Sons had said they'd "think about it"—a phrase that was the kiss of death in the sales world.

"I work in architectural software," I explained to the group. Then I steered the conversation to Nick's work in plastic surgery, a topic that generated much more interest than my low-producing, seriously-in-jeopardy sales job.

Nick gave me a grateful smile. My husband, at least, believed I'd won this round.

When the caviar dishes were cleared away, I excused myself to go to the bathroom before the next battery of discreet interview questions came our way.

The bathroom had a tiny white fireplace, where Joanne had placed a dazzling array of lit candles. I found the glow somewhat eerie. I used the commode and washed up, then clicked open my evening purse for my compact. My eyes landed, instead, on my silver cell phone. I'd turned off the ringer before dinner, and the display now read, *You have 3 missed calls.*

I dialed my voice mail. The first call was from Kit. "Hey, Rach, thanks for helping my mom out. She's doing okay, relatively speaking." Kit gave a short, cold laugh. "Now they're talking a bone marrow transplant or more chemo. I don't know what's going to happen. Anyway, call me."

I sighed. Poor Kit. When would the suffering end for her and her mom? I moved to the next voice mail. Kit again. "Rachel, you haven't called me back. What's up? Partying with more of your new friends?" I looked at the phone, surprised at the mean edge to her voice. I lifted the phone back to my ear. "Alain, that bastard. He hasn't called me, either. My best friend and my supposed boyfriend, neither will call."

Ah, that's what it was. She was hurt about Alain. I almost dialed her number, but decided to listen to the third message. Kit again. Her voice was bitter. "Rachel, I don't appreciate the lack of return phone calls. You're going to call me back. Right. Now."

Kit's icy and demanding voice angered me. I was at a dinner party. I'd call her back when I could. I clicked the phone shut and placed it firmly in my purse.

When I got back to the dining room, black-jacketed waiters were serving the main course, a flaky-looking white fish sautéed to a golden-brown.

Nick kissed me discreetly on the cheek. "Everything all right?"

"Everything is just fine." I took a bite of the tender fish.

"So, you two," I heard from across the table. It was Trevor, Joanne's husband, a blond bear of a man, who reportedly did little but spend Joanne's trust fund, which was much larger than his. I wondered how many scotches he'd had that evening. "Are you going to board the rugrat train any time soon?" He made a pumping motion with his arm. "You know, choo, choo!"

There was an uncomfortable silence, which was thankfully filled by Valerie's smooth, cultured voice. "What Trev is inartfully asking is, will we hear the pitter-patter of little feet soon?"

Nick and I smiled at each other. The pitter-patter was what we'd always wanted. Hopefully two pitter-patters. But Nick's affair and our teetering on the edge of marital oblivion had stalled all that. We hadn't discussed it since, but I still wanted kids. What's more, I wanted them with Nick. I wanted a little boy with his sweet nature and a little girl with his quick mind. I wanted kids with his wavy hair and freckles.

Nick squeezed my hand under the table, and I squeezed back, sealing an unspoken decision.

"Yes," Nick said. "We hope to have kids soon."

"To little angels," said Valerie, raising her glass again.

"To little angels!" everyone answered.

Nick and I toasted. We kept squeezing our hands together, and I felt a rising excitement, a feeling of being on the brink of something altogether new and wonderful.

The only thing that marred my mood was when I put my glass down and glanced inside the purse on my lap. There I saw the flashing red display of my cell phone: *Incoming call—Kit.*

* * *

I'm going to be pregnant. I told myself this constantly the day after the Weatherbys' dinner party. Hopefully it would be soon. Who knew? After last night, I could already be pregnant.

I smiled at the thought, absently brushing olive oil on chicken breasts, Nick's favorite grill food. A pan of stuffed mushrooms was in the fridge, alongside a salad, ready to toss. Nick would be home soon, and we'd take advantage of the break in the August heat. We'd sit in our tiny back garden and talk about baby names.

The phone rang. Probably Nick. But something made me check the caller ID first.

Kit.

I covered the chicken and turned the phone on. "Hey, Kit," I said.

"It's over with Alain."

"Oh, no." I held myself back from pointing out that it was probably over when he'd reneged on his promise to help her mom.

"Oh, yeah."

"I'm sorry. I'm really sorry."

"Yeah, well. He bailed when it got bad. Just like so many people. Speaking of which, why didn't you call me back?" Her tone was as hostile as in her messages.

I took a breath and stared out the kitchen window at the short willow tree in our backyard and the little table underneath. I considered saying I'd been busy, but I didn't want to lie to her. "To be honest, your messages didn't make me feel like speaking to you."

Silence.

"I know how much you're going through," I continued, "but you don't have to talk to me like that."

"Are you kidding me?"

"What's to kid about? Kit, I'm just asking you to be a little nicer. I want to be there for you, but you're making it hard."

She laughed. To an outsider, it would have sounded like a melodic laugh coming from a beautiful woman, but I knew that laugh. It was one of scorn. Usually reserved for people she thought were terrible actors.

"You're asking me to be nicer," she said.

"Yes, I'm—"

"You're asking *me,*" she said, interrupting. "Well, I'm telling you. I'm the one who knows about the Rome affair."

My stomach churned. I heard the rumble of the garage door opening. Nick was home. "What did you say?"

"You heard me."

I saw Nick's BMW pulling into the garage. My pulse seemed to twitch in my neck.

"Just don't forget that," Kit said, before she hung up.

It took me two days to quell the anger and shock Kit's threat had caused. Once calm, I called her and asked if she'd meet me in the atrium of the department store that Chicagoans would always call Marshall Fields. I was hoping a little shopping might ease the tension between us and remind Kit I wasn't her enemy. She'd agreed, her tone cool.

But she was late.

I checked my watch again—12:10. Kit was supposed to have been there at noon. Normally, I wouldn't have cared—normally, I could take all the long lunches I wanted—but Laurence had been right, and my sales for this month weren't good. A fact he kept reminding me of. I needed to get a dress for the Glitz Ball, a charity fashion show Nick and I had committed to this weekend, and then I needed to get back to the office.

At 12:15, my irritation grew. Damn Kit. Damn her, and her comment about "the Rome affair." Why threaten to expose one of my biggest mistakes? She knew I'd decided not to tell Nick. She knew I thought we couldn't deal another blow to our relationship. And she knew I thought I was right to handle it that way. Things were better than ever with Nick. So why was she tormenting me?

The shoppers around the fountain grew in number. I was bumped by a woman toting numerous shopping bags.

I stood. Forget Kit.

But suddenly there she was, stepping through the sunlit doorway, waving at me. She wore a summer dress of tan linen, her lavender chiffon scarf wrapped loosely around her neck. She looked beautiful, happy, and for a second, I was simply happy to see her.

"Hi," she said.

"Hi." Neither of us charged into a hug like usual. "You look great."

She grinned. "Thanks. They're having open calls at the Goodman all week, so I thought I'd give it a try."

"An audition?"

"Well, yeah, for me and the rest of the unemployed actors in Chicago."

"Wonderful! Good luck." We sounded formal, but it felt good to be talking about pleasant things.

"So you said you're looking for a dress?" Kit asked. "What's the occasion?"

"The Glitz Ball."

Kit whistled. "Running with the high-society crowd, huh?"

"No, not really." I shifted my purse to the other shoulder. There were more and more people in the atrium, and the noise level had risen.

"Sure you are. Nick being on *the board* now, and all that."

"Well, like I told you, he's not a full member yet, and I wouldn't say 'high society.'"

Kit said nothing. There was still a smile on her face, but it looked false.

"It's really not like that," I said, then stopped. Why did I feel so defensive? "Look, this thing is black tie, and the women dress to the nines. Apparently they're ultra-fashionable, so of course I thought of you. I need your help."

The compliment seemed to do the trick. Kit's face relaxed. "Let's go upstairs and look," Kit said.

For the next half hour, Kit and I were our old selves, the way we were that first day in Rome. We combed the store, and we gathered dresses made of satin and beads. We packed ourselves into a single dressing room. As I tried on one gown after another, Kit sat on the padded bench and called out proclamations—*Horrible bow. Way too long on you. Very hoochy mama. You go, girl. Sexy but slutty.*

When I tried on a tangerine silk dress with a beaded halter that tied behind the neck, I thought I'd found it. The dress was tight around the breasts and had a sexy diamond cutout that displayed a slice of cleavage. It was daring, but it seemed perfect for the Glitz Ball.

"I love it," I said, twirling around.

"Ugh," Kit said. "That color makes you look like you have malaria."

I stopped twirling. "Really?"

"Orange is not your color."

"It's tangerine."

"Well, that cutout thing makes it look a little…I don't know…cheap."

"Cheap?"

She shrugged apologetically.

"Are you sure?"

"Positive."

I sighed. I took off the dress and tried on a more classic lavender gown with tiny spaghetti straps. It skimmed my waist and landed exactly at my feet. Normally, I had to shorten everything, but this dress fit me perfectly.

Kit looked me up and down, and said, "That's it."

"Isn't it a little boring?" I studied myself in the mirror.

"The color brings out your Snow White side."

We laughed. Kit used to tell me in high school that I looked like Snow White because of my dark hair and pale skin.

"That's it," Kit repeated. "Ring it up."

I breathed with relief. Task done, and Kit and I were getting on so well. Exactly what we needed.

I began to slip the dress off. "How's your mom doing?"

Kit had been hanging up one of my discarded dresses, and when I asked the question, her body froze slightly. I realized for the first time that having Kit help me shop for a fancy dress, when she had little or no money herself, was insensitive and stupid.

"She's out of the hospital," Kit answered.

"That's good. Right?"

Kit shrugged. "Sort of. We couldn't pay for her to stay in. And it's too soon to tell for sure, but they don't think the treatment helped."

"I'm sorry." It seemed I said this all the time to Kit. I moved to her side and put my hand on her shoulder, but she brushed it off.

"I think I'm losing it sometimes," she said. "I see

what she's going through, and I look around at our crappy apartment, and then I think of what other people have, and I don't know... I just feel like I'm going to lose it."

"Sweetie," I said, trying again to hug her.

She stepped away. "Look, I was going to talk to you about this."

"About your mom?"

"Yes, and... well, our finances."

I lifted the lavender dress and slipped it on the padded hanger. "Okay."

"Did you tell Nick about that money you gave us?"

"No."

Kit nodded. "I was wondering if you could help us out again."

"Give you more money?"

"She's going to need regular chemo. We can't afford it."

"How much?"

Kit bit her lip. "Five."

"Five hundred?"

She scoffed. "No."

"Five thousand?"

Kit made a barely perceptible nod. "To start with anyway."

I blanched.

"I just need the first five thousand now," Kit said.

"I don't think I can."

Her face remained impassive. "Don't you have it?"

I thought of the money in my savings, where I'd drawn the three thousand for Kit only a few days before. There was at least fifty thousand there, saved penny by penny since the day I'd started working for a clothing store in high school. Nick and I had talked about merging the money into our other accounts or investing it somewhere, but I told him it was my nest egg, something I wanted to use for our kids, for our family, for when we really needed it. I couldn't just give that away without talking to Nick.

I opened my mouth to say no, but I caught Kit's look—her lips pressed together as if she was reining in some words. I thought of her words the other night—*I'm the one who knows about the Rome affair.*

"Why are you doing this?" I asked her.

"We need help."

"But why are you asking me like this? Why did you threaten me the other night?"

"I wasn't threatening you. I'm just reminding you of a certain fact that I happened to know."

There was a mean gleam in her eyes that I'd never seen before. It scared me.

I lifted the lavender dress and picked up my purse, dropping my eyes from Kit's gaze. "I'll have it for you by tomorrow."

Nick laughed as we moved around the kitchen, cleaning up after our dinner. "So the office manager told me my cases would start at eight," he said, "and I had twenty patients, right?" It was darkening outside with the twilight, but our house was bright.

"And?" I said, wiping down the counters. I could tell Nick was warming to his story, happy about the busyness of his medical practice and the kudos that kept coming from the partners.

"Then the surgical nurse called and said my surgeries would start at eight-fifteen, and I had five of those." He chuckled again as he dried a washed pan with a cloth. "Can you believe that?"

"But you handled it," I said, pleased for him.

"I called Miller, and I said, 'Hey, someone's got to cover me.' And then I told them I'd probably need even a little more coverage after we get pregnant."

"Nick, you didn't."

He put down the cloth, and wrapped his arms

around me from behind. "Any chance it's already true?"

We'd stopped using protection on the night of the Weatherbys' dinner party earlier that week, and we'd had sex every day since. "I suppose it's possible," I said.

"Well, let's get back to work, just to make sure." Nick lifted my hair and kissed the back of my neck. His body pushed mine into the counter, making me arch.

The counter phone in front of me rang. I could see the caller ID: *Cellular Call: Katherine Kernaghan.*

"Who is it?" Nick said, his mouth on my ear.

"Kit." I was filled with an irrational fear that he'd answer it, *just to say hi,* and she would tell him.

"Let me talk to her for a second," I said.

Nick groaned and lightly bit my earlobe. "Make it fast." He picked up the cloth again and began drying a glass.

"Hey, Kit," I said, answering the phone, trying to make my voice cheery and light. I was keenly aware of Nick, quiet and in the room with me.

"Why didn't you get me the money today?"

"I had a lot going on at work." That was the truth, but what was also true was that I'd spent a large portion of my day trying to decide if I should tell Nick about Roberto and tell Kit to go to hell. But Nick and I were so good right now, and hopefully we were about to be parents. If I rocked our marriage with my news, we'd be back to square one. And square one might be the end of us.

"I need that money," Kit said.

"Yes, so you've said."

"You're a smart girl. Don't mess with me."

I wanted to say, *like you're messing with me?* But Nick was only a foot away. I stayed silent.

"Rachel, look. I've got nothing, and you've got everything. God, don't you get that? You've got your beautiful house and your beautiful husband putting away the glasses."

I froze. I glanced over my shoulder. There was Nick, reaching high into the pine cabinet, placing a sparkling wineglass on the rack.

"Where are you?" I turned toward the window over the kitchen sink, which looked into the back-yard. It was black outside now. Anyone could be in our yard.

"It's almost like watching a movie."

My heart thumped. There was a scrape behind

me as Nick opened a drawer, then a jingle of silver as he slid forks inside.

"I could come in for a visit," Kit said. "Maybe tell Nick some stories about Italy."

"No, don't do that."

My voice was loud, and I heard Nick laugh behind me. "What are you telling her not to do? Is she dating that French guy again?"

I turned around quickly, a fake smile on my mouth. *Don't lie to him,* I thought. *Not again.* "Kit has an audition at the Goodman, but it's an open casting call. She's wondering if it's worth it."

"Ah, she should do it," Nick said, waving a hand. "You never know what will happen."

"That's true," Kit said in my ear. "You never know what will happen."

8

The lights blazed outside the Chicago Theatre and hip-hop music blared. A line of limos stretched around the corner. Men in tuxes strutted down the red carpet and into the theater. The women on their arms were dressed in colors of the rainbow. The marquee proclaimed *The Glitz Ball!* in large gold letters.

"Jeez, a red carpet," Nick said, in a jokey tone. "We're in the big time now, baby."

I laughed and gave his arm a squeeze and concentrated on walking in the four-inch heels Valerie Renworth helped me purchase that afternoon. She'd phoned in the morning, wanting to chat about the ball, what we were wearing and who would be there. I sensed, again, the testing nature of her questions, but I also felt relieved by her kindness. When I confessed that I had no idea what shoes to pair with my new lavender gown, she insisted I meet her at her favorite shoe store on Oak Street. She'd watched me try on several pairs, offering subtle comments— *elegant; interesting; a little ordinary, don't you think?*—that made it so different from shopping with Kit.

I went with the elegant shoes. Bone-colored sandals by Yves Saint Laurent with tiny crystals across the toe. They cost more than the dress, but I hoped that owning them would make some of Valerie's aristocratic calm and charm rub off on me. The fact was, the shoes were a bitch to maneuver in. I gripped Nick's arm tighter as we stepped into the gold-laden foyer of the theater.

Inside, the music was even louder. Cocktail bars had been set up on either side of the foyer, and the crowd mingled, holding martinis and champagne glasses.

Joanne Weatherby swooped in front of us. "There you two are!" She was wearing a strapless gown as pink as her flushed face. "You look wonderful!"

She kissed us on our cheeks, and I marveled at how easily Nick kissed her back, complimented her on her dress and offered to get her a drink. He had slipped into this world so quickly. The tricky part would be whether we could sustain our positions here, whether Nick would become a full member of the board. We had less to offer than many people—we weren't old money and we had relatively little new. We would have to fight for an official place in this world by showing the character we had as a couple and by giving, over and over, the right answers to the ever-present questions. Nick had asked me to be part of this crowd, though, and I'd given him my word. After what I'd done in Rome, making nice with board members was the least I could do.

I smoothed down the front of my dress and shifted on my high heels. I saw Valerie standing with a few people about twenty feet away. She wore a backless black gown, her hair in a high twist. She caught my eye, made a show of looking me up and down, and gave me a discreet thumbs-up.

I smiled gratefully. "Thank you," I mouthed. I took a glass of champagne from Nick, although I hadn't been drinking lately in case I was pregnant, and began listening to Joanne.

"God, *everyone* is here," she said.

We were jostled from behind by more people pushing into the theater.

Joanne led us a few feet away, under an eave of

gold leaf. "Now, see that gentleman with the blonde?" She pointed to a man of at least sixty with steel-gray hair, standing with a much younger woman with a white-gold mane that swirled in large waves down her back. "That's Marvin Frankel. He owns a media conglomerate, and he's one of the board's biggest contributors."

Nick perked up. "Really? Can I get an introduction?"

"Of course," Joanne said. "But let him have one more cocktail first. Or maybe we'll wait until the after-party. He's easier after a few gins."

Nick sent me a questioning look. I knew he was wondering if Joanne was brushing him off.

Our little group sipped their drinks and huddled closer as the crowd grew.

"Let's see, who else is here?" Joanne said, gazing around.

Her husband, Trevor, stepped over to our group and boomed a hello.

"I was just pointing out the glitterati," Joanne said.

"Oh, yes," Trevor answered. "Lots of glitterati at the Glitz Ball. Did you see the Chimners?"

"*They're* here? God, you'd think after last year they wouldn't show their faces."

"What happened last year?" I asked.

Joanne shook her head. "Total mess. The wife, who was an associate board member at the time, got absolutely schnockered and starting making out with a bartender at the after-party. The husband found them and punched the bartender."

"About twenty times," Trevor said.

"Needless to say, she didn't make full member."

Nick put his hand on my shoulder. "So, Rachel, you'd better watch the sauce."

I made a comical show of moving my champagne glass away from me. Everyone chuckled.

"Yes, there're the Chimners." Joanne pointed to the upper balcony packed with people. "See her? Green dress—a mistake—and streaked hair."

I followed her finger. Out of the corner of my eye, I saw the rest of the group nodding. I heard Nick mention a cardiologist he knew who was also in the balcony.

But I was immobilized. Because there, next to the Chimners, was Kit.

I narrowed my eyes and peered. What was she doing here? And what was she wearing?

"Isn't that Kit?" Nick asked.

"Who's that?" said Joanne.

"A good friend of Rachel's." He pointed.

"The one in that tangerine-colored dress?"

"That's her," I said, finding my voice.

"Now, that's a great dress. That's the kind of dress women under forty should wear to these things."

"Yes, she looks very nice." I raised my glass and took a gulp of champagne.

Kit had told me the dress looked cheap. But the price certainly hadn't been, so how had she afforded it?

Then I realized she hadn't. *I* had. With the money order I'd given her yesterday.

The lights flickered, and the music dimmed.

"Ooh, show's starting!" Joanne said. "Let's find our seats."

Our seats, courtesy of the Renworths, who'd spent almost a thousand dollars on each, were first row, center. In front of us, a heavy white curtain hung over the stage.

Valerie slipped into the seat next to mine, but I barely had time to say hello before haunting music began pulsing around us, louder and louder until it seemed deafening. I looked at Nick, who gave a happy shrug.

When the music reached a near screaming pitch,

the white curtain was ripped away. It broke into different pieces and disappeared, revealing models, each attached to hanging silver stars, clouds and moons. One by one, a star or moon descended to the stage, letting off its passenger, who strutted down the runway, a blue carpet dotted with more silver stars.

"Michael Kors," a male voice announced, and the crowd went crazy.

I looked at Valerie. "I've never been to a fashion show," I said, essentially screaming in her ear.

"Enjoy!" she said.

I tried. I wanted to ooh and aah over the different fashions, and I wanted to applaud when a new designer was announced. But I kept thinking of Kit. Was she in the theater somewhere? Was she watching me? But that seemed nuts, and why would she do it? I had no answer, nor did I know why she would sit outside my house or show up at an event wearing a dress I'd almost bought.

For the fourth runway show of the evening—a new designer named Kyra Felis—the stage was transformed into a garden, and the female models pranced forward in fifties-style, full-skirted dresses. A white garden table had been set up at the very front of the stage, and the models each stopped there, sitting on the table or posing near it, while more models filled the stage. The pool of light over the table fell on the first row as well.

"We're part of the show!" Valerie said happily in my ear.

Nick grinned and sat up straighter.

But I ached for that light to be off. Because all I could think was that somewhere in this theater, Kit might be sitting in the dark, studying me. I scooted around in my seat. I kept my head down. The feeling of being observed was so strong I wanted to bolt. I squeezed my hands together and made myself be still. After a long few minutes, the spotlight went off, and forty minutes later, the show was over.

"One more drink in the lobby bar," Joanne announced. "Then the after-party."

We followed her dutifully to the foyer and took our previous spot. As if the night had been rewound, there in the top balcony was Kit again, in the tangerine dress. Now she was looking squarely at us.

"Excuse me," I said to the group. "I'll be right back."

I made my way through the crowd and up the wide, velvet stairway.

Kit was near the bar, now talking to two men, her cleavage on display in the cutout gown, her red hair swept away from her face. If I hadn't been so angry at her, I would have told her how gorgeous she was.

"What are you doing here?" I asked quietly.

"Hi, Rachel," Kit said, smiling widely. "How are you? Robert, Tony, this is my best friend, Rachel."

I shook hands with the two men but offered no pleasantries.

"What are you doing?" I said again.

Kit blinked a few times. "Guys," she said, "can you give us a few seconds?"

The man named Tony—a big man, with black eyes and stylishly choppy black hair—gave Kit a look full of longing. "I won't leave you alone for too long."

"Good," Kit said, then whispered something in his ear.

He chuckled and turned to talk to a friend.

Kit crossed her arms. "Is there a problem?"

"Aside from the fact that you're fleecing me for money, you're watching my house, you bought the dress I wanted and now you show up here?"

"Are you saying I don't belong?"

"What? No, of course not. Kit, look, I thought you needed money for your mom. But did you spend it on this dress?"

Kit shifted her tiny evening bag to her other

hand. "Sounds like you think I should stay home while you're out at parties with your new friends."

"Jesus, that's not it!"

"You can't stand to see me happy."

"You're crazy."

I said it lightly, but Kit's hand shot out and gripped my forearm.

"Kit," I said under my breath, "that hurts." I tried to wrench my arm free, but to no avail.

"What did you just say to me?"

Some kind of rage seethed in my gut. I'd wanted to be kind to my friend; I'd wanted to say, *Tell me what's wrong with you, and we'll figure it out.* But as her nails dug into my skin, my sympathy drained away, leaving something nearing fury.

I leaned forward and enunciated my words. "What I said was—You. Are. Crazy."

Her eyes flashed and then dimmed. She pulled her hand away and wilted a little, looking around the crowd. "Maybe you're right. Sometimes I don't know what's wrong with me." She turned her gaze to me. "All I know is my supposed best friend gets everything. *Everything*. And now she's moving on without me into some big, beautiful new life."

I sighed, that sympathy rushing back. "I'm not

going anywhere, and I want you to be happy. I want to help you."

She shook her head and gave a laugh. "I'm helpless."

"That's not true. Just tell me what you need, what's going on with you."

She said nothing.

"Kit, tell me what I can do. I mean, I'll give you more money if I have to, but I don't think that's what's going to make you happy. I think you need—"

Something seemed to shift in her at the mention of money. She straightened up and interrupted me. "No, you're wrong. Objective achieved. I'm very happy tonight."

I crossed my arms tight over my chest, waiting. There was a feeling of more to come.

"I should warn you," Kit said, a sort of rueful smirk now on her face. "My mom's going to need another round of chemo soon."

"Is that true?" I asked softly. "Or do you need another new dress?"

"I'm just looking for some financial assistance, Rachel."

"And?"

"And you're going to give it to me."

Kit stood on her toes and peeked over the balcony. "Now, who's that Nick is talking to? Joanne something, right? Joanne Weatherby?"

I was silent.

"I've heard she knows everybody who's anybody," Kit continued. "I've also heard she controls the social scene in this town. I'd better not slip up and tell her anything too juicy, huh?"

We heard someone say Kit's name. It was Tony, signaling to the stairs.

"Looks like I'm going," Kit said. "I'll have to find Joanne later. See you, Rach."

She turned and left me alone, jostled by the crowd, a growing pocket of fear inside me.

"Let's make a baby," Nick said later that night. He said this all the time now. He seemed to love the sound of it, the way it inevitably led to fast, intense sex.

He laughed and undid his bow tie, tossing it on the bed.

I slipped one lavender strap from my shoulder, then the other. "Are you sure you're up for it? You had a lot of martinis at that after-party."

Nick made a face. "Is my wife implying that I might have some operational problems?"

"I'm not implying anything, dear husband. Just asking."

"Well, I can hold my liquor and still perform husbandly duties." Nick looked at me lasciviously as he removed his tuxedo coat and began unbuttoning his white shirt.

"Then, I think I'll put on something special." I had a short, lace nightie I'd bought a few weeks ago and never worn. Nick and I were too eager for each other these days to wait for a costume change. But now seemed like the right time.

"Just hurry up," Nick said.

I went into our master bathroom, shut the door and grabbed the nightie hanging from its brass hook. I took off my bra and panties and slipped the nightie on. I gave myself a quick spritz of perfume and opened the door again.

And there was my husband, the one who could hold his liquor and still perform husbandly duties, now sleeping facedown on top of the comforter. I smiled and sighed as I threw a blanket over him.

With the sexual energy drained away, I hung up our clothes and tidied the bedroom, left alone with my thoughts of the night. Thoughts that mostly concerned Kit. In many ways, I felt terrible for her. Things never seemed to go right in her life, not with her family, certainly not with the men she dated. But then I remembered her demanding more money, her implied threat to tell Joanne about my affair, her previous threats to tell Nick.

I suddenly felt the desire to remind myself of everything Nick and I had. Not bothering with a robe, I went downstairs to the living room, turned on a lamp and looked at the bookshelves with the stained glass doors that had drawn us to the house and at the leather sofas we found on sale and the green vase we bought in Mexico. I walked into the kitchen and stared at the hardwood floors we had refinished ourselves and the circular table we thought would be perfect for kids.

I went back upstairs and watched Nick, sleeping contently, dreaming of becoming a father. I placed my hand on my belly. I wondered if I was in danger of losing all this.

9

On the morning after the Glitz Ball, Nick and I found ourselves in the basement with the Sunday papers. He sat in the big chair, with me on a floor cushion between his legs. I adored that spot, tucked away in the room Nick had made, just the two of us, no phones or pagers, no board members or balls.

No Kit.

"Listen to this," Nick said, ruffling my hair.

I put down the travel section and leaned my head back.

"Luxury Lake Shore Drive Condominium," Nick read. "Four bedrooms, five baths on twenty-second floor of Mies van der Rohe–style building. Formal living room and dining room with stunning views of Lake Michigan. Rehabbed kitchen with granite countertops, Sub-Zero appliances and butler's pantry. Spa facilities and parking in building."

"Sounds nice," I said absently. I picked up the travel section again, and started reading an article about Melbourne. "Nick, we should go to Australia sometime."

"Yeah, sure." I felt him shifting around in the chair behind me. "But maybe we should go to this condo, too. You know, just check it out."

I swiveled to look at him. "Why would we want to look at a condo on Lake Shore?"

"Well, with a baby hopefully on the way, we might think about getting a different place."

I felt alarm ring in my body. "What are you talking about? We love *our* place."

"But it's small, Rach. There're only two bedrooms here. If we have more than one kid, we'll have to put them in the same room."

"So what?"

"And then we won't even have a guest bedroom," he said.

"It's not like we have a lot of guests these days." Since my parents had found out about Nick's affair, neither visited often, and Nick's parents were busy with the political life in Philadelphia.

"C'mon, honey, think about it. This place is going to be too small when we have kids."

I turned and raised myself to my knees, so that I

was eye level with him. "We love our house, Nick. Why are you even talking about this?"

"Oh, c'mon. You heard Joanne last night. It's a lot easier to entertain when you've got a larger space, and when you're in the Gold Coast."

"Well, Joanne can afford to live in a huge condo in the Gold Coast."

"So can we." He put the papers on the floor. "Rach, I've got something to tell you."

I went cold. I hated phrases like that—*I have something to tell you.* Or *I have to talk to you about something.* They always scared me with their ominous overtones, and ever since Nick had used them that night when he'd told me about Napa, they scared me even more.

"It's nothing bad," he said. "C'mere." He pulled me up and onto his lap. "Honey, I think I'm going to make partner. They'll vote sometime this month, but it looks good."

"What?" I said, relief rushing in. "That's amazing! Congratulations." I hugged him tight around the neck.

"If it happens, I'll be making a lot more money," Nick said. "Which means we could get a bigger place. Someplace really amazing."

"Nick, our house *is* amazing. I don't want to move. And I can't believe you do, either."

"I didn't think I'd ever want to leave here, but it's a step in the right direction."

"It sounds like a step back. We would miss this place so much. At least *I* would." I tried not to sound hurt.

"No, I'd miss it, too. I just think we should at least consider a move, and now with the partnership, we can."

"I wouldn't want to spend your whole salary increase on a new place."

"Well, we've got your income, too. And we have your savings if we need it, right?"

I hoped he didn't notice how my body froze in his lap. "My sales haven't been very good lately," I said halfheartedly. "And look, Nick," I charged on, not wanting to discuss my somewhat depleted savings account, "I don't want to move. I love this place. It upsets me just to think about it."

He sighed. "We'll talk about it another time."

"I don't want to talk about it at all."

Nick studied my face. A slow grin came over him. "I don't want to talk either. Do you know what I want to do?"

I shook my head, but I had a feeling.

* * *

Mary, the receptionist, stuck her head in my office and said breezily, "Hi, Rachel. Kit's here to see you."

"What?" My hands froze on the sales report I was editing. I'd been struggling to pretty it, but the numbers were inflexible. And now with Mary's announcement, things had just gotten worse.

"That redhead, Kit," Mary said. "She's at the front desk."

"Tell her I'm not here."

"Oops. I already said you were in. I know you guys are friends."

"We were." Once the words were spoken and hit the cool air of my office, I felt them for what they were. A mean truth. I'd felt sorry for Kit at first, then confused by her actions, then annoyed, then angry. Now, the thought of her made something deeper inside me resonate. Loss. The loss of her.

Mary blinked. "Oh, God. Sorry."

I stood. "It's all right, Mary. I'll see her. I'll be right there."

I put on my suit coat, as if I were getting ready for a formal meeting with a client. As I walked down the hallway, I thought of Kit's other visits here, when I was thrilled at the break from work, a visit from one of my oldest and dearest. I remembered the time she'd come straight from the airport when she'd learned my father had to undergo heart surgery. She'd flown home for her friend, because she knew I needed her. I thought of how I'd traveled to L.A. for her improv shows in a Santa Monica theater, bringing roses to wish her luck. I thought of how I'd raced to L.A. at other times because of Kit's disastrous relationship breakups.

I kept walking, drawing ever nearer to the reception area, and I recalled how Kit had been the only person who'd supported me when I decided to stay with Nick after his affair. Both my parents had been so enraged with him they couldn't believe I would let my own anger go. They were divorced, and each had remarried and moved away in the past few years. Between their new relationships and their inability to understand mine, we'd grown apart. Kit had been the friend, the family member really, who'd stuck by me. "Make him work hard to keep you," she'd said. "But eventually, you have to forgive him. Really forgive him." It had been good advice.

I stepped into the reception room. Kit was gazing at a painting on the wall. She turned when she heard me enter and had the gall to smile. She wore tortoiseshell sunglasses, pushed back on her red hair. She adjusted them and opened her mouth to speak.

I took a step closer to her. "Please don't say a word," I said, under my breath. I didn't need Mary or, worse, Laurence overhearing anything Kit had to say.

I led her through the glass doors into the elevator foyer. "What do you want, Kit?"

"Gosh, I haven't seen you in almost a week," Kit said. "Since the Glitz Ball. Did you have fun?"

I said nothing.

"The after-party was great, wasn't it?"

I stared at her, still silent.

"It doesn't have to be like this," Kit said softly.

"Doesn't it?"

"No, and seriously, I am sorry." She bit her lip. "I don't know how to explain it, Rachel. I just feel like I'm not myself sometimes. I get so… I don't know, mad, I guess, about how everything's turned out."

"What do you mean, how everything's turned out?"

She shrugged. "It's just been so easy for you. And I don't know why it's not like that for me. It makes me insane sometimes when I think about it."

I felt a twinge of sympathy for her again. "Kit, you need help."

She blinked, then scoffed. "You're right. My mom and I are going to need more help."

"I'm talking about seeing someone, Kit. Like a psychiatrist or a counselor. I can find someone for you. I'll go with you if you want."

Her face went hard. "We need financial help, Rachel. And you're going to give it to us."

"Right. Help," I said bitterly. "For your mom."

"Yeah, she's starting up another round of chemo, and—"

"Is she really?" I interrupted. "Or is that all a lie?"

Kit's eyes narrowed. "I would *never* lie about that. My mother is dying, and I'm trying to help her."

"Sure."

"Do not push me about that."

I stepped even closer so that our faces were only inches apart. "And do not push *me* too far, Kit. Because I'm not taking your shit forever."

"What are you going to do? Tell Nick about the affair? Now? Don't you think it's a little late?"

The fact was, I did think so. Nick and I were so very good right now. We were enjoying each other—and enjoying trying to get pregnant—like never before. A confession on my part would stall all that wonderfulness. It might very well end. I moved back, away from Kit. "What do you want?"

"Six thousand."

"You're incredible. How long are you going to bleed me? Just tell me what you really want, and let's be done with it. I'll give it to you, and then we'll never talk again, okay? You can see a shrink or not. I don't care. Let's just be done with this. With us."

A chagrined expression crossed her face. "Look, I am sorry. I didn't want it to be this way. We're friends."

I laughed.

Her features grew hard again. "You and your fabulous life. You kill me." She paused; she seemed to be thinking. "Thirty thousand."

A startled breath escaped my lungs.

"That's it," she said. "Then it's done, just like you said."

"How do I know this will ever end?"

"I promise."

I laughed again. "Your promises mean very little to me."

"I'm serious, Rach. Look at me."

I met her eyes. Neither of us flinched or backed away this time.

"I want this over, too," Kit said.

Was there something in her eyes? Some flickering of the old Kit?

"This is the last time," she said. "I promise." There was a resignation in her voice I hadn't heard before.

I put my fingers to the bridge of my nose and did the math. It would leave only twelve thousand in my account, the account that had taken me decades to save. Luckily Nick never saw the statements. And maybe it was the price I had to pay for this part of my life to be over. Maybe in some ways, I thought I deserved the punishment.

I looked at Kit "My bank is in Lincoln Park."

From the deck, we heard the doorbell ring at precisely seven o'clock.

"Shit," Nick said, "they're on time." He wiped his hands on his grill apron. "Do we have everything?"

"You get the door, I'll make sure all is ready." I kissed him on the nose. "Nick, it'll be great."

He snaked an arm around my waist and bit my neck. "It'll be more than great."

The doorbell rang again. Nick kept kissing my neck.

"Go!" I said, laughing, pushing him away.

While Nick went to welcome the Weatherbys and the Renworths, I surveyed our deck. A copper drinks tub was filled with ice and held white wine, sodas and assorted beers. The red wine was in the kitchen, along with the Cornish hens and vegetables, waiting to be grilled. The August night was warm but quickly cooling as the sun slid behind the city. The deck table was set with a red tablecloth and a bouquet of tropical flowers—perfect for an end-of-summer gathering with new friends. I hoped the night would show them, and maybe more importantly show Nick, that we could entertain in our little bungalow on Bloomingdale. There was no reason to move.

"Rachel, hello," Valerie Renworth said, stepping through the French doors. She wore crisp, white slacks and a pink camisole. Her black hair was tied back with a pink band.

"Hi, Valerie. Welcome." We embraced, the first time we'd done that, and I felt grateful. I needed the friendship. Yet I knew this friendship came with strings, ones that could be quickly severed.

"What a great place," she said.

"Thank you. We love it. What can I get you to drink?"

As I poured Valerie a glass of white, Trevor

Weatherby came outside, along with his wife, Nick and the others. "Quite a place, quite a place," Trevor was saying. "I've lived in this city almost all my life, and I don't think I've ever been this far out in the sticks."

I saw Nick bristle at the remark.

"Trevor," Joanne said disapprovingly. She made a face and shook her head, then greeted me with a kiss on the cheek.

"Nick," I said, "why don't you grab the appetizers?"

"Right, great," he said. "And would anyone like a glass of Shiraz?"

Soon, some cool jazz wafted from our outdoor speakers. The group gabbed and cocktailed, while Nick went to work on the grill. By the end of the first hour, he had a pleased grin on his face, and I knew the night would be a success.

When the sun was almost down and the sky was a rich rust color, our neighbor, Melanie Green, came across the lawn and up the deck stairs. Melanie was a mother of three. She was married to a consultant, who was almost always on the road.

"Hello, Melanie," I said. "Is the music too loud? Would you like a glass of wine?"

"I would," she said. "In fact, I'd kill for a glass of wine, but I've got to get back to the kids. I just wanted to let you know that a friend of yours was here earlier, looking for you."

Despite the warmth of the day, I went cold inside. "Really? Who was it?"

"Kit, I think she said her name was. Red hair?"

"Did she say what she wanted?"

Nick called hello to Melanie from across the deck. She waved. "I saw her waiting on your front step, and then I saw her come around and into the backyard."

"What time was this?"

"Around four, I guess."

"We were at the grocery store."

"Yeah, I'd seen you guys leave," Melanie said, "so when I saw her in your yard, I came out and asked her if I could help. Then I remembered I'd met her at that party you had. She said she just wanted to say hi."

"Did she say anything else?"

"No, she left after that."

"Oh." The water glass in my hand felt slick. I could imagine it slipping and shattering on the wood.

"Look, I should go," Melanie said. "I just wanted to let you know."

"Of course, thanks." I set the glass on the railing. "Thank you for coming over."

She turned and made her way through the yard, while I looked around wildly, wondering if Kit was still here. Was it possible she was behind the tree or the garage? What in the hell did she want? More importantly, why had I believed her?

A voice behind me gave me a start. "Everything okay?"

I spun around. "Yes. Valerie, hi. Just a neighbor of ours. Everything is fine. Can I get you another wine?"

I poured more chardonnay for Valerie, I helped Nick grill the vegetables, I invited everyone to sit. When the night grew dark around us, I lit the candles we'd set along the railing, and soon our deck was aglow with candlelight, our yard a dark carpet below us. It would have been so easy for someone to slip in that yard and watch us. I knew this. I was aware of it the whole time, and my eyes kept darting into the night, wondering.

"Everything is fine," I whispered to myself, wishing it were true.

"And back into downward-facing dog," the yoga instructor said. She made a loud exhale sound, encouraging us to do the same. A few people around me sighed with supposed yogic pleasure. I would have rolled my eyes, except that my head was already hanging upside down.

This class—ridiculously called Mommies-to-Be Yoga—entailed a good deal of uncomfortable moves and hanging-upside-down poses. The point, as far as I could tell, was to shake loose your fertility organs and hopefully make them more hospitable to visitors. It seemed silly that I would even be here, but Laurence Connelly's assistant had said she was sure this class—along with "yoga" with her husband—had gotten her pregnant. I figured since I wasn't pregnant yet, it couldn't hurt to try, and besides, wasn't yoga supposed to reduce stress? Maybe it could also shake loose the feeling that Kit was always following me, always waiting around the next corner.

But the fact was I'd heard nothing from Kit, and I reminded myself of this on the El train going home. Although Melanie had seen her in our yard, I hadn't actually seen or heard from Kit since that day she visited my office three weeks ago, when we had cabbed to the bank and I'd given her a money order for thirty thousand dollars. Maybe her promise had meant something.

And now it was a new season. Fall had arrived, and the leaves were beginning to paint themselves in shades of yellow. I walked the six blocks from the El train and smiled as I always did when I saw our house—a welcoming bungalow lit by old-fashioned streetlamps. I had a bottle of champagne in the fridge, and I planned to put it on ice while I waited for Nick to get home.

"Today could be the day," he'd said that morning. He was nervously tying his blue tie. "Partnership meeting."

I hugged him and wished him luck. The rest of the day, I waited for his phone call, which never arrived. I hoped this meant he wanted to officially give me the news tonight.

I slipped my key in the lock and stepped through the front door. I turned on the hallway light, and walked through the living room, turning on lamps along the way until there was a warm blush to the room. In the kitchen, I unearthed a silver bucket from under the center island and filled it with ice. I plunged the champagne inside.

I trotted up the stairs and into my bedroom. I threw my yoga bag on the bed. I stripped off my pants, T-shirt and my workout bra. A glance at my nightstand clock told me it was only six forty-five. Enough time for a quick shower.

I flicked on the bathroom light, and I screamed.

Kit. There was Kit, sitting on the toilet seat. She looked at me oddly, as if my shriek hadn't reached her ears.

"Jesus, Kit!" I yelled. "What are you doing?" My heart hammered. I clutched my chest, as if that would calm it.

Her eyes appraised my naked body. "You don't look pregnant."

I looked down at myself, then back at her. I grabbed a towel off a nearby rack and wrapped it around myself. "What in the hell are you doing here?"

She looked down at her lap, and it was then I noticed she was holding something. A pen, I thought. Then I saw it was pink, shorter. And that's when I recognized it. She was holding the pregnancy test I'd taken that morning—a stick I'd urinated on, which had boldly declared itself Negative.

"Yeah, these things must really work," Kit said, her voice soft. "No baby for you."

I took a breath. "How did you get in here?"

"You gave me keys when I house-sat last spring. Before we went to Rome, remember?"

I said nothing. A small part of me wanted to hug her, and say, *Honey, what's wrong with you? Why are you doing this?* But a larger, more logical part began to figure how long it would take to get down the stairs, grab a coat and put on shoes. I felt an intense desire to run from this woman whom I had once trusted with my house, my friendship.

"Not that it would be that hard to walk right in here," Kit continued. "Have you taken a look at your downstairs windows?" She made a derisive sound. "Anyone could jimmy those up and climb right in. You should do something about that."

"Thanks for the tip."

"Sure," Kit said, crossing her legs. She wore jeans and light blue sandals. She looked like a normal woman, an everyday person you might see on the street.

But she was fingering the pregnancy test, touching it all over as she looked at me.

"Kit, don't do that," I said, reaching for the pregnancy stick.

She yanked it back, as if it were a precious gem. "I'll do what I want." She looked at her watch, just like a normal person would. "Where's Nick?"

Nick! I thought. God, Nick would be home any minute.

"I'm not sure," I said, feigning nonchalance. Apparently not well enough.

Kit smirked. "Maybe I should just wait until he gets home. It would be interesting to know that the woman who's going to bear his children will fuck any Italian guy she comes across."

"We had a deal, Kit. You promised the thirty thousand would be the end of it."

"I'm not asking for money, am I?"

"So what do you want?"

She smiled and shrugged.

"Why are you doing this to me?"

"Oh, Rachel," Kit said, her voice low now, and eerie-calm. "You've done this all to yourself."

She stood, still holding the pregnancy test. It was tight in her fist now. She took a step toward me. I willed myself not to flinch. Not to run. Then she took another step. In those sandals, and with me in bare feet, she was several inches taller. She peered down at me with her violet eyes; she turned her head this way and that, like a scientist studying an interesting specimen. Her perfume was cloying—a pungent cinnamon smell.

"See you soon," she said. "Very soon."

She brushed past me, and I heard her footsteps on the wood stairs. The front door opened, then

shut, surrounding me in a pocket of terrible silence.
I sucked in air. I tried not to move, as if by staying
frozen I might soon wake up and find this had been
a dream, maybe a yoga-induced hallucination. Then
I shot into action. I dressed quickly and ran down
the stairs. I bolted the front door and pushed a chair
in front of it. I checked the windows. Kit was
right—some were so old and their locks painted
over so many times, they wouldn't lock properly. Or
if they did lock, the connection could be easily broken by jiggling them back and forth. I put tiny, glass
bud vases on the sills with the broken locks, hoping the vases would fall and the glass shatter if
someone tried to break in.

When Nick came home half an hour later, I was
sitting in the living room with the drapes drawn. I
mustered a beaming smile when he told me he'd
made partner. I hugged him and I poured champagne, just like I'd planned. And when he'd given
me all the details, I told him congratulations one
more time. Then I said, "Nick, let's go look at that
condo on Lake Shore."

He raised his eyebrows in delight. "You'd do
that? You'd think about moving?"

I looked around the living room. I took in the rest
of the house in my mind's eye. I thought of our

walk through the neighborhood, when we'd first stumbled upon this place. I thought about all the plans we'd made here and the future we'd imagined here. I told myself not to get sentimental. It was just a house. Our marriage—our *safety*—was more important.

"Yes," I said. "I would think about moving."

10

"The countertops are granite, of course," the real estate agent said. She ran her hand over the counter—soft black speckled with rusts and taupes. "It's called Sierra Pesca. It's very hard to come by."

Nick squeezed my hand. "It's great."

"Seems like there are a lot of upgrades in this place," I said. We'd already been awed by the living room with its fourteen-foot ceilings, restored parquet floors and intricate moldings, not to mention the wall of windows and balcony with astonishing views of Lake Michigan.

The agent, a tiny woman in a smart navy suit, turned toward us, her eyes open wide. "Oh, *everything* you see in this condo is top-of-the-line. The owners thought they'd stay here forever, but the wife got transferred to Scottsdale. I mean, look at these appliances." She made a grand gesture with her arm toward the refrigerators—one for catering, one for everyday use—the hundred-bottle wine fridge, the restaurant-style range.

"It would be nice to have everything so new," Nick commented.

I nodded. He was right. Our house on Bloomingdale had been built in 1923 and was forever in need of maintenance. No matter how we rehabbed, there was always the crumbling foundation to repair or the electrical wiring to update. And then there were the windows. The fact that they were old and didn't lock well had never really bothered me before, but it was now on my mind all the time.

"Come see the master bedroom," the agent said.

She led us down a parquet-floored hallway and swung open a heavy maple door.

"Oh, wow," Nick said.

We stepped inside, our heads swiveling. The room was huge—fourteen-foot ceilings again and more windows overlooking the lake—with a raised nook for a large bed on one side and an expansive sitting room on the other. The agent showed us a refrigerator, bar and coffeemaker hidden in the papered wall of the sitting room.

"We could read in here before bed," Nick said.

"And make coffee in the mornings," I said, excited despite myself.

We viewed the other bedrooms, the plethora of bathrooms, the butler's pantry.

"Any questions?" the agent said

I got a flash of Kit sitting in our house, clutching the pregnancy stick. "Can you tell us more about the security system?"

"Ah, I'm glad you asked." The agent led us to a wall in the foyer. She pushed a hidden latch and a small door popped open. "Here's your security center. The fact is you probably don't need it, since you've got a twenty-four-hour doorman downstairs, but this is fully loaded." She pushed a series of buttons, showing us how the alarm monitoring worked. I looked toward the living-room windows as she talked. They were plate glass and twenty-two floors up. No one was going to jimmy those windows.

Next we viewed the building's spa and fitness facilities, available exclusively to condo members. The place was laden with yellow marble. There were hot tubs, cold plunge pools, steam rooms and saunas. White, plush towels were stacked everywhere. The attendants outnumbered the spa's guests.

"We could get massages every week and work

out every day," Nick said, studying the gym's fitness schedule. "Look, there are yoga classes for you."

When we were on the street, we said goodbye to the agent and stood on the building's front sidewalk.

"What did you think?" Nick asked.

"It's fantastic." I didn't have to ask what he thought. I could see the excitement in his eyes, the look of having come upon the next big thing in his life. "But do we need all that? Four bedrooms? Five bathrooms? A gym?"

"It doesn't matter if we need it. We can afford it now that I've made partner."

"We need to save money, too." I'd been telling him I couldn't expect a big bonus this year, at least not at the rate I was going, and then there was the thirty-eight thousand to Kit, which he knew nothing about. But Nick wasn't worried. He was sure he could take care of us now.

"We can buy this place and still save," Nick said. "God, didn't you love that kitchen?"

I nodded. Of course I did. "But there's no lawn like at home."

"There's a balcony overlooking Lake Michigan."

"There's no real neighborhood."

"You're two blocks from the Mag Mile."

I studied his face. "You love it, don't you?"

He nodded. "Don't you?"

"I like it. I love the place we have now."

Nick took my hand. "I do, too, baby. But we're outgrowing it."

"I'm not sure."

"Let's give it a few days, all right? We can come back and see it again if we want. We'll think about it. Deal?" He didn't say what I knew he was thinking—this place would help him get an official spot on the board. I was growing quickly tired of all this board business, but I knew how important it was to Nick.

I thought how it was both great and horrible that this condo was so different from our Bloomingdale bungalow. Then I couldn't help but smile at the eager look in Nick's eyes. The freckles on his face seemed to stand out, now that he was losing his summer tan. Despite his overeagerness about the board, despite his faults, more than anything, *he* was home to me. "Deal," I said.

My mother called me on a Saturday morning, just as I'd come in from another yoga class where I'd spent much of the time in a backward bend, letting the blood flow to my head and, supposedly, my

ovaries. It was the first week of October, a time I
loved, and a time that was making me feel that I
could never leave our house on Bloomingdale
Avenue. It helped that there had been no word from
Kit for a while. But I knew my husband, and I knew
he was already in the Lake Shore Drive condo, already decorating rooms and having board members
over for drinks. I didn't know how to tell him I
wanted to stay. So when I saw my mother's name
on our caller ID, I snatched up the phone.

"Ray Ray," she said. "I miss you."

I sat down at the kitchen island. "God, Mom, I
miss you, too." I gazed outside. The willow tree
hung heavy. The others were dripping red leaves
onto the green lawn.

"Honey, I hear you might have some news."

"Like what?"

"Well, first off, I hear you might be moving."

I groaned. "Who did you hear that from?"

"Nick's mother."

"You talked to Nora?" Nick's mom was not
someone my own mother had ever warmed to.

"She called me out of the blue, wanting to talk
about you two. Of course, I didn't have much to offer.
You and I haven't spoken much lately, Rachel."

I was quiet. I hadn't talked to my mother lately

because she didn't want me to stay with Nick after he cheated. But I missed her.

"I was embarrassed when she called," my mother continued, "because I didn't know you had all this news."

"There's no news, Mom. We've looked at a condo, but we're only thinking about it. Well, Nick's thinking about it."

"Nick's mother mentioned something else as well."

"What's that?" But I could guess.

"She said you're trying to get—"

"Pregnant," I said, finishing her sentence for her. "Yes, that's right. But no luck yet."

"Honey," she said. Just that one word. "You'll be such a great mother."

My throat felt thick. I fought tears. "Do you think so?"

"I know so. You're kind and generous and loving. You have so much to give a child."

"Thanks, Mom." I kept gazing at our backyard. I'd always thought we'd put a swing under the willow tree when we had kids. I'd imagined family barbecues and a sandbox in the far corner.

"And just think," my mom said, "you can teach the kids how to paint."

I told her about the basement room Nick had made for me, and how I'd been too busy lately to paint. I decided right then I would spend the afternoon downstairs. Nick had an emergency surgery and wouldn't be home for another hour or two.

My mother and I talked for twenty more minutes. Then I fixed myself a sandwich, imagining myself with our kids in that kitchen—packing lunches, sending them off to school, having the neighborhood children for sleepovers. How could we leave this house? And what would it be like to raise kids in a high-rise condo building? I had to talk to Nick. I had to tell him I couldn't move.

I padded down the stairs to the basement, pleased with my decision, filled with anticipation of a few solitary hours in my room. But the minute I switched on the light, something felt wrong. We hadn't been down there in weeks, so the place was tidy, no Sunday papers scattered by the big chair, no paint rags or dirty brushes on my workspace. Yet it seemed as though someone had been here. Something was out of place.

Then I saw it. Roberto's painting.

It was hanging above my table again. It had been in the back of the closet since Nick and I had taken it down. I'd meant to throw it away, just as I put behind me that horrible mistake in Rome. But now there it was, the red paint of the woman's portrait looking like blood.

"Kit?" Her name hung in the air. I felt light-headed with fear. Had she put up the painting? Was she still here?

"What do you want?" I said. Was I talking to no one? Was I crazy? And why hadn't I changed the damned locks? But I knew it wouldn't have mattered. There were the windows. And even more, there was Kit, who possessed a fierce determination when she set her mind on something.

The red painting seemed to pulse from across the room. *Beware*, it seemed to say. *I'll never forget. You'll never be safe.*

"Kit!" I yelled. Again her name lingered.

Maybe she was in the closet. Maybe she was upstairs in my bedroom, waiting for me. I gulped for air, my breath too shallow.

I looked at the painting one last time, then bolted up the stairs. My eyes searched the kitchen—the pantry, the door to the hallway, the bathroom. Kit could be anywhere.

I grabbed my purse from the counter and ran out the front door, not even bothering to lock it. What did it matter? Kit would get in, anyway.

I ran down the street, which was dusted with fall leaves. I stopped when I came to the coffee shop. Inside, I ordered a "calming tea," praying it would work. My hands were shaking as I spooned honey into the tea. I burned my lip trying to sip it. I changed seats three times, until I felt secure in the rear of the shop, my back against the wall. Finally, I called Nick and left him a message to meet me when he was done at the office.

I sat there for an hour, watching the door, but mostly thinking about a day when Kit and I had lunch last year, shortly after she returned from L.A. I was happy to have her back, and I'd wanted to treat her, so I took her to Bistro 110, and we requested a window seat, where we could watch the shoppers streaming toward Michigan Avenue. We had a wonderful time, exchanging stories that had gotten lost from living so far apart. During our dessert, a tall woman with blond hair stopped outside the window to dig in her bag. She found her cell phone and answered a call, standing in front of us for a few minutes.

Seeing her, Kit launched into her guessing game at someone's background, their life. "She's over forty, even though she looks thirty," Kit said, studying the woman. "She's been married twice, but she's unhappy with the second marriage."

"How do you know that?" I said.

"Look at her ring. It's huge. That's not a first marriage ring. But she answered that phone too fast. It's a guy. Someone she's seeing on the side."

We watched the woman, and sure enough, the woman laughed and smiled a sexy smile. She covered her eyes for a moment, in a coy, embarrassed way.

"Maybe she's talking sexy to her husband," I offered.

Kit tsked. "No. It's a boyfriend. Rich, older, who she's hoping to make husband number three." Kit shook her head. "She doesn't deserve it."

"What?" I laughed and gave Kit a joking shove on the arm. "You can't say who deserves something and who doesn't."

She turned and looked at me, her face expressionless. "Why not? Don't you think *I* deserve to find a husband and have a great home and a ring like that on my finger?"

"Of course."

"Then you *do* believe that some people deserve their lives while others don't."

"No, I believe everyone deserves happiness."

Kit tsked again and shook her head. "Rachel, you can be so naive. Some people deserve to have it all taken away."

Now, alone at the coffee shop and waiting for Nick, I couldn't help wonder why Kit had decided that I didn't deserve my life anymore. What had I done to incur her wrath? I tried to be a good person, and I tried not to hurt anyone else along the way. I tried to be happy, and I tried to make my husband happy. Was there a sin in that somewhere, one that Kit felt the need to address? Or had she really lost it? Had the stress of her mother and her failed ambitions pushed her into some sort of psychosis? Or, even scarier, was it all of these things?

By the time Nick arrived an hour and a half later, I was still shaken. He waved when he saw me and crossed the room. "Hey, Golden Girl." He kissed me and slipped into a chair. "What's up?"

"I want to buy the Lake Shore condo," I said, without hesitation. "I want to move."

11

Over the next few weeks, I slid into a slump. That was true professionally, certainly, and something my boss, Laurence, reminded me of at least a few times a day.

"How're your numbers?" he'd ask. He'd lean his shoulder against my doorway and give me his patented I'm-disappointed-in-you face.

But no one was more disappointed in me than I was. And I didn't need Laurence lording it over me.

"You've got access to a company computer, don't you?" I said to him one day. "I think you know how my numbers are. So why ask me?"

He seemed ready to give one of his usual sarcastic answers, but he only gave me a small smile. "Seriously, Blakely, I want to see if you need help."

He sounded genuine, which made me feel worse. "I'm sorry. I'm just stressed about something personal."

This was true. Although Kit hadn't shown herself in the past few weeks I always felt her close. I
forever had the feeling of being chased, of being
watched. I tried to keep busy with the multitude of
tasks that went into closing on the sale of two homes
and getting ready to move. Since the owners of the
Lake Shore Drive condo had already moved to
Scottsdale, they were eager to sell fast. We went
through a quick bidding process, and the bankers
said we could close in two and a half weeks, at the
beginning of November. The fast timing was just
fine with me. There was entirely too much to do, yet
I didn't think I could linger in our house on Bloomingdale too long. It would only remind me what
we'd had there—worn, comfortable, wonderful
roots I thought we'd have for years to come.

So I cleaned and I organized and I sorted. I dis-
mantled our old life. I felt a sort of unraveling inside
me as the once stable parts of my life seemed to drift
away. Our house on Bloomingdale—gone. My parents—off leading their own lives. My job—teetering
on extinction. And Kit, or the Kit I used to know?
Gone.

It was the Kit part that bothered me the most.
How had we turned so sour? I thought about what
Kit had said that night I found her in my bath-

room—*Oh, Rachel. You've done this all to yourself.* Was she right? I wondered again what I had done to cause such rage and hatred in her. It couldn't have been just my night with Roberto. Was it simply that I'd led a life much easier than hers, at least up until now? Though that might have been true, I had always been aware that tragedy was only a breath away. My parents might become ill, Nick might be in a car accident, I might never get pregnant. Or worse. I had always known inherently there was the potential for much worse. And Kit's actions had made the "worse" seem to loom silently above me. As if waiting.

"Please be careful with that," I said to the movers.

"Got it, Mrs. Blakely. No problem. We're almost done here."

I watched as two burly men picked up our shelves with the stained glass doors. They moved through the house and down the front porch stairs, carrying the hutch easily. Almost too easily. In fact, the move was going too well. How was it possible that we could slip so seamlessly from our dream home without calamity? I kept expecting a disaster, maybe even a tornado or a swarm of locusts, some sign from the gods that we weren't meant to leave

Bloomingdale Avenue. Instead, it was a sunny fall day, the movers had shown up on time, and our house was speedily being drained of all traces of Rachel and Nick Blakely. Nick had been pleased, of course, not morose and increasingly depressed like me. So when he got a request from the hospital to assist an emergency replantation surgery, I told him to go. Now it was just me, the movers and the empty shell of our home.

I went from room to room, checking that the movers had taken the correct items and left the few pieces of old furniture and other discarded bits, which would be picked up later today by a refuse service.

In our empty bedroom upstairs, I stood for a full five minutes, thinking of the joyful night we'd moved in, only a month before our wedding. I let myself remember the awful times we'd had in that room, too—when we reconciled after Nick's affair and I found lying next to him agonizing. I thought of the past few months, how I'd slept in that room with guilt, but with a man I loved, a man I was trying to have a baby with.

I went next to the guest room, then downstairs to the living room, the kitchen. I looked out on the lawn, now covered with brown leaves. I sighed and crossed my arms. There would be children on that lawn some day, but not ours.

Saving the hardest for last, I opened the basement door. I stood on the landing, not wanting to see the room—the special room Nick had created for me—forlorn and nearly empty. I knew it would be just a basement now, a basement with papered walls and a straw mat floor. I felt a catch in my throat. *Do not cry,* I told myself. *It's just a room.*

But it wasn't just a room, and I would never be convinced it was. It was a refuge, a symbol of devotion, a safe haven.

Slowly, one drawn-out step at a time, I descended the stairs. I would only stay a minute, I decided. I would take in the room, I would remember the time we'd spent there, I would say goodbye and then I'd be done.

When I reached the bottom of the stairs, I took a breath and reached toward the light switch. At the same time, I heard a soft voice say, "Hello, Rachel."

One of my hands flew to my neck, as if protecting myself. My breath stopped. I forced my other hand to move. I flicked the switch, flooding the basement with warm light.

Kit was sitting in the middle of the floor, legs

crossed. Her violet eyes blinked, trying to adjust to the light. She'd been here in the dark for how long?

I opened my mouth; it was dry, as if coated with sand. I couldn't find words. My heart hammered.

Without taking her eyes off me, Kit reached behind her and lifted something blood red. Roberto's painting. I'd put it in a box and left it for the refuse service. But here was Kit, displaying it for me, in both hands now.

"Aren't you forgetting something?" she said.

I ran up the stairs, past the puzzled-looking movers, and sprinted from the house. I stopped three blocks away, doubled over and panting. I paced the neighborhood, looking over my shoulder, expecting her behind me at any minute.

When I went back to the house an hour later, I asked the movers if they'd seen a woman with red hair. Neither had. I asked one of the men to go through the house with me. There was no sign of her. It was as if Kit had slipped in like a ghost and evaporated just as seamlessly. And taken the painting with her.

That image of her sitting cross-legged in my basement tarnished the house on Bloomingdale

Avenue. I now couldn't think of the place without seeing her there.

But seeing Kit that day also allowed me to lock the door that last time without tears, without remorse. It allowed me to embrace the condo on Lake Shore Drive in a way I hadn't been able to before.

Nick and I painted the walls of our new living room a light, soothing gray, wanting nothing to detract from the view of Lake Michigan—sometimes calm and blue like the Caribbean Sea, other days frothy and white capped. We got a huge, new four-poster bed for our master bedroom, along with a chaise longue and round glass table for the sitting area. The kitchen already boasted stainless-steel appliances, but we filled the rest of the room with the vases and dishes we'd collected over our years together.

The condo became a stylish urban apartment, just as Nick had wanted. As soon as the dining-room table and chairs we'd ordered arrived, he planned to have a large dinner party with ten board members. I'd told him, half jokingly, that we should have an "LSD Party," because of the way some people called Lake Shore Drive "LSD." People could dress up in freaky costumes and we'd play Jimmy Hendrix tunes. Nick gave me a confused look and said that he was thinking of an invite that said something like, "Join us in our embrace of Lake Michigan…" We would place the table in front of the windows, set it with blue cloths and have Lake Michigan whitefish.

But the board was Nick's domain, so I shrugged and gave up the image of myself in crystalline Elton John glasses and platform shoes.

I didn't love our new place the way Nick did, but I had to admit, I liked it. I especially liked the security system. I enjoyed the *beep beep beep* that sounded whenever someone came in the door. I liked the feel of the touch pads under my fingers as I typed the code to arm our system. I loved the sense of safety the alarm gave me at night, knowing that if someone somehow unlocked our door and came into our apartment while that alarm was armed, a series of short tones would sound, and if the correct code wasn't entered in exactly forty-five seconds, the system would erupt into piercing screams that would draw the doorman and neighbors and eventually the police.

We got a new phone number, and I made sure it was unlisted. I didn't send out new-address cards, even though that made my socially graceful mother cluck her tongue in disgust. I told her I was too busy with work and with the move. I couldn't tell her about Kit. I couldn't tell anyone.

I took the remaining money out of my once-healthy savings account and closed it. I put the money in my joint account with Nick. It was something I could contribute to the one thing that made me happy these days—my marriage.

I was still looking over my shoulder—Kit had made sure of that—but I started breathing normally again. Within the safe confines of our apartment, I didn't go to bed scared anymore.

Beep beep beep, the alarm sounded. "Honey, I'm home!" Nick called in a kidding way as he opened the door.

"Hi, babe."

I heard his keys clatter on the front-hall table, and the sound of his footsteps down the hall and into the kitchen.

"How did it go today?" I asked. Nick had handled a complicated hemangioma surgery and been nervous about it all week.

He opened the fridge and pulled out a beer. "You know what? It wasn't bad. A few anesthesia problems—we had to keep the patient under a lot longer than expected—but we got it done." He kissed me. "How about you?"

I groaned.

"Another bad day in the world of architectural sales?"

"Bad doesn't cover it."

"Thompson & Sons come around?"

"Nope."

"Any hope?"

"Doesn't seem like it. And Laurence is forever letting me know how bad I'm failing."

"What an asshole." Nick shook his head. "Are we ordering sushi, by the way?"

"Already done." Since we'd moved to the condo, we seemed to cook very little. We either went to a function or out to dinner with board members, or we ordered in.

I eyed Nick's beer. I wanted a glass of wine desperately after my day, but since I was trying so hard to get pregnant…

Nick saw me staring, and looked down at his beer. "Want me to put it away? I don't have to have one. Not if you can't."

"No, it's okay."

"Any news on that front?" He put the beer on the

counter and slid his arm around me, rubbing my belly as he did so.

I shook my head. "I think we need to buy stock in the companies that make ovulation and pregnancy tests. I'm going through those things like crazy." I laughed a little. "Maybe that's why I'm doing so poorly at work."

"Maybe you should just quit."

I pulled away and gave him a sharp look. "What?"

"Only if you want to, but hey, now that I'm a partner, we can afford it."

"Nick, you're making a great salary, but we've got a brand-new home with a brand-new mortgage. A *big* brand-new mortgage." *And I had to give Kit $38,000 so she wouldn't ruin us.*

"But when we have kids…"

I kissed the tip of his nose. "Let's get me pregnant first, and then we'll decide if I should leave work."

"Let's try and get you pregnant right now," Nick said, his voice lowering.

I smiled. I slowly leaned into him, and kissed him, this time full on the mouth. Nick's cell phone rang.

He took it out of his pocket. "Shit, it's Bill." Dr.

Bill Adler was the head of Nick's practice group. "Sorry, hon, but I'd better talk to him. And I've got to dictate my surgical report. Can I take a rain check?"

"Of course. I'll let you know when the sushi is here."

Nick mouthed his thanks as he answered the phone. He picked up his jacket and went down the hallway to one of the guest bedrooms we'd made into a study, closing the door.

I gazed at Nick's beer on the counter, then stuck it in the fridge. I thought about trying another ovulation stick, but it was just a waste of money. I either was ovulating or I wasn't, and ultimately that knowledge hadn't mattered, anyway. I simply wasn't getting pregnant.

I got out the plates for the sushi. I poured water for myself. I called Valerie Renworth and left her a message, asking if she wanted to have lunch the next day, something we'd been doing regularly. Although Valerie was almost ten years older than me and different from me in many ways—she'd had her children already, and she hadn't worked in years— she was a friend, in a time I really needed one.

A few minutes later, while I was in the bathroom, the phone rang. "Valerie," I said to myself. I washed my hands and ran to the phone, but it had already gone silent. I looked at the caller ID. It was an unfamiliar cell phone number with a 312 area code. Probably Valerie's. I dialed it.

I heard the phone being answered, but then there was silence.

"Hello?" I said.

"Well, hello, Rachel."

My whole body went cold. "Kit."

"Thanks for calling me back."

"I didn't recognize the number."

"I got a new cell phone. My other one wasn't working very well." She said this snidely. "My friends couldn't seem to get through."

"I thought I was calling someone else."

"Why do you have to be like that?"

I looked over my shoulder. The door to the study was still closed. "Kit, leave us alone," I said fiercely. "Just stay away from us."

"Us, us, us," she said tauntingly. "Aren't you lucky to be part of an us?"

"Yes, I am," I said. "I know I'm lucky. I don't need you reminding me, and I don't need you as a friend any longer. So just stay the hell away."

I raised my arm and crashed the phone back on the cradle. When I took my hand away, it was shaking. I checked the study door once more. Still closed. One glass of wine wouldn't hurt, I decided. I sat on a stool in the kitchen, slowly sipping a glass of sauvignon blanc, and within twenty minutes, I felt calmer, more contained, as if the phone call had been cathartic.

I was walking down the hallway, thinking about the cozy pair of pajamas that were waiting in our new walk-in, cedar-shelved closet, when the phone rang. I froze, but when I reached the phone I saw it was the doorman downstairs.

"This is Hector," he said. "Did you order sushi?"

"Yes, send him up, please."

"Nick!" I yelled at the closed door of the study. "Sushi's here."

When a knock came at the front door, I opened it and paid the delivery guy.

"Thanks," he said, pocketing the tip. He turned and left.

Before I could close the door, someone appeared from around the corner.

I gasped. Kit.

With fluid speed, she moved forward and shoved me hard, making me drop the bag. She stepped inside and slammed the door closed with such force it sounded like a gunshot. I wrapped my arms around my chest instinctively.

She pushed past me and strode into the apartment, looking this way and that. She wore a black pencil skirt, high boots, and a short charcoal jacket. She struck a pose in the living room. One leg jutted out, one hand on her hip. She wore an angry expression on the face I once thought so lovely.

"Miss me?" she said.

12

"What are you doing here?"

She huffed. "Did you think I could just leave our conversation like that?" she scoffed and shook her head. "More importantly, Rachel, did you think I wouldn't find you? Did you think you could just move up and on in the world, into this fancy new high-rise and leave me behind?"

I tried to stay calm. "I think you did the leaving, Kit. You left our friendship *way* behind."

"Oh, it was me? You didn't leave me alone after you got married and wanted to hang out with all your couple friends?"

"No, I didn't," I said quietly. I wanted to scream at her, but more than anything I wanted her gone. And before Nick came out of the study. I shot a look down the hallway.

Kit caught it. Her expression shifted from anger to amusement. "Is Nicky boy home?"

I pursed my mouth. "Kit, get out, and leave me alone."

Her smile was cold. "I need more money."

"What? I gave you *thirty thousand*, and that was on top of what I'd already given you before. You said that would be it."

"It's really not open to discussion, Golden Girl. I need twenty grand."

I half laughed in astonishment. "You're absurd. For one thing, I don't have it."

She looked around. "Nice place. I'd say you can afford it."

I heard a door creak and Nick's footsteps down the hallway. "Hey, Kit," he said. "Didn't hear you come in."

That cold smile graced her face again. "Hello, Nick. It's been a long time."

"Yeah. How are you?"

"Nick," I said, nearly jumping between the two of them, "could you give us a sec? Kit and I have to talk about something." I grabbed her arm, led her through the living room and out onto the balcony, shutting the door tightly behind me. It was chilly but clear outside.

"Great view," Kit said. Across the lake, lights from a distant town twinkled. Twenty-two floors below us, cars streaked along Lake Shore Drive.

"Kit, like I told you on the phone, this is done. *We're* done. I want you to go away and stay away." I stopped myself from saying *please*.

"Maybe you weren't listening. Twenty grand."

"You drained my savings, Kit."

"Bullshit."

"It's true, and I closed the account. I don't have any money I can take out without telling Nick."

"Well, maybe we need to tell Nick, then."

"Jesus, Kit, haven't you done enough? Isn't it enough that you killed our friendship? That you've ruined my trust? That you've stolen money that took me years to earn?" I trailed off. Why was I even asking such questions? She was insane, and there were no answers.

"Aren't we high-and-mighty?" Kit leaned in, mere inches from my face. "How convenient that you can go off and sleep with whoever you want and then come home and expect to have the perfect little relationship and the perfect little life."

"I messed up, Kit!" I was yelling now.

"Well, Rachel, sometimes when people mess up, they mess things up for everyone around them."

"And you're saying I did that?"

She shrugged. She opened her mouth as if to say more, then shook her head.

"Kit, I know I screwed up, and I'm trying to make it up to Nick—"

"Oh, so you've told him?" she snarled.

"That's none of your goddamn business!"

She smiled. "Twenty grand, Rachel."

"Nothing!" I said, spitting out the word. I leaned in even closer. "I will never give you anything again."

I heard the scrape of the door behind me, then Nick's voice. "Everything okay out here?"

Kit looked at Nick, then back at me. She crossed her arms, her expression defiant.

I frantically wondered what to do. I opened my mouth, but nothing came out. Then I made my decision. I would tell him. Now, and in front of goddamned Kit if I had to. It would ruin our marriage. It would be the nail in the coffin, but it would be my nail.

I took a breath, and in that one instant, Kit's words rang out. "She cheated on you, Nick. She fucked some guy while we were in Rome."

I cringed, despite myself, then I made myself look at my husband. His eyes narrowed and blinked rapidly. "What?" he said.

"Kit, shut up!" I yelled.

"What do you think about that, Nick?" Kit said, also yelling. "How does that make you feel?"

"Shut up, shut up!" I was desperate to stop her now.

I turned to Nick, and took another breath. "Nick—"

But he cut me off. "Is this true?"

I nodded. "I'm so sorry. I only did it because…well, I guess I was trying to get back at you. I was calling you and calling you from Rome, and you weren't answering. I thought you were with someone else. And then when I came back to Chicago, we were doing so good. I didn't think I could tell you."

"Rachel," Nick said, his voice sad but calm.

"But Kit knew," I said, rushing in, frantic to tell him the rest of the story, the whole horrible story. "And she threatened to tell you. So I started giving her some money."

Nick's mouth dropped open slightly. He stared at me as if in shock. His gaze turned to Kit and then back to me again.

I kept talking. I had to explain it all. "So, I gave her some money a few times. A lot of money actually." I felt on the verge of tears now that it was all bursting out into this cool fall night. "And God, I'm so sorry about all this Nick. But now my *friend* here wants more money, and I told her I won't give it to her, and…and…I was going to tell you."

Nick's face shifted from shock into some kind of understanding and then into pure fury.

"You've been blackmailing her?" he screamed at Kit. "You're blackmailing my wife?"

His voice was so loud, so forceful, that I instinctively looked at the other balconies to see if anyone else was out there. To my right and one floor down, I could see a guy standing with a beer in his hands, staring out at the lake. Could he hear us? Did it matter? It was all coming out now.

I glanced back at Nick and saw him moving closer to Kit. "You're blackmailing *her?* Are you fucking kidding me?"

Kit's expression was taunting. "That's right, Nick. She screwed around on you. Feel good?"

"I can't believe you."

"Yeah, I bet. Don't you wish she'd told you? Or maybe you wish she'd kept giving me money so you could both keep your heads in the sand."

"You bitch!" Nick shouted, real hatred in his voice. He took a step closer to her. "You fucking bitch!" He reached out and grabbed Kit around the neck. She opened her mouth as if she meant to laugh at him, but then Nick squeezed. Her expression became startled, her eyes wide and unblinking.

"Nick, don't!" I cried.

He seemed not to hear me.

Kit fought back, shoving him and kneeing him in the groin. Nick bent over for an instant, losing his grip on Kit's neck. Then he charged, his hands on her shoulders moving them both across the balcony in one ultra-fast, blurry moment until Kit was backed against the railing.

"Nick, stop it!" I tried to grab him, but he seemed not to hear me.

He roared in anguish, and with one more massive shove, Kit was lifted off her feet. Her feet were dangling, kicking. Her face was contorted in panic and shock.

And in the next instant, Kit was gone, over the balcony, and all I saw were those distant lights, that faraway town.

There was a moment of silence when Nick and I were alone on that balcony. No cry from Kit. Nothing at all except silence. Then reality rushed in, and there was screaming, screaming in my head.

I must have been screaming out loud, as well, because Nick began shaking my shoulders. My head rocked back and forth. I couldn't seem to hold it up. I saw Nick saying something to me, but I couldn't hear his words.

"What?" I said. It was silent again for one long moment, and Nick and I stared at each other, both of us mute. Then came the sound of a siren, not an unusual sound in the city, but then there was another and another, and there was no doubt they were coming closer.

I started for the railing.

"No, don't," Nick said.

Did he think I was going to jump? "I have to see," I said.

"No." His voice was forceful. He turned me and held me by the shoulders again, this time gently. "Rachel, listen. We have to tell the same story."

"Story?" What was he talking about?

I looked at the railing. Kit, poor Kit.

"We have to say the same thing," Nick said. "Do you understand me? We have to tell the police what happened, and we need to say the same thing, or it's going to look bad."

I coughed. "Look bad?" I repeated stupidly. Was that all he cared about? How things appeared to others? "Nick, why did you push her?"

"I did not push her." He enunciated each of these

words distinctly. "Listen to me, Rachel. You saw it. She came after me. She attacked me. She pushed me. She kneed me in the groin. And then I had to do something. I was only defending myself. You saw that, right?"

"You had your hands around her neck."

"No, that was only after she attacked me. Remember?"

I shook my head. I didn't think that was how it happened, but I couldn't be sure. His struggle with Kit now seemed like a dream, moments I'd remembered clearly upon waking but ones that were quickly losing their sharp edges.

"Oh, my God, Kit," I said, moaning. I covered my mouth. I felt intensely nauseous.

The sirens grew louder.

"Why were you so angry, Nick?"

His face went hard, but only for a second. "I just found out that my wife slept with someone else."

I felt bile rise in my throat. I swallowed against it. "I'm sorry. I'm so sorry. But…I've never seen you like that."

Nick took my hand away from my mouth and cupped my face. It seemed for a second as if he might kiss me. "Rachel, listen to me. Kit hasn't been acting like herself for a while. You've said that yourself. She came over, and she started getting on you for having stayed with me after my affair."

"It was *my* affair," I said.

He shook his head. "Does anyone else know about Rome?"

"No. But, Nick, we have to call the police."

"We will. Just one second." He took a breath. "Look, don't tell anyone about what happened in Rome."

"Why?"

"It will look like you were mad at Kit because she knew about Rome and because she was blackmailing you. It will make you look guilty."

But you're the one...

"Listen," Nick continued, "just say Kit was mad on your behalf because of *my* affair. She's always been protective of you. She thought you should leave me, and she was taking you to task about it."

I thought of how Kit had been the one person who'd understood when I forgave Nick. It wasn't the other way around. Still, I felt relieved that Nick was taking charge like this. And I wanted no one else to know about Rome.

I nodded.

"I heard you two fighting, and I told Kit to mind her own business," he continued. "We argued about it, and it got heated. Kit has been acting crazy lately with her mom dying, and suddenly, as we were arguing, she attacked me. She came at me, trying to hit me. Then kneed me in the balls. Are you getting this, Rachel?"

I nodded again.

"After she kneed me, I fought back to protect myself. I shoved her too hard, and she went over the railing. That's how it happened. She charged at me. I was defending myself."

The sirens were shrill. We both looked up Lake Shore Drive and saw three police vehicles heading south toward us.

My head swirled with a thousand thoughts— *Kit's gone; Nick knows about Rome; he pushed her; no, he pushed her after she attacked him; Kit is gone; oh, my God.*

"Let's go talk to the police," Nick said. He took my hand and led me toward the front door. With his free hand, he picked up his apartment keys and pocketed them. He led me into the hallway. We walked to the elevator in silence. We said nothing during the ride. I could hear my heartbeat. My whole body pulsed. Nick squeezed my hand, and I gripped back. I kept seeing Kit in front of me, then disappearing over the balcony railing. The doors opened, and the sound of sirens pierced the lobby.

Kit's red hair was fanned out on the sidewalk, her red lips open in an O, her violet eyes still open as well. A red pool lay behind her head, growing larger as we watched.

I began to shake, then sob. "Kit," I said. I took a step toward her, but a policeman grabbed me by the arm.

"Miss," he said, "please don't go near the body."

"We're her friends," Nick said. "She fell from our balcony."

The cop, a short Hispanic guy, looked at Nick and me. "This way please."

He led us a few steps away to a cop car with its blue lights swirling. He got on the radio and said a few words. He opened the back door and motioned us inside. "Wait here. A detective from Violent Crimes will be here in five minutes."

My heart was beating so thunderously I wasn't sure I heard him right. "Crimes?" I said.

13

"So Ms. Kernaghan didn't call before she came over?" the detective asked. His name was John Bacco, and although he was a homicide detective he was surprisingly young, with short, shiny brown hair and bright brown eyes. His navy-blue suit looked as if he'd purchased it yesterday, yet he had a worldly, unhurried air about him that spoke of experience.

"No, I told you that already." I looked around, sure that at any minute this white room, and the long, hard bench on which I sat, would disappear. Some reality vortex would swirl in and I'd learn that none of this existed; this night hadn't happened; Kit hadn't come over; I hadn't screamed at her; she and Nick hadn't fought; she'd never fallen over our balcony.

The problem was a small but ever-growing voice

in my head that told me my reality had changed forever.

The detective sat on a similarly uncomfortable looking wood chair across from me. He moved it closer. There was nothing between us. No table, nothing. It seemed intimate somehow, overly personal. Yet the setting was, in a way, my own fault. Detective Bacco had tried questioning Nick and me in our apartment, but I couldn't bear it. There were people crawling all over, radios squawking, and I couldn't stop staring at the balcony.

"Can't we do this somewhere else?" I'd said, watching a policeman take measurements on the balcony. I heard the edge of hysteria in my voice.

Detective Bacco shrugged. "You can come to the station."

"Fine," I said, standing, "let's go."

"I'll have a squad car meet you downstairs."

"No," said Nick in a forceful tone. "No way. We'll drive."

And now here I was, in this bleak room, afraid to leave because it might make Nick and I look guilty.

"Do you know how Ms. Kernaghan got by the doorman?" the detective said.

"I'm not sure. Did you ask him?"

Detective Bacco gave me a kind smile. "I can't tell you that."

"What *can* you tell me? How long have I been here?" I glanced around the room. No clock. I looked at his wrist. He wore no watch, nor did I, since I'd taken mine off when I'd gotten home from work that night. How long ago that seemed. I couldn't remember if it had been an hour or a day since Kit fell. There was no natural light in this room, nothing to tell about the outside world.

"I'm not sure," the detective answered. "Just a few more questions."

"You said that before, and I've told you everything I remember." *Everything except how furious Nick was. How he charged at her first. How his hands were around her neck.* But now I doubted my own memory. Maybe it *had* happened like Nick had said. Kit had charged at *him*. He was only protecting himself.

The detective studied me, then looked down at the notes in his hand.

"Where is my husband?" I said.

"He's being questioned down the hall."

"Is he all right?"

"Is there any reason he wouldn't be?"

I blinked. I shook my head. "Why are we being

questioned at all? My friend just died in a horrible accident." I went quiet. Saying it out loud had made me see Kit again on the sidewalk, the pool of blood behind her. Confusion rushed in. I dropped my head in my hands.

"Give me a minute," Detective Bacco said. He stood and left.

The white room closed around me, stifling me. I stood and paced, but it only made me aware of how trapped I was. *Leave,* I thought, *just leave.* But was I allowed to? Was the door locked? No, he'd said I was only being questioned. *So get the hell out.* But wouldn't that make it seem like I had something to hide? Would I look guilty? But guilty of what? Kit had fallen. It was an accident. It *was.*

The detective came back in. "Here's the thing," he said, taking his seat.

I stayed standing.

"Your husband is saying something a little different from what you are."

"What?" The word came out loud. Harsh.

He gave me a sympathetic look. "Take a seat, Mrs. Blakely."

I did.

"The way he's describing the incident," the detective continued, "just doesn't match up with your description."

I heard Nick's words on our balcony. *We have to stick together, Rachel. Listen to me. It was an accident. She charged at me.*

"Well, what...what's he saying?"

"Maybe we should just go over it all again, because I have a few more questions."

I felt hot along my scalp. I felt an intense desire to wash my hair, wash my face. To be gone from here. There was nothing to feel guilty about, was there? So why did I feel so culpable?

I nodded at him. "Okay."

"Let's start at the beginning. You were in your condo. Now, Mrs. Blakely, what's the usual protocol with the doorman at your building? I mean, when someone comes to visit you."

"I told you, they call upstairs."

Detective Bacco nodded. He perused his notes for a moment. He was in no hurry, and his patience unnerved me. "Mrs. Blakely, why were you on your balcony on a cold night?"

"I told you earlier. Why are we going over old material?"

"This isn't 'old.' We talked earlier about the fact that you were on the balcony. We all know you were all on the balcony. Now I'm asking *why*. Especially when it was cold tonight."

I felt a grip of nervousness. Nick and I hadn't talked about this part. Was there something I was supposed to say? *Tell the truth.*

"Kit and I were arguing," I said. "I didn't want Nick to hear."

"You were arguing about his affair?"

I was thankful that the detective had provided me with an answer, even if it wasn't the right one. *Don't tell anyone about what happened in Rome.* I nodded in assent.

"Why would your girlfriend be arguing about your husband's affair?" he asked. "Isn't that *your* job?"

God, what to say? The truth was that Kit had been supportive of my need to forgive Nick and move on with my life. I tried to think of some way I could tell the truth without messing up the story. "Kit was always protective of me," I said finally.

"So you two were quarreling about your husband?"

I nodded. It was a true statement.

"And you didn't want him to hear, so you took her outside on the balcony?" the detective asked.

"Right."

"Why did your husband come outside?"

"I guess he could see that we were arguing. He wanted to know if we were okay."

"What I don't understand is how it got so heated that she attacked him."

"We were arguing, and Nick was getting defensive, and it just got louder and more intense."

Detective Bacco seemed to think for a second. "It's odd that Ms. Kernaghan would attack your husband over something that was really none of her business."

I said nothing.

"Mrs. Blakely, why would your friend get so upset about your husband's affair?"

I remembered what Nick had said. "Kit has been a little off lately." Again, this was the truth, and I warmed to it. "Her mother is very sick," I continued, "and she hasn't been herself lately, not at all."

"What do you mean by that?"

"She's been under a lot of stress by moving back to Chicago and taking care of her mom. And she's just been acting strange. I don't know exactly how to describe it." *She blackmailed me. She broke into my house. She sat in a dark basement and waited for me.* "She's been doing and saying odd things, and getting very upset lately. Tonight was no exception."

Suddenly I thought of Kit's mom, and felt the urge to weep for the woman. Nearing death, and now her daughter had preceded her. "Does Mrs. Kernaghan know about Kit?"

"We dispatched someone to her house a few hours ago, so I'd say she does."

The door opened behind me. I turned to see a man with trim gray hair, wearing khakis and a blue shirt rolled up at the sleeves. "Mrs. Blakely?" the man said. "Rachel Blakely?"

I nodded.

"I'm Tom Severson. I've been retained by your husband to represent you both."

Detective Bacco seemed slightly deflated by the sight of Tom Severson. The two men shook hands.

"How are you, John?" Severson said. "Haven't seen you in a while."

"Yeah," Detective Bacco said, "that Muller case."

"Let me talk to my client outside, all right?"

Bacco shrugged, as if to say it wasn't all right but he couldn't stop us.

Tom Severson led me down the hallway to a quiet corner.

"Thank you so much for being here," I said.

"No, problem. It's my job. I'm a criminal defense lawyer."

I flinched at the implication that I was a criminal who needed defending. "How do you know my husband?"

"I don't actually. He called Joanne Weatherby, who called me."

I tried to process this. My husband had turned to Joanne Weatherby, the president of the board, in a time of crisis? Well, maybe he'd been right to do so. Tom Severson looked unruffled by the fact that a homicide detective was questioning his new client.

"Where's my husband now?" I asked.

"He's just down the hallway."

"Can I see him?"

"Yes, you can. You're not being charged with anything so far. I'm pulling you both out of here."

"But the detective said he had more questions."

Tom Severson shook his head. "You don't have to answer anything if you haven't been charged or arrested."

"But I don't want to be charged. I want to cooperate."

"Trust me. There's no cooperating with these guys. Just tell me what you've told them so far."

I explained to Tom what had happened on the

balcony, giving the same story Nick had asked me to, although I couldn't help thinking, *Is this the same version Nick told? Did he ask me to give one story and then tell another himself?* I was relieved when Tom Severson seemed to think that mine was a perfectly reasonable rendition of the events. And maybe it was. Maybe that *was* how it happened. Lastly, I told him exactly how I'd been questioned by Detective Bacco and how I'd answered.

We walked back to the interrogation room.

"Detective," Tom said, "it's late. Unless you're bringing a state's attorney in to charge her, I'm taking my client out for now."

Detective Bacco looked at Tom, as if trying to make a decision. Finally he nodded. He turned his gaze to me. He seemed to be peering into my mind, sifting through the contents for real truths. I felt a growing panic, as if he might be successful. I tried to scramble my thoughts, though I knew this was ridiculous. I put a look on my face I hoped was pleasant.

"Mrs. Blakely, you're free to go for now, but I'd like to question you again."

"Why?" Tom said.

"This investigation is still open." The detective's gaze never left mine. "Wide-open."

* * *

The lights were still on in the apartment, as if there'd been a party and everyone had just left a moment before. Nick's keys clattered on the hall table, just like they had earlier that night. But everything was different. I stood there, looking into the living room and toward the balcony. Our apartment no longer seemed a stylish, urban place, but more an empty hull where something dreadful had happened. Instinctively, I craved our house on Bloomingdale Avenue, but I quickly realized that was tainted, as well. I thought about the time before Rome, and decided I would gladly go back to the moment I found out about Nick's affair, because although there was pain and uncertainty, we still had everything then. We just didn't know it.

Nick came behind me and put his hands on my shoulders.

I turned around. His normally expressive eyes looked exhausted, almost dead. "Nick, I am so sorry."

He shook his head.

"Nick, about Rome—"

"I don't want to hear about it."

"Why?"

"It doesn't matter." His voice was lifeless.

"Of course it matters. Everything happened because of what I did." I buried my head in his chest. "Nick, I have to tell you it was only one night."

"Please. I don't want to hear about it."

"Why? Don't you care?"

"Of course I care." Nick lifted my head up with his hands. They felt large on my cheeks, like they were shielding me. "Rachel, I love you." He said those last few words fervently, and I nearly wept with relief. I realized I had been waiting for them since Kit blurted out my sins.

"But," Nick continued, "I deserved it."

"That's not true. You made up for what you did in Napa. You told me you were with someone else. And I wanted to do the same, but... I don't know. I guess I wasn't sure we could handle it."

Nick gave me a sad smile. He shrugged.

"Do you think we can handle *this*?" I asked.

The silence was devastating.

Nick squeezed me tight. "We can do this, Rach. We're a team."

"So if we're a team, we have to tell the same story. Like you said tonight, right?"

He peered down at me. "Of course. Didn't you tell them what happened? The way we went over it?"

I nodded. I bit my lip. "But the detective told me

that you were saying something different than I was."

"What?" Nick exploded. "What was different?"

I shook my head. "He wouldn't say. But I told the exact story, just like you told me."

"You told the truth, then."

I said nothing.

Nick took a breath and pulled me back into a hug. "I told the truth, too. That detective is full of shit. And we'll get through this. We'll show them that we're strong. We'll show everyone that nothing—" he seemed to be struggling for the right phrase "—nothing bad happened here."

I nodded into his chest, but something in his words caught me. "Who's everyone, Nick?"

"Well, you know my partners…"

I took a step back. "Nick, why did you call Joanne Weatherby from the police station? I mean, if you're concerned about what people would think, she's probably the last person to tell you're getting questioned for murder."

That word *murder* shocked both of us. I saw anger flash across Nick's features.

"I'm sorry," I said, "but you know what I'm saying. Why bring Joanne into this?"

He breathed out hard. "Because she'd find out,

anyway, and I knew it'd be best if she heard the version I told her."

Like the version you asked me to tell the police, I thought.

"But more importantly," Nick continued, "she's connected. I knew she'd hook us up with the best attorney in the city, even if it was only so that she could tell everyone the story of how I called her."

So many stories, I thought.

Nick cocked his head slightly. "Does anyone know about the money you gave Kit?"

I dropped my eyes. "No."

"Good. We can't tell anyone about that. It would look terrible."

"What do you mean?"

"It would give you a motive for wanting to kill her."

But I didn't! I thought. *You...* But my mind was distorted with confusions. This was unreal.

Nick put his head in his hands and sighed heavily. I'd never seen him look more tired, even during his residency all-nighters.

"I'm sorry," I said, thinking a litany of if-onlys. If only I hadn't gone to Rome. If only I hadn't taken that phone call from Roberto. If only I'd been able to stop myself.

"This is not your fault," Nick said, raising his head.

"But—"

"What happened on the balcony—" He stopped abruptly. We looked at each other. I knew we were both reliving it. Kit's angry words, Nick's hands on her neck. But the exact sequence was getting more and more blurred. I could only remember clearly the story I'd been telling all night.

"It's not your fault," Nick said. "It was Kit's. This is Kit's fault."

I gave a small, unsure nod. What he was saying didn't seem quite right, but this night was so bewildering, and so terrible.

"Don't blame yourself anymore, okay?"

I nodded.

He gave me the saddest smile and pulled me to him once more.

Minutes later, I stripped my sweater off over my head and washed my face the way I did every night, knowing sleep would never come. I thought of how I'd always known that tragedy was in my future. Very few people, it seemed to me, were spared some unspeakable awfulness in their lives. I had just been waiting in the queue for mine. When Nick cheated it was certainly a blow, but it wasn't tragic. But tragedy was here now.

And somehow I knew it was going to get worse.

14

I heard Nick showering the next morning. He had a surgery that couldn't be rescheduled. I heard him sigh as he searched for a tie to wear. I could have gotten up and hugged him. I could have made him a cup of coffee. But then we would have to talk, and what was there to say now? The mundane chat we used to make—*Honey, do you think we should get a new light fixture for over the dining-room table? Should we go visit my mom in Florida this year?*—seemed impossible. Kit was the only topic on our minds.

I heard the front door open, then close as Nick left. I heard the distant ding of the elevator bell. I knew I should get out of bed. But what was a person supposed to do when her ex-best friend had just fallen to her death from her balcony?

I picked up the phone and dialed the number for

Kit's mom. No answer. Again. I'd called twice the night before. I left another message.

Beep, beep, beep—the sound of the front door opening again. "Nick?" I called, irrationally frightened. Who else would it be? And really, what was there to be scared about? Kit was gone.

Nick came into the bedroom, carrying a newspaper. His face looked white, as if he'd been out in the cold for a long time. Wordlessly, he tossed the newspaper on the bed. It landed at my feet. Without moving, I could clearly see a headline on the bottom half of the page: *Woman Dies in Fall From High Rise Condo.*

I looked up and met Nick's eyes. He shook his head, as if to say, *This isn't good.*

I picked up the paper and read the first few paragraphs.

Chicago, IL—A River Forest, Illinois, woman fell approximately 300 feet to her death from a condominium located in the 1200 block of Lake Shore Drive. Katherine Kernaghan, 35, died from injuries after she fell from a friend's twenty-second-floor balcony, where there had been a "skirmish," police say. Kernaghan was pronounced dead at Chicago General Hospital.

Kernaghan's friends, Nicholas and Rachel Blakely, were questioned by police and re-

leased. Authorities are not calling Kernaghan's death a homicide. However, the cause of death is pending an investigation.

"What are we going to do?" Nick said.

"What do you mean?"

The phone rang. I picked it up, half hoping it was Kit's mom, but dreading the conversation just the same. "Hello?"

"Rachel, it's Joanne Weatherby."

"Hi, Joanne." I looked at Nick, who mouthed, *Let me talk to her.*

"Thank you for recommending Tom Severson," I said. "We really appreciated his help."

"Of course," Joanne said soothingly. "I'm so glad Nick called me. This is just awful, what's happened."

"Yes, it is awful. Joanne, Nick would like to talk to you."

I handed Nick the phone. He sat on the edge of the bed and thanked Joanne; he talked about how wonderful Tom Severson had been.

When he hung up, some of the color had come back into his face. "She was very nice."

"Who cares about Joanne right now? Kit is dead." I said these words in a flat tone, but Nick looked surprised, as if I'd slapped him.

He opened his mouth to say something, but the

phone rang again. He answered it. "Yes, this is," he said. "No, I can't this morning. Yes, my wife is available. I can be there at two this afternoon."

He hung up. "That was Tom. He wants to meet with each of us individually. The police are making noise about wanting to question us again."

To get ready for my meeting with Tom Severson, I dressed in a black straight skirt, light green shirt, black pumps and a black wool jacket.

I tried to simply call in sick to work. The usual protocol was to leave a message with the receptionist, Mary, who would tell Laurence. We were professionals at our office. If you couldn't get in—for whatever reason—no one thought twice about it, as long as you pulled your weight eventually. Maybe the problem was I hadn't been carrying mine. Or maybe it was the newspaper article. Because Mary put me on hold as soon as I said my name. And then Laurence came on the line.

"Saw the paper this morning, Blakely," he said. "Sorry to hear about your friend."

"Thank you. As you can imagine, I won't be in today." I felt guilty that I was inadvertently blaming Kit's death for my absence from work when the real, absolute reason was I had to meet with my criminal lawyer.

"Anything we can do?" There was a momentary kindness in his voice. It nearly made me cry.

"No. Thank you, though. I'll probably be out a few days."

I hung up reluctantly, if only because I knew I had to try Kit's mom again.

She answered right away this time, as if she'd been sitting there, hoping Kit might call to say she was late, she'd be home soon, just as I'd heard her do a million times in high school.

"Mrs. Kernaghan," I said. "It's Rachel."

She started to cry. Softly at first, then her cries turned into wails. I stood frozen in my hallway, the cool grays of our oh-so-stylish apartment now cold and unsympathetic. Each cry from Kit's mom tore into me like a scythe.

After what seemed like hours but was probably three minutes, Leslie Kernaghan gulped air and became silent. "I'm sorry, Rachel."

I still couldn't move. I held the phone in one hand, my black bag in the other. I wanted to fling the bag against the wall. I wanted to shriek and sob. But Mrs. Kernaghan deserved more than hysterical displays.

"No, *I'm* sorry," I said.

"What happened last night?"

What had the police told her? Had she seen the papers? "Kit and I had a fight."

"Honey, why? You were her best friend."

I was. We were.

I told her the story I'd told the police. I could repeat it in an almost removed, unfeeling way now. It had begun to resemble reality, for some stealthy part of my mind was erasing the other version with each retelling.

"But I don't understand," Mrs. Kernighan said. "How did she fall over the balcony?"

I continued with the story. I told it quickly, my words almost pushing past one another because I thought if I paused I might not be able to finish.

Mrs. Kernaghan sighed when I was done. She broke into a sob, then caught herself. "Kit was my everything."

"I know."

"She was taking care of me."

"I know," I said again. I thought of telling her that we would pay for her cancer treatments, then I hated myself for thinking how this would look to the police.

"I don't want a wake for her," Mrs. Kernaghan said.

At last I dropped my bag on the parquet floor of

our foyer. "What's that?" Somehow I hadn't thought about Kit's wake, Kit's funeral, Kit's burial.

It was more than I could stand. I sank to the floor. My sobs sounded strangely like Mrs. Kernaghan's only moments before.

"Oh, honey," she said, soothing me, which made me feel guiltier. "It'll be okay. I was just saying that I'm going to have a graveside service and that's all. I can't afford more."

"We could help you with that."

"No, honey, Kit would want it simple."

That made me stop crying. *Kit would want…* Who knew what Kit would have wanted? What had she wanted from her life? What had she wanted last night when she'd come here?

"Will you read it?" Mrs. Kernaghan was saying.

"I'm sorry, what's that?"

"I have a poem I know Kit loved. And she loved you. Would you read it at the service?"

I swallowed hard. I squeezed my eyes to stop more oncoming tears. "Of course," I managed to say.

Tom Severson was a partner in a small but obviously successful firm, called Brandt & Severson. Their offices were on the seventeenth floor of a building on Dearborn Street, near the Daley Center.

The elevator opened onto an elegant reception room with mahogany moldings, burgundy silk wallpaper and plush carpeting. The receptionist showed me to a similarly well designed conference room, where trays of refreshments and bakery rolls awaited me.

I stood up when Tom entered the room. He wore a gray suit, with a green-striped tie.

"Good morning, Rachel," he said warmly. "Is there anything you need? Coffee?"

I smiled. "No, but thank you. This place is a far cry from the police station last night."

He laughed. "They do that on purpose, you know. They give you only that hard bench and sit right across from you so they're in your face."

I nodded. It would all have been interesting, amusing even, if it wasn't about me.

He gestured for me to sit. "Any questions?"

"Nick said they want to question us again."

Tom poured coffee into a gold mug with the Brandt & Severson logo. "That's right, but as I mentioned last night, if they aren't charging you or your husband, you don't have to speak to them at all."

"But we do want to be cooperative."

"Yes, but I don't want you to incriminate yourself, so I'm going to try and put off any further questioning."

I thought about this. "Did any of our statements last night incriminate us?"

Tom shook his head. "They didn't bring in a state's attorney to charge you, so obviously there was nothing that would stick."

"Detective Bacco told me that my husband said something different from what I said. Nick says that's not true."

"They're allowed to lie to you during interrogation."

"Isn't that entrapment?"

"Nope. They do it all the time." He took a sip of his coffee. "I spoke to Detective Bacco this morning, and he doesn't believe Katherine would fight your husband like that."

"Kit," I said.

"Excuse me?"

"We called her Kit."

"I see. Well, Bacco's got one of his famous gut feelings. He thinks there's something strange about the whole thing, and he's going to keep looking. Of course, that's his job. And as long as there's nothing to find, we don't have to worry."

The lawyer seemed to be waiting for me to comment. I stayed quiet.

"Rachel, is there anything I should know that Detective Bacco might discover as he starts digging?"

I thought hard. "There was a man on his balcony last night at the same time we were out there."

"Do you think he heard your argument?"

"I don't think so. He was one floor down."

"But obviously he could see you. I mean, if you could see him."

I felt my stomach flip. "I'm not sure how much he could see. Part of his view would have been blocked, but yes, he might have seen some of the fight."

"The cops will probably find him, then. Anything to be worried about there?"

I tried to remember the man, his hand holding the beer bottle, his body facing out at the lake. Had he turned around and looked up at our balcony? Had he seen Kit and Nick fighting? "I don't know. I don't think so."

"They're interviewing the doorman today. A guy named…" He looked down at a yellow legal pad. "Hector Vanzuela. Do you know him?"

"Not well. We just moved in three weeks ago."

"Does he usually call before he lets someone up?"

I nodded. "Usually, but I've seen him wave people through if he thinks they look familiar. He did call about the sushi guy. I don't know if Kit snuck in somehow when the delivery guy was giving his information to the doorman. I wouldn't put it past her."

Tom studied me. "How are you holding up?"

I met his eyes. "Am I holding up? It doesn't feel like it."

"One day at a time," he said. "That's what they told me when I quit drinking, anyway. Don't think about getting through this week or this month. Just get through today."

"It's just that I don't know how to act. I don't know what to do. Should I go to work? Should I stay home? What do I *do?*"

"Those are good questions. And my advice is to act like the typical mourner. Your friend died. You are allowed to mourn her death. You *should* mourn her death." He dipped his head to one side, as if about to hedge what he'd just said. "Now, unfortunately the media seem to have taken some interest in the case. Whether they'll stay interested depends on what happens and what the cops find. But anything you do, you should think about how it would seem if it appeared on the five o'clock news."

I blinked. My life had become surreal in the span of twelve hours. Then again, I knew how to act when I was being watched. Kit had been watching me for months.

"Okay," I said to Tom.

"I mean, I want you to see friends—you need support after going through something like this—but Rachel, I don't want you or Nick talking to anyone about what happened last night. No one. You should assume everyone is wearing a wire."

"Is that possible? I mean, would the police do that?"

He shrugged. "Again, it depends on what they find. This whole thing might be over in a day or two. Then again, it could drag on for months."

"Months?"

"Years, if there's a trial. So let me reiterate. It's you and Nick on this. Feel free to talk to each other about last night, but no one else, got it?"

I nodded. Just me and Nick. There was a small relief in it. I was so used to keeping secrets by myself, sharing them only with Kit, who'd used them against me. Now, at last, I'd have Nick.

For the next few days, Nick used his patients and his surgeries as excuses to work feverishly. He even took on the kind of cases he normally avoided. He covered for any partner who asked. Yes, he seemed to be saying, my wife's once-dearest friend died at our apartment this week. Yes, we're being questioned in her death. But hey, I've got a rhinoplasty from Dr. Taylor and a breast augmentation that's really going to make a difference in this sixteen-year-old's life.

I felt terrible for thinking such things. Nick loved his work, and more than anything he loved the surgeries that did help people. I couldn't blame him for keeping food in our mouths and for continuing to do what made him happy. There wasn't anything to be done at home except wait for a call from Tom Severson, and I envied how Nick's job pulled him from the apartment.

As for me, I called in sick. I couldn't get myself to work. I couldn't get myself to do much of anything, except wonder what Detective Bacco was thinking. Was he working on other cases, pushing aside Kit's death the way I did end-of-the-month paperwork? Or was he reviewing, over and over, the notes from interviews Nick and I had given, seeking discrepancies and unbelievabilities? According to a recent newspaper, there was still an "ongoing investigation," but it said little else.

Finally the afternoon before Kit's funeral, after sitting on the couch and staring at the choppy waters of Lake Michigan for at least two hours, I decided there was one thing I could stand to do—paint my photos. I hadn't done any painting since we'd moved to Lake Shore. But where to set up? I no longer had my basement room on Bloomingdale. I decided on the dining-room table.

I covered the table with a big sheet and pushed all the chairs away. I set up my paints and my palette, then I had to decide what photo to use. I almost always painted landscapes. I liked taking a black-and-white photo of a suburban field and turning the grasses a bright orange-yellow, making the pine trees behind the field almost electric-green, muting the sky to a soft gray-blue. The possibilities were endless. But as I flipped through the stack of photos, none of them inspired me.

I put the photos aside, left the dining room and went into the sitting room off our bedroom. On a glass table next to the chaise longue was our wedding album. It contained a mix of color photos and black-and-whites. I paged through it until I found the one I wanted—a black-and-white solo shot of Kit wearing her spaghetti-strapped bridesmaid dress, her hair artfully arranged on top of her head.

She was holding a bouquet of daisies, making a comically demure face for the camera.

I took the photo into the dining room and taped it to my desktop easel. I mixed my paints—rusty-red for her hair, wine-red for her mouth, lilac for the dress, orange for the huge gerbera daisies, powdery blue for the sky. By the time Nick came home, I had worked on the painting for more than three hours. I had almost brought her back to life.

"What's all this?" Nick asked when he walked into the dining room at seven o'clock.

I didn't answer right away. How could I? I'd come to despise Kit, to fear her. And yet, I think I wanted to bring her back in some small way, so that neither Nick or I would be responsible for her demise.

Nick came behind me and stood with a hand on my shoulder, silent.

I pointed with my brush. "I can't seem to get her eyes right. I mean, you know how her eyes are purple sometimes? And when she's wearing a dress that's lilac, her eyes would definitely be purple, don't you think?"

Another gap of silence. "Rach, you're talking about her like she's still here."

"Well, she is right here. Right now." I had no idea

what I meant by this. I just knew that it had felt okay for a few hours while I was painting Kit's photo. But now the painting was nearly done, and Nick was breaking the spell.

He took the brush from my hand and placed it neatly on the sheeted table. "Let's get something to eat."

"You want to go out?" I was still staring at Kit's face.

"We'll go to that sandwich place around the corner. You need some air."

"Well, I could get some air on the balcony." I heard the near hysteria in my voice.

I looked at Nick. His eyebrows were raised.

"What's that look?" I asked, my voice loud. "Jesus, Nick, how can you be so cold? Why aren't you freaking out like I am?"

A disbelieving look crossed his face. "I *am*, Rachel. Do you think I've slept? Do you think I've thought of anything else since it happened?"

"It seems like everything is back to normal for you."

His expression softened. "Baby, I'm trying. I'd love us to be back to normal. I want it for both of us, don't you?"

I nodded, said yes, a tear slipping down my

face. What I didn't say was, *How can we ever be normal with what happened, what you did?* Because I was no longer sure what exactly did happen that night.

Nick reached out a hand and brushed the tear away. "I love you."

"I love you, too." That I was sure of.

"Then let me take you out for a bite. Let's get out of the house."

"Thank you," I said. "You're right."

I stripped off the white jacket I always wore to paint—an old lab coat of Nick's. I didn't look at the photo. I let my husband lead me away from Kit.

But there were other photos of Kit at her funeral on Friday. It was crisply cold and very sunny as Nick and I pulled his BMW into the parking lot of the small graveyard. I hadn't been to a cemetery in years, probably a decade, and it seemed horrific that I was now here for Kit, when the only funeral any of us had envisioned was her mother's.

Nick turned off the car, and we looked past a few rows of headstones to where Kit's mom sat in a wheelchair. Nearby, other women were busy arranging enlarged photos of Kit on four easels surrounding an open grave site. And lying next to the grave, on a small platform covered with lurid green AstroTurf, was a coffin. Kit's coffin.

We got out of the car and walked slowly to the grave site. I averted my eyes from the coffin and instead stared at the photos. They were professional studio shots, obviously taken while Kit was in L.A. In one, her hair was huge and crazy, and she was laughing, her mouth open and sumptuous. The second showed her in an evening dress, another in jeans and a camisole, her arms wrapped around her knees. The last photo was a close-up of Kit's face. In it, her hair had been styled straight and slicked back. A red flower, so deep in color it was almost black, was tucked behind her ear. Her eye makeup was smoky dark. She was leaning forward, her mouth slightly open, and she seemed to stare through the camera at the viewer, at me. The photo was so well taken I could *feel* Kit here. I could sense her. I could hear her murmuring, *Golden Child.*

I stopped twenty feet away from the grave site. "I can't do this," I whispered to Nick, looking away from the photos. "I cannot do this."

"What are you talking about?" he whispered back.

"This is impossible. This is obscene."

He took me by the shoulders. "Rach, listen.

We're here. This is happening. And I know it's hard, but you're strong. I'm here for you."

"But I'm supposed to read, and I…"

"You will, and you'll do a fine job. Look at me when you're up there, okay? Just look at me, and I'll get you through it." He smiled and for a brief second, I felt okay. But then I turned my head and saw what awaited me, and I felt a rising panic at the thought of walking toward those pictures, toward Kit in a wooden box.

I knew Kit was dead. I'd seen her body. But I'd been enveloped in a depressive fog the past few days that made everything seem off-kilter and dreamlike. This funeral was real.

"Let's go home," I said.

"We're not going home. People will notice if we're not here."

"God, Nick," I whispered fiercely, "what is it with you and *people?* Why do you care so god-damned much about how we act and what everybody thinks?"

"Because in case you haven't noticed we were questioned for Kit's murder." His eyes darted past me to Kit's mom. He waved at her, then turned back to me. "And someone is here who will be watching how we act."

I turned and saw Detective Bacco and another man walking toward the grave site.

"Oh, God," I said. The detective hadn't called to question us again. He hadn't even called Tom Severson, as far as I knew, but I felt him circling around our life.

"Take a deep breath, Rachel, and let's go. You can do this."

I did as he instructed. Nick grabbed my hand. "Remember what I said the other night. We're a team."

I nodded. I squeezed his hand back and walked toward Kit's mother. Thirty minutes later, my legs trembled as I stood up from a metal folding chair and made my way to the lectern near Kit's open grave. I tried not to look at the coffin, but it was impossible. The casket was wood, with a reddish cast. I had a strange thought that Kit would have appreciated that; it suited her coloring.

I felt an intense desire to throw up. I bit my lip and steadied myself. I took a few more steps until I was behind the lectern.

There were only about thirty people at the service—Mrs. Kernaghan's sisters and their kids, a few people from high school, a few others from the Goodman Theatre where Kit had been working.

And of course the detectives, who stood at the back of the group like sentries.

I looked to Nick for support. He nodded. *You can do this.*

I glanced at Mrs. Kernaghan. The poor woman had once been a robust, ribald woman who told raunchy jokes, even to the kids in the neighborhood. She was thin and waiflike now, her skin gray, her blond wig ill fitting and hanging too low over her teary eyes. She blew her nose when she saw me and tried to smile.

The reading was printed out on computer paper and folded a few times. I unfolded it and tried to focus on the words. It was Robert Frost's "The Road Not Taken."

"It always made me think of Kit," Mrs. Kernaghan had told me. And as I read it, I could picture Kit, too. She had taken the road less traveled, that was sure. Our lives had been nearly identical when we were young, but instead of finding some nice boy and settling down, Kit headed to L.A. She followed her passion.

I didn't look up as I read the poem, because I was thinking that Kit had taken the road less traveled with me, too, someone who was supposed to be her friend. Instead of the known path of friendship—of keeping counsel and dishing out supportive words—she had instead exploited our relationship. And I didn't know if I could ever forgive her for that. Even now.

Did a glimmer of anger cross my face as I read the last words, thinking of the last few months with Kit? Did I somehow reveal, with a hard syllable or a minuscule but dismissive shake of my head, how I had really come to feel about Kit and her road less taken? I wonder. Because when I finally raised my head, the eyes I met were those of Detective Bacco, and I sensed a question there—*What are you hiding, Rachel?*

15

Saturday. At last, Saturday. I didn't have to call work to report I wouldn't be in again or pretend to be productive at home. I could stay in bed.

When Nick left for the gym at nine in the morning, he bent over me and brushed my bangs from my forehead. "You all right?"

"I don't feel well."

"Do you want me to stay?"

I shook my head and buried myself deeper in the covers.

"I'll be back in a few hours. Call me on my cell if you need anything."

"Thanks."

It wasn't hard to sleep. It was a blissful escape.

When Nick came home, I murmured hello, then tucked myself into a ball and slept again.

Later Nick woke me up by gently shaking my

shoulders. He felt my forehead. "You don't feel warm," he said. "Are you all right?"

I blinked and struggled to sit. "What time is it?"

"Four o'clock. You've been in bed all day. How do you feel?"

"Better. A little. I should get up." I realized I was ravenous. "Do we have any food in the house?"

"What do you think?"

"Right. Empty fridge. What should we do for dinner?"

"Well…" His voice died off.

I looked at Nick. The waves of his light brown hair were combed close to his head. He wore a French blue shirt I didn't recognize. "You seem dressed up for a Saturday afternoon."

"There's that dinner party at the Renworths' to-night."

"What?"

"You know, that party Valerie is throwing to get people assigned to the board's literacy committee."

I stared at him in shock. "Who cares about the literacy committee?"

"I know it sounds stupid, but I care about it. I want to make it as an official member of the board. And they're voting sometime next month."

I fell back onto the bed, staring at our muted

gray ceiling and the ivory moldings. "I can't believe you."

"You can't believe I want to go on with life?" Nick's voice was loud. "You can't believe that I don't want Kit to rule us? Look, Rach, I get it. I know you think the board is a bunch of bullshit, but it means something to me."

"What?"

"If I'm a member, it means I've made it in this town. By myself. Without my parents' connections. It means I can take care of you. I can take care of our family."

"We don't need it."

"I do, Rach. It's a goal I set for myself, and I don't want Kit to take it away."

I turned my head. "She just died, Nick. It's only been days."

He was silent for a moment. "I know that. But she ruined your friendship, and she blackmailed you. She made your life hell for months. I'm not saying you shouldn't grieve for her, but I am saying it would be a shame if she took away any more."

I squeezed my eyes shut, as if by doing so, I could close out the whole world.

"Tom Severson said we should see friends when we need to," Nick said.

"He also said we should act like typical mourners. Partying is not a typical mourning activity."

He cleared his throat. "More than anything, Rach, I think this is a good opportunity for us to get out of the house. You need to get out, babe."

I heard the concern in his voice, and it softened me. It made me think of all the grief I'd brought into our lives by not dealing with Kit sooner, better.

"We'll just go for a few hours," Nick said. "Everyone will understand." He leaned over and kissed my forehead. He smelled clean, soapy. I suddenly desired a hot shower and fresh air.

"Okay," I said. "I'll go."

In the lobby, we saw Hector Vanzuela, the doorman who'd been there the night Kit died.

"Dr. Blakely, Mrs. Blakely," he said, scooting around the desk.

"Hello, Hector," Nick said. "How are you?"

He coughed. "I was hoping to see you."

Both Nick and I stopped. Nick tightened his grip on my elbow.

"You see," Hector said, rubbing absently at his fleshy, pleasing face and adjusting his green cap, "I got called into the police station this week."

"Yes, we heard," I said. *What had he told them? What did he know?*

I made myself take a breath.

"How did that go?" Nick asked.

"I wasn't there too long, but I just wanted to tell you both how sorry I am."

"Why is that?" Nick said.

"Well, I guess I let her up. I mean, it's like I told the police, I called up about the delivery man, but I don't remember seeing any lady, but sometimes I do let people through. You know, if I think they're a resident or a friend. I'm just real sorry. I feel responsible." Hector's eyebrows drew together. "I'm real sorry," he repeated.

Nick put his hand on Hector's shoulder. "Please. This is not your fault."

I looked at Nick, and I wondered, whose fault is it? Did Kit bring this on herself? But it was me who'd given Kit the money, who'd kept the secret from Nick. The secret Nick had forgiven so easily. And yet it was Nick's hands that had been around Kit's neck and on her shoulders. It was his force that sent her soaring.

"We're just sorry that you had to get involved in this," Nick continued.

"Oh, no, sir, like I said, I want to apologize."

Hector put on an overly bright smile. "So anyway, where are you two off to tonight?"

I shot Nick a look. *Do not say a party.*

"To see a few friends," Nick said. "We'll be home soon."

Outside, I blinked at the November cold. Nick put his arm around me, while Hector hailed us a taxi. In the cab, I rolled down the window and breathed in the chill. It pierced my lungs. The pain made me feel a little bit alive.

The Renworth house on Astor Place was a city mansion—a heavy, old residence made of stone, lit with street-side lanterns and the buzz of something wonderful inside. It was the kind of place Kit and I used to study when we first moved to Chicago. We'd leave our Old Town basement apartment and cut down Astor on our way to the Division Street bars. We'd stand in front of such houses—this might have been one of them—and we'd talk about the day we'd be invited to parties in places like that. Or even live there.

The bell was antique brass. Nick pushed it with a determined finger.

The door was opened by a man in a black suit. The tinkling of music and conversation rushed outside. "Welcome to the Renworth residence," he said. "May I take your coats?"

Nick thanked him and helped me off with my wool coat. My black dress underneath felt too light. I smoothed down the front and looked around at the party. Most of the people seemed to be gathering in the great room, where a massive stone fireplace roared and crackled.

Did the music dim for a moment as guests started to notice us? Or do I just remember it that way, mixing the moment with one I'd seen in a film somewhere? I caught the glance of one person, then another. No one looked familiar.

Just then, Valerie Renworth approached us. "Nick, Rachel," she said. "Welcome."

There was no warm hug, like the kind she'd given me at the Glitz Ball or when I'd met her for lunch and shopping. Just a dry kiss on each of our cheeks. She stepped back and her eyes moved from me to Nick and back. "What can I get you to drink?"

I hadn't had alcohol in a while, due to our efforts to get pregnant, but nothing was the same as it had been days ago. I wanted to ask for vodka. I restrained myself and asked for a glass of cabernet. Nick ordered a Scotch, something he'd been drinking since becoming an associate member of the board.

"Wait here," Valerie said. Was she afraid that we

would somehow enter her party and infect it? Or was I being paranoid?

I glanced at Nick and saw mild panic on his features. "There's Charles and Toni." He pointed to a couple a few years older than us, whom we'd met at a few functions. They were a striking black couple, both tall and lean and animated. They always gave the slightly breathless impression that they'd just hopped off the tennis court or golf course.

Nick led me to them. "Charles, Toni," he said. "I don't know if you remember us."

They turned, and it was clear they not only remembered us but had read the papers, too.

"Hello," Toni said. "We heard the dreadful news about your friend. We're so sorry." Her husband hung back and took uncomfortably long sips of his drink.

"Thank you," Nick said. "It's been a tough week. We thought we should get out of the house for a few hours."

Except that you've been gone all day, I thought.

"Of course," Toni said. "Of course."

Valerie came toward us. A waiter followed with our drinks on a tray. "Here you go," Valerie said stiffly.

She looked at Toni, and they exchanged a glance I couldn't read.

"How has everyone been?" I asked. It was a weak conversation opener, yet I was desperate to change the awkwardness of the situation.

But instead of launching into a breezy chat of the weather or the new car someone had bought, Toni turned to me and shook her head. "It doesn't matter how *we* are. How are *you*? This has got to be awfully trying."

This, she'd called it. As if Kit's death and our being questioned by the police could be swept into that one vague word.

"It's been hard," I said, just as vague.

"What happened that night?"

There it was—the specific question they'd wanted to ask. Valerie, Toni and Charles all drew toward us. I could already imagine how they would tell this story to friends the next day. *You know that couple who the cops think killed that actress? Yes, you know, she went over the balcony on Lake Shore? Well, I talked to them at a party last night and...*

I looked at Nick, who had lost his words for once. I pictured Tom Severson's face, warning that anyone could wear a wire, that Nick and I should only speak to each other about Kit's death.

I saw Nick open his mouth, and I suddenly feared

what he might say. He wanted the approval of this crowd so badly. I jumped in. "It was a tragedy," I said. "Our friend accidentally fell, as I'm sure you heard. We're both trying to get over it."

They nodded, clearly disappointed by my lack of specificity. Two women stepped into our circle and extended their hands to Nick and me. "Hi," one of them said, "I'm Erica Selene, and this is Karen McConnaghy. We just wanted to introduce ourselves."

"Nick Blakely," Nick said, shaking their hands, "and this is my wife—"

"Yes, we know," Erica said, her eyes gleaming. "Rachel. And we wanted to tell you how sorry we are for your loss."

I shook her hand and tried to smile. This was the other part Kit and I used to dream about on those nights when we stood outside such a house. "We'll be famous in a good way," Kit would say. "You know, when people know who you are and respect you just by looking at you."

Nick and I were clearly known in this room, but I doubted there was any respect here.

"Rachel? Tom Severson. Sorry to call you on a Sunday."

I felt a jolt travel through me. I sat up from my

prone position on the couch, the place I'd been most of the day. Nick had bought the Sunday papers, but there didn't seem to be the right place to read them in this new apartment. Nowhere as cozy as my old basement room.

"It's no bother." Neither Nick nor I had heard from Tom since our meetings at his office the day after Kit died. I think we were both hoping we might never hear from our criminal defense lawyer again. I think both of us knew better.

Nick entered the living room, and I signaled him to come over. I mouthed, *Tom.*

"I got a call from John Bacco. He's the detective who questioned you."

I swallowed hard. "Yes. I remember."

Nick sat on the couch, and I angled the phone so he could hear.

"Well, they're making noise about wanting to question you and Nick again. I was able to put them off for a while, but now they claim they've got new information, which makes me nervous. I have to apprise you of this, but I say we continue to refuse."

"What if we don't answer their questions?"

"If they really want you in for questioning, and they think they have enough, they arrest you and press charges."

"Charges?" Nick said. "Tom, look, we can't let them do that. It would be a disaster for our careers, our lives. Why don't we just talk to them?"

"I wouldn't recommend it. They're probably just fishing for information. Let them arrest you if they want."

At the second mention of the word *arrest,* Nick's eyes closed for a minute. "I can't do that," Nick said. "I can't sit around and force them to arrest me just so they can question me. Let's talk to them. We didn't do anything, anyway. We have nothing to hide."

I kept looking at Nick when he said that. He didn't meet my eyes.

"Ultimately it's your call," Tom said, "but I don't like it. I don't like not knowing what we're getting into. Have you two heard anything new?"

Nick and I looked at each other. "Nothing," Nick said.

"Would we have to go to the police station again?" I asked. I hated the thought of that cold room, that hard bench.

"No, we can make them come to my office. But again, talking to police is against my recommendation."

"I won't be arrested," Nick said. "Let them talk to us."

"You're sure you guys want to do that?"

"Yes," we both answered.

"All right," Tom said. "Nine o'clock tomorrow work for you?"

"I'll have to reschedule a surgery," Nick said, "but that's fine."

I sank back onto the couch and closed my eyes, knowing I wouldn't sleep all night.

Detective Bacco looked exactly as I remembered—blue suit, brown hair, a youthful appearance that made you underestimate him and a glint in his eye that said he hoped you'd do just that.

"How are you, Mrs. Blakely?" he said, as he entered Tom Severson's boardroom.

"Rachel," I said instinctively. We shook hands. He extended his hand to Nick, who shook it but said nothing.

"Where's your partner today?" Tom Severson asked, referring to Detective Carlos Negga, who'd interrogated Nick at the police station.

"We had a triple last night, so it's just me."

Tom nodded. He wore a brown suit and a ivory shirt. I had to admit I felt ever so slightly better just seeing him. He instilled confidence and calm.

Tom gestured for the detective to help himself to

the coffee set up on the side table. "John, I'd like you to question Dr. and Mrs. Blakely together this morning." This was something Nick had suggested, and although Tom said it was unusual, he'd explained that we were within our rights to ask. I held my breath now, because as scared as I was, I would feel infinitely more relaxed being with Nick. And knowing what he said.

Detective Bacco halted on his way to the coffee. "No. No way, Tom."

"I think that's all we've got time for today."

The detective crossed his arms. "Absolutely not. I question one witness at a time. You know how it works."

"It can work this way, too."

"I won't do it."

The two men stared at each other, sizing each other up. "Let me talk to my clients," Tom said.

He waited for the detective to leave the room before he turned to us. "Look, guys, he didn't bring his partner, and that's a good sign."

"Why?" Nick asked.

"He's making a nice show about a triple homicide last night, but believe me, the Chicago PD has enough detectives. If they were serious about pressing charges in this case, they'd both be here. We'll let him question each of you for a short amount of time, and hopefully that will be the end of it."

I moved forward in my chair. "Tom, would you be able to tell the second person what was said by the first? I mean, if one of us was questioned first, could you tell the next person what they were asked and what they said?"

Nick looked at me curiously. I wondered what he was thinking. I wondered if he knew that I very much wanted to be the second person questioned.

"Sure," Tom said. "Ethically, I can't tell you exactly what to *say*, but I can tell you what was discussed with the other person."

"Nick has to get to the hospital," I said. "He should go first."

Nick nodded, still giving me that curious look.

"Let's do it, then," Tom said. He opened the door and called to Detective Bacco.

In the waiting room, I paged through the morning papers. Occasionally, I glanced up and smiled at the receptionist, but every time I did, it seemed that she was already staring at me. Was I imagining it? Or did she have yesterday's morning paper at her desk, the one that mentioned the continuing investigation into Kit's death and stated, "*The police are*

*still speaking to Kernaghan's friends, Dr. Nicholas
Blakely and his wife, Rachel Blakely.*"

Thirty minutes passed, then another. What was
going on in there? What was Nick saying? I kept
leaning my body toward the conference-room door,
hoping for a peep, a hint. I heard nothing.

At ten-thirty, I called my office. There were at
least twenty-five voice mails, most of them from
last week. I returned the few that seemed like cri-
ses, then dialed again and asked for Laurence.

"It's Rachel," I said.

"Well, hello, Rachel, nice to hear from you."

"You know I've been out because of what happened to my friend." *And I'm about to be questioned by the police. Again.*

"Yes, I know. And I'm sorry. I really am. But I
need you in here, Blakely."

"I'll be there in an hour or so." I looked at the
closed door and amended my statement. "Definitely
by this afternoon."

"This is a job, in case you forgot."

"I haven't," I said too loudly.

The receptionist looked at me inquiringly.

"You sure?" Laurence said.

"I haven't," I repeated more quietly and through
gritted teeth. My job had taken a back seat to ev-

erything else in my world lately, but it was the one bit of normality I had left. I hadn't forgotten the joy my job used to bring me.

The conference-room door opened. It was my turn to be questioned.

"Laurence, I have to go. I'll see you in a few hours."

Nick came out, a relieved expression on his face. "Walk me to the elevator, Rachel."

"How did it go?" I asked when we reached the elevator bank.

He nodded. "Well, I think. He asked a lot of questions, but it was mostly the same stuff they asked me at the police station."

"And?"

"I told him the same thing I told the other guy. The truth."

I nodded. The *truth*. Until this past week, I'd never realized how fluid a concept that could be.

"He asked a few things about Kit's mom," he said, "and personal stuff like that. But I didn't know much. You'll probably be able to tell him more."

"Okay." I straightened my jacket collar and told myself to breathe.

"Hey, you'll be fine." Nick smoothed my hair.

"It's going to be okay, baby. Just go in there and tell them the truth."

That word again.

Tom Severson appeared in the hallway. "Rachel, can I speak with you?"

I said goodbye to Nick and followed Tom into an empty office.

"Are you ready?" he said.

I nodded. "Nick said there weren't many new questions."

Tom Severson's brow furrowed. "I guess that's true, but Bacco is fishing."

"What do you mean?"

"He's asking a number of pointed questions about Kit's finances, her boyfriends, her employment. I get the feeling he's circling around something." He frowned at me. "Any reason for me to be nervous?"

My stomach clenched. "I don't think so."

"Let's do it, then."

Detective Bacco sat at the end of the conference table, Tom and I together on one side. We went over the events of that night, and it was a strange solace to tell the story again, the same way I'd told it that night at the police station. It seemed to make more sense with each retelling.

After twenty-five minutes or so, Tom asked the detective to "move things along."

Detective Bacco glanced at the yellow pad in front of him. "How did Kit make her living?" he asked.

"She was an actress in L.A. When she came back to Chicago, she was working at the Goodman Theatre."

"Was her acting career successful?"

"She landed a few commercials, and she was in a few theater productions, but mostly she was struggling."

"And how about her job at the Goodman? Did she make a decent amount of money?"

I felt a whisper of fear, as if someone had lightly blown on the back of my neck.

"I'm not sure what you mean by decent," I said. "I don't know exactly how much Kit was making, but I don't think it was a lot."

"Did she do anything else to supplement her income?"

"John," Tom said, "is this important?"

Detective Bacco didn't take his eyes from my face. "Yes," he said simply.

"I'm not sure what you mean," I said.

"Did Kit Kernaghan get money from any other sources?"

The whisper of fear grew into a roar that filled my ears. I felt my breath become shallow.

"She might have," I answered. "I'm not sure."

"You're not sure?"

Detective Bacco's tone was sharp, and Tom looked back and forth quickly between the two of us.

"It seems that a woman like Kit Kernaghan might have gotten desperate," the detective said. "She might have turned to her friends for help. She might have even gotten a little greedy and pushed those friends too far."

"All right, enough," Tom said. "Ask a question, John, or we're done."

"Did *you* help your friend out financially?" the detective said, his voice a little louder. His eyes were still locked on mine.

Tell the truth, I thought. *The truth.*

"Yes," I said. "I gave Kit money."

Detective Bacco sat back in his seat and gave me a cold, satisfied smile.

Tom Severson pulled me out of the conference room and into the empty office again. His face was somber. "You want to tell me what we're getting into here?"

I put my hands behind my back and squeezed

them into fists to stop them from trembling. "I gave Kit money on a few occasions. I lent it to her. She was supposed to use it for her mom, who's going through chemo."

Tom's eyes narrowed. "Supposed to?"

"Well, we ran into her once at a party, and she was wearing a very expensive dress, which I assumed she'd bought with the money I gave her."

"Did you fight?"

"We had a discussion."

"Did anyone see you?"

I squeezed my hands tighter. The trembling was crawling from my hands and up my arms. "There were hundreds of people at the event, but it would have looked like we were just talking."

Tom Severson shook his head. "Rachel, you should have told me this earlier."

My husband told me not to tell anyone. "I'm sorry. I didn't know it would be important." I wondered now if I should tell the whole truth about how Kit had blackmailed me. What had Nick said? *It will make you look guilty.*

The delicate task of sorting half-truths from real ones, keeping parts of stories aside while telling others to the world, exhausted me. I sank onto an office chair and covered my face.

"Are you all right?" Tom said.

"Fine." I rubbed my forehead as if to erase the doubts, then sat up straight. "Should we go back in there and finish this?"

"I'm not sure. How much money did you give Kit?"

I didn't have to do the math. I knew exactly. But I took a moment and pretended to add it up. "Thirty-eight thousand."

"Damn it. All at once?"

"No. Different payments."

"What kind of payments?"

"The funds came from a savings account. I couldn't write checks, so I gave her money orders."

He looked at me. "This could be a mess."

I almost wanted to laugh—*could be?*

"Here's what we're going to do. You're going to answer a few more questions to keep Bacco happy," Tom said, "then we're closing up this shop. Tell him you gave her money, tell him why—for her mom's chemo—and then we're done."

But it wasn't that easy. Detective Bacco had smelled something interesting. "So they were loans?" he asked once we were back in the boardroom and I told him the basics. He said the world "loans" incredulously.

I nodded and clenched my hands together under the table.

"If you were going to give her thirty-eight grand, why not just do it all at once?"

"I didn't plan to give her that much. She asked for money to pay for her mom's chemo, then she asked for more later."

"And you just kept giving it to her?"

"She needed help. She was a friend."

"Sounds like she was shaking you down."

A shot of fear pierced me.

"Whoa," Tom Severson said. "Ask a question, John. We're about done here."

Detective Bacco never took his eyes from me. "Was Kit Kernaghan shaking you down?"

"I don't know what you mean."

"Was she blackmailing you?"

"No." I shook my head and forced a bewildered expression onto my face. It wasn't hard. I was terrified.

"You're sure?"

"Kit and I were friends. What would she blackmail me about?"

I kept the confused expression on my face. I listened to the pummeling of my heart against my ribs. Could they hear it, too? I shot a glance at Tom, who was studying me cautiously. He gave me a slow nod as if to say, *You're doing okay.*

Detective Bacco crossed one leg over his knee. "I don't know. I was hoping you'd tell me."

"There was nothing to blackmail me about. I helped out a friend who needed it, just like anyone would. I don't know why I should have to defend friendship." The lies mixed with the truth and came out sounding plausible.

Detective Bacco watched me in silence. I tried to return his gaze confidently. Inside, everything was trembling now.

"Anything else?" Tom Severson asked. "Otherwise, I think that's it."

Detective Bacco was still silent. He looked at Tom, then me. Finally he stood and gathered his notes. "All right, we're done."

Why didn't it feel like the end?

I could feel the air shift when I entered the reception area of Randall Design. The receptionist, Mary, who was talking to one of the sales assistants, leaped to her feet when she saw me.

"Rachel," she said, her voice high, "how are you? I mean, gosh, I know you're not good, with your friend and the police and all, but I mean how are you? How is everything?"

She glanced at the sales assistant, a woman named Janet I didn't know well. Janet's eyes were a little wide, and she looked nervous.

"I'm okay. Thanks for asking." I began to head to my office, but Mary stopped me.

"You got a call from the *Sun-Times*," she said.

"When was that?"

"About an hour ago."

I tried to appear unruffled, but the fact was the few articles about Kit's death in the papers hadn't mentioned where I worked. Apparently, someone had found out.

"Did you put them to my voice mail?" I asked.

"I said I would, but they asked to talk to a superior, so I gave them to Laurence."

No, no, no, I wanted to say. I managed a tight, "Okay. Thanks. I'll go see him."

I threw my purse on my office chair, ignoring the pile of messages and unopened mail. I steeled myself, then headed straight to Laurence's office. Best to deal with him now, apologize about the *Sun-Times* bothering him and tell him I was back and on board. I couldn't guess what was going to happen with the police. I didn't have a clue what was going to happen at all, but I could start from here. I could throw myself into work like Nick had done and hope to get my life rolling again.

I rapped on the open door to Laurence's office and stepped inside. He was seated behind his desk and talking on the phone, while pulling on one of his suspenders, one of his trademark moves. When he saw me, his eyebrows rose. He waved me inside.

I stood there while he spoke on the phone. His volume seemed to have gone up since I'd come in.

"Our software has 3-D modeling and rendering," he was saying, obviously talking to a customer. "You've got full editing capabilities that act like pencil and paper. The way it works is far superior to that of our competitors." He paused. "Yeah, sure. Tell you what, I'll be out there tomorrow, and you'll try it for two months, all right? If you like it, we'll get everyone in your company set up and running."

He smiled smugly as he hung up. "That was Lake Architectural."

"Hello to you, too, Laurence."

He crossed his arms.

"Why are you calling on my customers?" I asked.

"Because you apparently can't do it."

"You know I've been working on Lake," I said in a patient voice.

"Well, they called and wanted to see the product, and you weren't here. Someone has to pick up the slack."

"Laurence, my friend died last week. At my condo."

"Yes, I know. Ask the papers. I've been doing your work and now I'm your publicist, too."

"What did the *Sun-Times* say?"

He sat behind his desk. "Have a seat, Blakely."

Dread filled me. There was something ominous about his tone. I stayed where I was.

"Not to sound like a bad breakup," Laurence said, "but this isn't going to work."

"Don't do this."

He shook his head. "Blakely, the company is struggling. You know that, and you've been struggling, too."

"I've had a bad couple of months. And now I'm having the worst month in my life, personally. Please don't fire me. Please, Laurence. This job is the last normal thing I have in my life. Don't cut me off."

He bit his lip. "We can't have this kind of PR.

Randall just got wind of this." He waved a hand as he spoke the owner's name. "He won't stand for it."

My desperation swooped into anger. I had worked my ass off for this company for years. I had made them an inordinate amount of money. The last two months shouldn't erase that. "Will he stand for a wrongful-termination suit?"

"Don't be that way, Blakely."

"Don't be that way?" My voice got louder with each word, and I felt the edges of my mind fraying.

"Hey, c'mon." He made his voice purposefully quiet. "You'd do the same thing in our situation. We can let you go for cause right now. You know we've had to let other people go for not producing. I was hoping you'd come around, but you haven't."

"You know I can get my sales up. You know it."

He shrugged. "Maybe, maybe not. You've got some other issues to deal with, it sounds like, and Randall doesn't want bad blood hanging around."

"Well, then tell him to expect a lawsuit—Bad Blood versus Randall Design." Even as I said it, though, I knew I wouldn't do it. I couldn't handle anything else in my life. Not one more thing.

Laurence said nothing. "I'll have Mary help you pack up your stuff."

I wanted to shout at him. Instead, I closed my

eyes for a brief second and pretended none of this had happened. Then I opened them and said, "Don't bother. I can do it myself."

Forty minutes later, I was in the back of a cab, leaving Randall Design for the last time.

16

"I was fired," I said when Nick walked into the apartment that night.

I sat on the living-room couch, next to the box of stuff I'd brought back from the office. Beyond the glass windows, I'd been looking at our balcony for what must have been hours, although I couldn't be sure of the time. I wanted to force myself to remember every second of that night. At least then, I told myself, I'd have that moment, the moment before it all shifted.

The problem was that I'd relived that night, that fight with Kit, so many times in my mind and out loud for Tom and the police, I could only clearly remember the story Nick had insisted on. I knew that version wasn't exactly what I'd seen, yet I'd shaded the events in my mind and now I couldn't seem to take out the tint.

"What happened?" Nick said. His keys jingled as he dropped them on the table.

"Laurence Connelly fired me today," I said.

Nick came around the couch and knelt in front of me. "Why?"

"He mentioned my sales, but the real reason was that the *Sun-Times* called him today, and he felt the firm couldn't risk any bad publicity." I turned my face down toward Nick's. His freckles looked darker, his face white with the cold outside. He must have walked from his office, something he enjoyed. Had his life changed so much since last Tuesday? It didn't seem so.

"That's unbelievable!" Nick said angrily.

Was he upset about my firing, I wondered, or the fact that the *Sun-Times* had called me at work? More bad PR for us, for the board to feast on.

"He can't do that," Nick said. "You're the best salesperson they have. We'll sue him."

"I threatened, but let's face it, Nick, that would just put more scrutiny on us. The papers would probably get a hold of that, too."

"I don't care. They can't do this to you."

"You wanted me to quit, anyway."

"Only if you wanted to. But this is ridiculous. I'm serious about a lawsuit. Should we call Tom?"

His expression was so earnest, so absolutely angry on my behalf, that some of my earlier questions melted away.

"No," I said. "C'mere." I pulled him onto the couch and buried my face in his chest.

He hugged me tight. "Jesus, Rachel, I'm so sorry."

"I'll be okay. We'll be okay. Won't we?"

Did he pause for the slightest second?

"Of course," he said.

The next few days bled one into another. I'd never known life could be like that—just a cavernous, forever-bleary moment spent wandering around the apartment, trying to avoid looking at the balcony again, wondering what other people— normal people—did when they didn't work, when they were depressed, when they'd lost someone, when they'd lost something from their life, when they didn't know if they were a murderer or if it was their husband or both or neither.

Nick came home in the evenings and appeared startled by me.

"What's going on?" he said one night, taking in the yellow cotton pajamas I'd worn since he left for the office.

He shed his cashmere coat in the hall closet and

loosened his yellow necktie. I stared at the tie, thinking that it wasn't appropriate for a November day at the office. It looked more suited for a wedding in May.

I sank onto the couch and I sensed, somewhere in the sane part of my mind, that I was acting depressed, strange, that I'd strayed from the me I used to be familiar with, comfortable with.

Then came the scary thought that maybe I'd strayed so far, mentally at least, that I'd never get back, that maybe this was me now, this creature moping around an apartment, haunted by a dead friend.

"Rachel," Nick said. Just my name with finality. No other words.

We looked at each other across the gleaming parquet floor.

"Did you get out today?" he said.

"Where would I go?"

He heaved a sad sigh. It was Friday, and we'd had this conversation every night. "For coffee. To look for another job, if that's what you want. To the bookstore. To see friends."

"Friends?" My voice croaked slightly. I'd talked to no one for twelve hours. "Nick, we don't have any friends."

Over the past few years, most of our buddies

from school or our early working days had slipped into their own lives, their kids, their houses in the suburbs. I'd still had Kit, even though she wasn't always around, and so the lack of others didn't bother me. But now they were all gone.

"Of course we have friends," Nick said. "Call Valerie."

"Valerie Renworth. Are you serious? You saw how she looked at us at her party."

"Don't say that," he said. He threaded the tie off his neck and tossed it on the couch.

I thought randomly, *Well, that's something I can do tomorrow. Pick up Nick's tie. Clean the house.* Then it seemed too much trouble. I couldn't imagine a day with purpose anymore.

"Nick," I said, "please tell me you see it."

"See what?"

"We're not *friends* with the Renworths and the Weatherbys. God, tell me you see that."

He looked at me sharply. "That's crap."

"No, it's not. Jesus, Nick!" It felt delicious to yell. "Don't be so naive!"

"Naive?" he shouted back. "What's naive? Assuming your friend, Kit, would blackmail you only once? Assuming she'd keep quiet about the fact that you slept with someone else?"

He'd meant his words to wound me, I could tell from his tone. After years of marriage, I knew nearly every nuance of Nick's expression and voice. But I was oddly glad he'd lashed out. It meant he wasn't as impervious as he'd seemed since Kit died.

I got up from the couch and moved to him. I embraced him. Lightly at first, then fiercely. "I'm so sorry, baby."

And then Nick gave way. He sagged into me and began to cry. Quietly at first, then the gulping sobs of a boy who has wanted to cry for years but couldn't let himself.

"It's okay, it's okay," I said, stroking his wavy hair, loving him for this release, which I knew he felt was weakness.

We stayed like that for a moment that seemed more real than any second of the past few weeks. When he straightened up and stared at me, he was surprised, I think, by his emotion. I felt an intense love. I kissed him. The first time we'd kissed since the night Kit died. His mouth was warm, minty, soft, full. I inhaled Nick's scent, a mixture he'd had since I'd known him, a scent of something rugged and yet clean and crisp. A combination of a young boy and a man who worked as a doctor. It was that scent that had made me feel sexual for years now, and I pushed my mouth harder into his. I raised one leg and wrapped it around his waist.

He lifted me up, so I was straddling him, my legs tightening around him. He bit my neck, then kissed me again. Nick sank onto the parquet floor and pulled off my clothes in a frenzied rush. And I felt alive.

17

On the day I learned I might be charged with the murder of Kit Kernaghan, I also found out I was pregnant.

When we were first trying to have a baby, I awoke each morning thinking, *This might be it. This might be the day!* I read books on getting pregnant and pored over baby Web sites. I made covert runs to the drugstore to purchase ovulation sticks and pregnancy tests, and I smuggled them into the work bathroom with me.

But since Kit died, I'd nearly forgotten about the baby we were supposed to have. The pregnancy tests had sat unused in my bottom desk drawer at work and now far under the cabinet at home.

And I wasn't surprised when I awoke that last week of November, feeling a strange nausea growing and rising inside of me. In fact, it seemed a relief. I had felt sick and twisted inside since Kit's death. When I opened my eyes and knew I was going to throw up, I thought, *Thank God.* I craved the purge.

It wasn't until I'd washed my face and was brushing my teeth that it hit me. Could it be? Could I be? I quickly spit out the toothpaste and rinsed my mouth. Not bothering to dry my hands, I reached under the cabinet. I stripped the foil packaging from the pregnancy test; I pointed it downward just like the instructions directed, instructions I now knew by heart. *Results in as early as two minutes.*

I stood naked in the bathroom, counting the seconds. Two minutes went by, then three. I picked up the test and squinted at the two boxes. Nothing. Had I done it wrong? Impossible after all this time.

I squeezed my eyes closed for one minute, not even sure what result I wanted to see. When I opened them, there it was—a pink plus sign in the round window. I felt a heaving in my stomach, half joy, half bile. I covered my mouth and waited it out. When it passed, I opened the door with a smile. I had an almost giggly feeling. I would tell Nick. This was what we needed, what we wanted, what was supposed to be.

But Nick was already awake and on the phone, probably with the office, an early surgical call.

I stood waiting, the pregnancy test in my hands behind my back. I couldn't wait to see his face when I told him.

He hung up the phone and turned around. His expression was one of shock. He was breathing short breaths, his eyes searching the room, finally landing on me.

"Nick, what is it?"

"That was Tom Severson. The police are talking murder charges."

An hour later, we were sitting in Tom Severson's private, corner office. He wore khakis and a brown cashmere sweater, and for the first time since we'd met him, he looked worried.

"Have a seat," he said, gesturing toward the two leather armchairs in front of his desk. Lining the wall were floor-to-ceiling bookshelves, loaded with files, legal books and picture frames, most of them showing Tom and three blond children at different stages of life.

"Your kids are beautiful," I said.

Tom smiled. "Thanks. Best thing I ever did."

I noticed there was no woman in any of the pictures.

Tom seemed to hear my unspoken question.

"Divorced," he said. "A long time now. Somehow, along the way, I got entirely too involved with my job."

Nick nodded. "Easy for that to happen."

I marveled at our banter, the kind of talk that could be heard at a country club. My eyes strayed to the pictures again, and I thought how badly I didn't want that—framed photos of just me and my child. I wanted the family pictures—Nick and I and our two kids, the four of us on a beach or a back porch in the woods. But then my eyes landed on a legal tome entitled *Illinois Criminal Procedure,* and I remembered why we were there.

"Tom," I said, "I need to get right to the point. Are we definitely being charged?"

Tom opened his hands wide. "Not officially. Not yet. However, the cops have written up a criminal complaint, accusing you both of Kit's murder."

You. Kit. Murder. Those words didn't go together. We hadn't done anything. I shot a glance at Nick, and thought, *I* didn't do anything.

"So if there's a criminal complaint, how is it that we haven't been officially charged?" I asked.

"Put simply, the cops believe you did it. They believe Kit was blackmailing you, Rachel. They think you got sick of it and told Nick about it, and you both decided to get rid of her."

"That's ridiculous!" I said. It was. Just sitting in that office and hearing those words was bizarre and otherworldly. I had to stop myself from gazing out the window or from looking again at those pictures of Tom and his kids. Anything to get away.

I thought of our baby. I had yet to tell Nick, but I knew it would mean the world to him. It was what we'd always wanted. And so we would have to face this situation. We would have to overcome it.

"How do you know all this?" I asked Tom. "I mean, if nothing is official."

"I have a couple contacts inside the Chicago PD. They gave me the heads-up. Basically, the police think you two lured Kit to the apartment and out onto the balcony, then got her in a shouting match so you could push her over and claim self-defense."

"Why would they think that?" Nick said. "What evidence do they have?"

"For starters, they have a phone call from your apartment to Kit an hour before her death."

Nick's eyes shot to me.

"The number was on our caller ID," I said. "I thought I was calling someone else back."

Nick shook his head, as if I had been monumentally stupid.

"They also have Kit's bank records from the past six months," Tom continued, "and they show deposits of money orders that came from Rachel's savings account at Lincoln Park Savings & Loan."

I looked at my lap, then made myself raise my eyes again and meet Tom's. A feeling of guilt washed over me. The evidence made me look as if I'd done something very wrong. "I was trying to help out her mother," I said softly.

"With all three payments?"

I took a breath. I had no idea how much to tell Tom. If I told my attorney about the blackmail, would I eventually have to testify about it? If I testified about it, my affair would be out there for the world to see. And wouldn't that implicate me in Kit's death?

Before I could answer, Tom spoke again. "There's also a witness named Anthony Palmazeri."

Nick and I shook our heads. "Never heard of him."

"He says he met Rachel at something called the Glitz Ball, and he overheard you saying that Kit was—" he squinted at a paper "—fleecing you."

I suddenly remembered the dark-haired guy—Tony, his name was—who Kit had introduced me to that night.

"Then there's another witness," Tom continued, "who says Kit had something on Rachel."

"Who?"

Tom shrugged. "My contact didn't know that. All she could tell me was that it was a Frenchman, someone who used to date Kit."

"Alain?" I said with surprise.

Nick's head swiveled my way again.

Tom stared at me, his mouth set straight. "Do you know this guy?"

"Yes…well, actually no. I never met him. Kit started seeing him during a trip we took to Rome." I shut my mouth. I didn't want to talk about Rome any more than I had to.

"He's apparently with the embassy," Tom said, "which brings a fair amount of credibility to a witness. Does that sound like the same guy?"

I nodded. I felt faint, then sick. "I think he lives in Paris."

"He's been transferred to the States. He apparently will testify that…" Tom stopped and leaned forward with his elbows on his desk. "Look, before

I go any further, I need to know if either of you want to retain separate counsel."

"No," Nick said. "Absolutely not."

"Think before you answer," Tom said. "I can only represent you if you both have the same interests. In other words, there are no secrets, and you both agree on what happened that night."

Nick looked at me, his green eyes searching my face.

"Are there any conflicts of interest between the two of you?" Tom asked. "If so, this is the time to speak."

I saw Nick's fingers on Kit's neck and shoulders. I saw her go over the balcony. But then I thought how Nick and I both had responsibility for this mess. Nick had been overzealous in his anger, but my affair had opened the door to Kit. It had opened the door to the money I paid her and the phone call I'd made that night. We had to stick together. It was the only way. To get separate attorneys could mean pointing fingers at each other, and that might destroy our tenuous marriage, the only thing left in my life.

I nodded. Nick did the same.

"We don't want another attorney," Nick said.

Tom sat back. "All right. Well, this French guy

apparently gave a statement stating that Rachel had an affair during a vacation she and Kit took. He knew about it through Kit, and he also has an e-mail Kit wrote him, talking about how she had you, Rachel, 'on the line' for your affair in Rome. She said you didn't want anyone to know. I guess this Alain person feels like he failed Kit in some way when he broke up with her, and so when he learned about her death, he decided to come forward with the e-mail. Now his statement is all hearsay, but when the cops heard it they asked Kit's mother for her recent bank records, and she gave them a few months of statements from a bank here in Chicago showing deposits of money orders drawn on Rachel's account."

My stomach tightened. I focused on relaxing my body, for the baby's sake. "As I mentioned, that money was for her mother's treatment."

Tom turned his gaze to Nick. "Are you aware of all this, Nick?"

"I didn't know about Alain, but I knew about the affair. Rachel told me when she got back."

My mouth went dry. Another lie. The stories, the lies, the shadings of the truth—they were all getting hard to hold on to.

"And did you know about the money?" Tom asked.

Nick nodded.

"Well, with the facts as they are, they can draw some pretty big conclusions about blackmail, whether it's true or not. But we can argue that as long as Nick knew about the affair, it couldn't be blackmail, because there was nothing to cover up. Of course, the police will argue that even if Nick did know, neither of you wanted it public. They'll argue you both tried to silence her." He folded his hands together. "Whatever evidence they've collected, it wasn't enough to pass felony review and convince an assistant state's attorney to file the official charges."

I felt the tiniest strain of optimism. "That's great."

"It would be, if the state's attorney rejected the case altogether. But they didn't. Instead, they ordered a continuing investigation."

"But if there's nothing else to find…" Nick said.

"In my experience, when they don't reject it, it's because they think there's a case, just not enough evidence yet. And quite often, the cops do find something."

We were all quiet for a moment, before Nick spoke. "What, exactly, would the charge be?"

"Murder. First degree."

I felt an overwhelming desire to scream, to pull

my hair. "What about a lesser charge?" I asked. "Like second degree, or whatever it is."

Tom shook his head. "We can ask for an instruction on that at trial, but the state's attorney will never charge you with that. They always go for the throat."

"But why charge both of us?" Nick asked. "I mean, it was me fighting with Kit."

"That's not how they see it. They think you both wanted her dead. They think you both planned it. They think you lured her there. So in their eyes, Rachel—" Tom stopped and pointedly stared at me "—you're every bit as responsible."

The morning after our meeting with Tom Severson, I called my mother.

"Mom, it's me," I said. "And guess what? I'm pregnant." I didn't tell her my other news. I couldn't. We hadn't been charged with anything yet, and we might not be. Despite Tom's warnings, there was a chance the detectives wouldn't find enough. I needed to believe that.

"You're pregnant?" My mother let out a holler that I'm sure awoke residents along eight miles of Florida coastline. "Oh, honey! Oh, Rachel. I'm so excited."

"You're going to be a grandma."

She groaned playfully. "My baby is going to be a mother."

"It's early, so don't tell anyone else yet."

"When did you find out?"

"Yesterday. I must only be a few weeks along, and I have to see my gynecologist, but—"

"But you just know, don't you? Every time I was pregnant I knew before the doctors did." I knew she was thinking not only about her pregnancy with me, but about the others she'd lost, too. My mother had suffered through four miscarriages—three before and one after me, and the legacy of the other children was never far from my mind.

"I'm getting a blood test tomorrow," I said, "but I had to tell you."

"Well, of course. You have to tell your mother. And what does Nick say?"

"We've been so busy—" *with our lawyer* "—I haven't found the right time to tell him yet."

She clucked her tongue, but I could tell she was pleased I'd confided in her. "Honey, how are you doing with Kit's death? Are you all right?"

Kit's death. *Kit's death.*

"I'm hanging in there," I said.

"So sad. So tragic."

"Yes, it is."

"Do you want to talk about it?"

"Thanks, Mom, but not right now."

"Well, you let me know."

"I will."

There was a small silence, during which I could hear my mother's mind work. She wanted to console me, but after the detachment of the past couple of years, she was afraid to push.

Finally she said, "Now, have you thought about baby names?"

We talked about names and strollers and foods to avoid while pregnant and foods to eat. And when I got off the phone, I continued my mental gymnastics. I watched any television show with a baby in it, and I read baby books. I pretended I was your average neurotic mommy-to-be, and for six hours that day, I succeeded. I couldn't wait until Nick got home and I could tell him.

But when he stepped through the door, he asked, "Did Tom call you?"

"I had the phone off."

"Okay, well, he's calling me back on my cell. He got some kind of news."

Immediately my hand flew to my abdomen. "What?"

"It's something he learned from his contact at the

police department. I'm not sure what, but we haven't been charged."

There it was—charges, Kit, lawyers—all back in the open, in my present.

Nick must have seen my expression. He crossed the living room to me. "How are you holding up, hon?"

I gratefully accepted a hug. I was about to tell him the news—I wanted to keep moving forward with my charade of being the average pregnant girl—but then Nick's phone rang.

He looked at it. "Tom." He answered and switched the phone to speaker. "Hi, Tom. We're both here."

"Hello, guys," Tom said. "Here's the latest. The woman I know at the police department tells me they questioned somebody today, a resident from your building."

Nick and I looked at each other over the phone. "The man on the other balcony," I said.

"It appears so," Tom said. "Have you seen him around?"

"We don't even know who he is. I'm not sure I would recognize him." I thought of the night Kit died. I tried to remember the man. I could see his hand holding the beer bottle, his other resting on the railing, his body facing the lake.

"If anyone approaches you in your lobby, please don't talk to them." Tom said. "If this man is going to be a witness, we don't want it to seem like you tried to sway him after the police investigation and before trial."

My insides cramped at the word *trial*.

I noticed that Nick's jaw was clenched tight now, and he was shaking his head slightly from side to side.

"We just have to hope the guy doesn't think he saw anything," Tom said. "You're sure you don't have any idea what he might have told the police?"

"No," Nick said quickly.

I was silent for a second before I also answered, "No." Because how could I know, when it was hard for me to remember myself?

I sat upright on the gynecologist's table, swinging my legs and trying to feign comfort in the paper gown.

The nurse, a motherly type in powder blue scrubs, stepped into the room with a chart. "Got your blood work back," she said with a smile. "It's official."

I jumped off the table and hugged her.

I left the office with a bottle of prenatal vitamins and at least fifteen pamphlets on everything from natural childbirth to cesarean section, prenatal healthy eating to postpartum depression. Nothing could get me down at that moment. I was pregnant, and such a gift had rendered me hopeful and wide-eyed. Even about the situation with Kit. She was gone, and we had a criminal lawyer, but we hadn't been charged with anything. That was the key. There was hope. There had to be, because I was pregnant.

Could people see it as I walked north on Michigan Avenue, heading back toward our apartment? Could the doorman in front of the Tiffany's building sense that I had a wonderful secret? Did the elderly woman who smiled at me know that I'd just received the best news in the world?

I made my way over to State Street and stopped at a grocery store. I loaded a cart with fruit and cereal and chicken and cheese, and just about everything else my eyes landed on. We hadn't cooked often in our Lake Shore apartment, but that was about to change. Before I checked out, I snagged a bottle of champagne from the cooler. Nick would want a glass when I told him tonight.

At home, I pounded the chicken and wrapped it

around asparagus. I made an arugula salad and a fruit tart for dessert.

When Nick walked in, the dining-room table was set with ivory linens and glowing white candles.

"What's going on here?" he said.

I stepped out of the kitchen, wearing a skirt and a silk blouse.

"You look gorgeous," my husband said.

I smiled. "Sit."

"Is this the last supper or something?" he joked.

We both stalled. My optimism dimmed.

"Sorry," Nick mumbled. "I don't know why I said that."

"It's the *first* supper," I said, recovering.

"Oh?"

"Yes," I said mysteriously, leaving it at that. I popped the champagne. I poured Nick a glass.

"What's the occasion?"

"You have to wait." I went in to the kitchen and came back with a cheese plate and our salads. Then I poured myself a tiny swallow of champagne and raised my glass.

Nick did the same, his eyebrows lifting in a question.

"Nicholas Blakely?"

"Yes, Rachel Blakely?" he said, gently mocking me.

I touched my glass to his. "Congratulations, you're going to be a father."

A grin spread wide across Nick's face. "What? What? Are you kidding me?"

"Nope. We're pregnant."

"Oh, my God! Oh, honey." He put his glass down and yanked me into a fierce hug.

"Hey, watch my champagne!" I laughed.

He placed my glass on the table. "Only a tiny bit for you from now on."

"I'm happy never to drink again."

He pulled me back in a hug. "This is it," Nick whispered, his voice muffled by my shoulder. "This is our future."

The next morning, Nick left at seven for the hospital. I bounded out of bed, took my prenatal vitamins and then stood, surveying the apartment. Something had to be done about the gray walls, I decided. They were too morose, especially for a child. I couldn't paint the whole apartment in one day, but I decided to tackle the living room.

I put on gray sweatpants and a T-shirt and pulled my hair back in a ponytail. I hadn't had a haircut in forever, and it was long and messy. But first things first.

By ten o'clock, I had taped the moldings and the baseboards, and I'd covered the furniture with sheets. I had paged through fifteen home magazines, studying the wall paint, and I had decided on a warm taupe color with a hint of gold.

I drove to the hardware store, where I spent thirty minutes with a salesman picking out just the right paint, along with drop cloths, brushes and rollers. When I got home, I set everything up. I was starving, but I wanted to get right to it.

Halfway through painting the first wall, I stood back and surveyed my work. The color had mellowed the room in that area. It gave the place a welcoming feel. I felt a burst of excitement. I hadn't done a home project since we'd moved to Lake Shore Drive, and I'd forgotten what joy it could bring me. I had splashes of paint on my sweats and my arms, but I didn't care.

I dragged the roller in the paint and lifted it again. And right then there was a rap on the door.

My breath froze in my lungs—old instincts Kit had brought into my life. But Kit was gone. Why hadn't Hector or the doorman on duty called up? Since Kit had gotten into the building, they had sent out notices heralding the ramped-up security in the building.

I carefully put down the roller and walked toward the door. "Who is it?" I yelled.

A pause, then another knock.

"Who is it?" I said more loudly.

One word was shouted through our thick wood door—"Police."

My breath stopped. I put my hand on my chest.

"Ma'am?" said a woman's voice from the other side of the door. "Please open up. It's the Chicago Police."

I put my eye to the peephole. In the distorted glass, I could see two people in blue uniforms.

I opened the door.

One of the cops was a young African American woman. The other was a big man who appeared to be in his forties.

"Can I help you?" I said.

"Rachel Blakely," the woman said.

I nodded.

"You're under arrest for the murder of Katherine Kernaghan."

My shoulders fell forward. I put my hand over my mouth, fearful I might vomit.

"Ma'am," the woman said again, "please step back inside and put your hands against the wall."

"Oh, God," I said, starting to weep.

"Step inside, ma'am."

I did so and turned around. I saw the half-painted wall, the open can of paint, the roller waiting in the pan. "I was in the middle of something," I said.

"Hands on the wall, please. Shoulder level."

I faced the foyer wall. Gray, like most of the others.

I felt one of my hands being securely gripped. My arm was pulled behind me, and my hand twisted away from my body. There was a clank, then a series of clicking sounds as a handcuff cinched my wrist.

I gulped and stopped crying. "I have to call my lawyer."

"You'll get a chance to do that at the station."

"What about my husband?"

Silence.

My other hand was pulled behind me. Another handcuff, those sinister clicking sounds again, and now I was fully cuffed. *I am handcuffed*, I said to myself, as if I could make myself believe it. *I am being arrested.*

"Can't you let me put on some decent clothes?" I asked.

The man gave a gentle snort. "We'll take a jacket for you." He went to the closet and took out an old jean jacket of mine.

"When will I be back?"

"It's hard to say," the woman said.

"But I'm pregnant," I said. "Can I bring my prenatal vitamins?"

"Sorry, we can't let you take anything. Once you're booked, they'll have you checked out by a doc. They'll give you something."

"Please," I said. "Don't I get to put on some shoes?" I nodded at the floor, at a pair of my running shoes near the door.

"No laces. Only slip-ons. Tell me where to find some other shoes."

"What? Just let me put those on. This is crazy. I have certain rights."

I was swiveled around. The female cop gave me a bland stare and shook her head. "Maybe you don't get it. You've been charged with murder one. I'm about to read you your rights, but aside from those you have very few at the moment."

"Oh, no, Mrs. Blakely!" Hector said as I was led through the lobby.

I tried to smile reassuringly, but it was impossible.

"I'm so sorry, Mrs. Blakely. They wouldn't let me call up."

"It's okay, Hector. It's fine." But, of course, there was nothing fine about being marched through my lobby handcuffed.

"Open, please," the female officer commanded Hector. She gestured to the glass door to the right of the revolving ones.

Hector scurried across the foyer and held open the door. He met my eyes and shook his head in sympathy.

Just outside the doors, I heard someone say my name. I saw a woman I knew only as Deb, someone I ran into at the building's gym.

"Are you all right, Rachel?" She eyed the police officers with great annoyance, which I appreciated.

"Just a misunderstanding."

"Please don't talk," the male officer said.

They grabbed the flesh of my upper arms tighter as we neared the police car.

"Call me if you need anything!" Deb said.

I tried to smile at her over my shoulder, but there was a gentle push as I was guided into the back seat of a white police car, blue lights swirling. I remembered the blue lights of that other police car, on the night Kit died, as the car sped down Michigan Avenue.

There was no speeding with this car. The officers got in the front, and began driving north. There was a Plexiglas shield between us, but I could see them chatting casually, like this was any other day.

I went to rap my hand on the glass, forgetting I was cuffed, and the steel cut into my wrists.

"Excuse me," I said.

Neither of them acknowledged me.

"Excuse me!" I said more loudly.

The female cop, who was in the passenger seat, twisted around and slid open a tiny window in the Plexiglas. "Yes?"

"Can you please tell me what's going to happen here? I mean, where am I being taken?"

"Area three. Violent crimes. The Belmont station."

"What about my husband?"

She shrugged. "I'm not in charge of him."

I thought of Nick at the hospital. How humiliating for him if they'd arrested him there.

Then a thought struck me. What if he wasn't arrested? What if it was just me? I *had* to call Tom.

"Anything else?" the cop asked. She gave me a short, sad smile.

"I need to call my lawyer."

"After you're booked." She slid the Plexiglass closed and turned away.

The car made its way north, heading up Lincoln, then west on Belmont, until it reached a police station I had seen occasionally when I was in that neighborhood. And never once had I suspected that I would be here. That *I* would be a suspect.

The station was a squat, brown-brick building on a hardscrabble piece of land. The car pulled around the back and into a garage.

I was helped out of the car and walked down a hallway, through two swinging doors. Inside was a check-in desk with cubbyholes behind it. Both officers greeted the clerk and handed their weapons across the desk. The clerk made them sign a sheet, then she placed their guns in one of the holes.

We pushed through another set of doors and walked down a linoleum-covered hallway.

"Where are we going?" I asked. The unknown nature of this place, these people, these handcuffs, began to overwhelm me. I felt woozy from fear, and from the fact that I hadn't eaten anything that morning.

"Booking," the male cop said simply.

"Could I please get something to eat? I haven't eaten, and I'm—"

"We know," he said, cutting me off. "You're pregnant. Got to book you first. Can't do anything else until we get that done."

"It doesn't take long," the policewoman said, not unkindly.

She was right. It didn't take long, but it was mortifying. My thumbs were shoved into ink and marked onto papers. I was asked to stand against the wall, in front of a camera. I hated myself for it, but all I could think was, *I have no makeup on. My hair looks awful. There is paint on my face.* Just as I opened my mouth to ask a question, the camera's flash boomed.

I blinked rapidly to clear the flash from my eyes. When my vision settled, the nightmare was still there.

18

I was in a cage, literally a *cage,* with greasy silver bars on all four sides and bars on the ceiling, as well. The floor was made of steel, stamped with tiny octagon shapes the size of my thumbnail. I know this because I was so strapped with a combination of terror and boredom, that at some point I crouched on the floor and measured my thumb against it. And I stared. I just stared.

"You're lucky," said the guard who'd brought me here, now standing again outside my cage. She was an obese woman with a platinum-blond wig and a cold, unpleasant stare.

"Lucky?"

"Yeah, you're pregnant, right?"

"That's right."

"Must be nice. You get your own cell. Otherwise, you'd be with those ladies." She jerked her head toward another cage. Inside, were four women, two sleeping on cots, two standing and looking at me.

"Yep, *very* lucky," the guard said.

I met the guard's stare. "I haven't been able to make a phone call yet. I have to call my lawyer."

She shook her head. "You'll have to wait until the detective gets here."

"When will that be?"

She shrugged, and the gesture of nonchalance scared the hell out of me. No one knew I was here.

I wanted to spit at the guard; I wanted to yell. Instead, I cleared my throat. "I haven't eaten all day. Can I please have some food?"

"Be right back." She turned and left without a word. Five minutes later, she came back and tossed a snack bar inside the cage, along with a small cup of orange juice with a foil top. I ripped open the packaging of both and ate as quickly as I ever had. I was still starving. When would I get to eat again? It must have been afternoon, but I had no idea what time. There was no natural light in the room, no clocks.

"Hey there," someone called in a crooning voice.

I turned to see one of the women in the other cage standing and waving at me. She wore jeans and a purple football jersey. "What are you here for?"

"I was arrested." I realized the obviousness and stupidity of this statement as soon as I said it.

The woman hooted and doubled over with laughter. The other women behind her chuckled.

"Oh, you arrested, huh?" she said. "What for?"

"Murder."

That stopped her.

"You playing with me?" she said after a second.

"No."

"Who'd you slice?"

"I didn't do it."

She laughed again. "Your man?"

"What?"

"You slice your man, your husband?"

"No. No, I think he's been arrested, too." But I didn't know that at all. I had no idea where Nick was.

I turned away from her and crossed my arms. I should be quiet, I knew. *Don't talk to anyone about that night,* Tom Severson had said to me more than once.

But then I realized this woman could help me. I turned back. "Do you know why they won't let me call my lawyer?"

"You lawyered up already?"

"Yes, I have an attorney." I hated how prim I sounded.

"They don't like that."

"Who doesn't?"

She snorted at my naiveté. "The cops. It pisses them off when you're already lawyered up. They'll make you sit here forever."

"Don't they have to let me have one phone call? Isn't that how it works?"

"They have to clear your prints first."

"How long does that take?"

"You been arrested before?"

"No," I answered.

"Can take up to a day, then."

"Are you kidding?"

She shook her head. I could see she was losing interest in the conversation.

"So I get to call my lawyer after the prints are cleared?" I asked.

She shrugged. "You're on their time now."

Time—it was a concept that took on a different meaning while I was in the cage. There was nothing to do, nothing to look at but those octagon shapes on the floor or the women in the other cell. Time became a taffylike object that stretched and stretched and never broke. Other women were brought into the cages around me. Three of the women in the original cell were led out at different times. And I sat and stood and sat and stood, and wondered where Nick was, whether I was in even deeper trouble than was already obvious.

At some point—some point that must have been hours and hours past the time I'd been arrested—two guards appeared and led me out of the cage and into the hallway. The lights were so bright I blinked and nearly stumbled.

"Let's go," one of the guards said.

"Where are you taking me?"

"Interrogation room."

I was shown into a white room with white-painted walls that looked identical to the one I remembered from the night of Kit's death. And sitting in a lone chair across from a wood bench was something else familiar—Detective John Bacco.

He stood when he saw me and had the gall to smile apologetically. "You can take the cuffs off," he said to the guards.

"Have a seat," he said, when they were gone. He gestured to the bench.

I remained standing. "I want to call my lawyer."

He nodded. "Fair enough." He took out a cell phone. "What's the number?"

I told him. He dialed and handed me the phone. The voice mail for Tom's office came on immediately.

"What time is it?" I asked Detective Bacco.

He looked at his watch. "One a.m."

"What? That's ridiculous!" Then I went quiet, listening to the voice mail, which stated that in case of emergency, Tom's cell phone should be called. I left a message telling him where I was, then asked the detective to call the cell phone.

"Technically, you only get one call," he said.

I glared at him.

"All right, all right. I don't want you complaining later."

He dialed Tom's cell phone, and I left another message with specifics about where I was and asked him to come immediately. "Please, Tom," I said. "Please get here as soon as possible."

"Why are you doing this?" I said, handing the phone back to Detective Bacco.

"Doing what?"

"For starters, why have I been sitting here all day?"

"You're not being treated any differently than anyone else. You're in here for murder, do you get that?"

"Yes, I *get* that. But Kit's death was an accident. So why are you doing this?"

"Look, Rachel, you seem like a nice enough

woman." He gave me a smile again. "Sit down, okay?"

This time I followed his direction. I crossed my legs and tried to smooth my lank, greasy hair.

"I didn't think there was much to this case," the detective said, "but I had to question everyone, and I had to look into it. And then I kept finding very incriminating things against you. You had an affair in Europe. Your friend knew about it and was blackmailing you. You called her that night and asked her to come over. A witness saw your husband struggle with your friend and push her over the balcony."

I heard Tom Severson in my head—*Don't talk about that night*. I bit my bottom lip until my teeth nearly pierced my skin.

"I know your husband did the dirty work that night," the detective said. "Maybe all of it. If you just talk to me about it, we can maybe lower your charges. Maybe get rid of them altogether."

I thought of Tom again. I heard him explaining how the state's attorneys would never file charges below murder one for a death they felt was intentional.

If I could explain...

Yet what would I explain? I *had* called Kit—accidentally; we hadn't lured her there—but really, that was the only fact the detective had wrong. And if I admitted that now, then I was admitting I lied to the police. Twice.

And what if Nick had doubled back himself and told the cops something different? What if he'd been saying different things every time he was questioned, the way Detective Bacco told me? *They lie,* Tom Severson had said. *They do it all the time.*

Too many voices swirled in my head.

Too many questions.

Too much fear.

"Seriously," the detective said. "I can get a guilty verdict right now. You're going to get forty-five to life. But if you tell me what your husband really did that night, I'll make sure the judge knows you cooperated. That can make a big difference."

"Where is my husband?"

He studied me. "He's here."

"What do you mean?"

"He's in the male lockup."

"So he's been arrested?"

"Yes."

I hate to say it, but I felt the opening of the tiniest window of relief. This was a dreadful dream, a horrible, lurid nightmare. And yet as far as I could tell, Nick and I were still in it together.

* * *

An hour later Tom Severson arrived, and we were given a short time together in yet another windowless room. I sat at a table, barely able to keep my eyes open, despite my fear. Tom appeared untired, unruffled.

"How are you holding up?" he asked.

I shrugged. I tried not to cry and was unsuccessful.

He put a hand on my shoulder. "I want to tell you what to expect, okay?"

I nodded.

"They're going to take you to Twenty-Sixth and Cal," he said.

"The criminal courthouse?" I wiped my eyes and sat up straight. I'd seen the place on the news, but I'd never been within a mile of it.

"That's right," Tom said.

"Why?"

"You have to be brought to bond court. I'll be waiting in the courtroom. Sometimes they do it via video, but because this is a big case, the judge will hear it and set the bond. I'd guess it will be about five hundred thousand to one million."

I put my hands over my mouth.

"You'll only have to pay ten percent of that," Tom said. "Can you handle it financially?"

I thought of the money I'd given Kit. The money that could now have paid for most of my bond.

"So that will be fifty thousand or a hundred thousand?" I asked Tom.

"That's right. For each of you."

"Oh, my God," I said. I felt a new surf of fear crash upon me. "So we'll have to pay a hundred thousand to two hundred thousand?"

Tom nodded again. I marveled at his ability to be so calm. But then, he'd done this before. He'd probably hardened himself to it.

"I guess we'll have to," I answered.

"How's Nick?" I asked.

"I wanted to see you first. I'm on my way there now."

"Tell him we'll be okay."

After Tom left, I was taken back to the cage. There was no use trying to sleep. I paced to keep myself alert. There was enough room for four steps. One-two-three-four. Turn. One-two-three-four. Turn. After another hour or so, a guard came to the cell.

"Hold your hands out through the bars, ma'am."

I quickly made my way to the guard, almost falling over with exhaustion. I put my hands out. Was she giving me food?

"Nice manicure," she said snidely.

I looked at the light pink polish. It appeared childish and out of place here.

"Turn your palms completely facedown," the guard said.

I followed her directions. She took a Sharpie marker and wrote 10034 on the backs of each of my hands.

"What is this?" I gazed at my white, marred skin as if it were someone else's.

"Your number," she said. "That's how you'll be called to court."

The numbers looked like they would never come off. My own version of the scarlet letter.

Minutes later, I was cuffed behind my back and led into a garage with a waiting bus. The bus was half-full of women, all of whom looked as exhausted as I felt. A number of them smirked when I got on. Others stared predatorily.

I don't belong here, I thought. I dropped my gaze then, embarrassed by the thought.

The woman with the football jersey was in the second seat near the window. I was pushed into her seat and landed half in her lap.

"Sorry," I said.

She grunted. I was apparently no longer as amusing to her as I had been earlier.

The bus rattled out of the garage and into a black night.

"What time is it?" I said, half under my breath.

"They never tell you," the woman said.

I longed to rub the sleep from my eyes. My scalp felt itchy and dirty, and I wished I could scratch it. My hands cuffed behind my back made me feel trapped and somehow short of breath. The heat was blasting. There were no open windows, not a breath of fresh air. I began to think that it had been years since I'd gulped real air.

The bus lumbered through sleepy neighborhoods and onto the highway. Twenty minutes later we pulled into another garage and were marched off the bus.

They led us through an underground bridge and into elevators large enough to hold cattle. Once upstairs, I was taken into a room with two guards. In contrast to the bus, it was freezing. My handcuffs were undone. Freed, I scratched my scalp and my face. I tried to push my hair out of my eyes, to smooth it somehow.

"Don't bother," one guard said. "You're getting a shower."

I nodded, surprised at how the littlest things could cause happiness.

"Remove your clothing," one said.

"Here?"

"Just do it."

I hesitated.

"Let's go, let's go," said the guard.

I stripped naked and stood shivering in front of them.

A guard pointed to a rubber-sheeted table. "Lean over the table," she said, "and spread your cheeks."

"What?"

"You heard me."

"Why?"

"We have to examine you."

"Why?"

One of the guards scoffed. "You can't believe what people will put up there. We're mostly just looking, not touching."

I felt a wave of nausea, but I welcomed it. Hopefully, it was morning sickness. It meant the baby had survived the night in the cage.

I turned around and breathed through my mouth, trying to get more air. *Just do what they say.* I bent over the table. My skin was cold in my hands. I squeezed my eyes shut, steeling my body for an invasion. I heard rubber gloves being pulled on.

Hands touched my buttocks, spreading them further. A quick finger was run through the area.

"She's clean," one of the guards said.

I curled my lips over my teeth, on the verge of whimpering.

"Stand up," a guard said. "You're done."

After the inspection, one of the guards directed me to stand near a drain set in the linoleum floor. She unlatched a large black hose from the wall and without warning directed the powerful stream of water at me. It blasted my thighs, my knees. It drew upward. I covered my abdomen with my hands.

"Turn around," a guard called over the water. "And spread 'em again."

I was getting used to taking orders now. I did as I was told.

I thought I'd been embarrassed in seventh grade when two boys walked in on me peeing. I thought I'd been disgraced when Nick cheated on me. But I knew nothing then. This was humiliation.

19

When they led me into the courtroom, Nick was already there, wearing the exact same thing he'd worn to the office the day before—black slacks and a blazer—but his face looked years older.

We were seated next to each other at a wood table. Tom Severson was already there, leafing though a stack of file folders and papers. Nick and I looked at each other, then we leaned forward and kissed.

"I can't believe this is—" I began.

"I can't either," Nick said, interrupting me. "Let's not talk here."

"Okay."

"I love you."

"I love you, too."

"Is the baby okay?"

"I think so."

"All rise," someone yelled.

Everyone in the crowded courtroom jumped to their feet. I wondered if the spectators were here for us for some reason, for our story. But then the bailiff called out ten different bond cases to be heard. Ours was first. People took their seats again. I glanced, embarrassed, down at my sweatpants and T-shirt, limp with old sweat. I felt like I'd been wearing these clothes for an eternity.

A judge stepped into the room and up the stairs to a high carved wood desk. She was a woman of about fifty with short, blond-gray hair and a shrewd gaze. She stared down her nose at us, while our case number was called and our charges read into the record. I tried not to flinch when I heard the clerk say "murder."

A man in his thirties with a ruddy complexion stood from the other table. "Good morning, Your Honor. Bill Zar on behalf of the State. Your Honor, we're here to set bond in the matter of State versus Nicholas Blakely and Rachel Blakely. The count against each is murder one. The couple is accused of luring their friend, Katherine Kernaghan—"

"I'm familiar with the case, Counsel," the judge said.

I shot a glance at Tom Severson, wondering if her

knowledge boded well for us. He studied the judge calmly.

"Bond recommendations?" the judge said.

"Your Honor, we're recommending bond be denied in this case," Bill Zar said.

"For what reason?"

"This is murder one, Your Honor. Nicholas and Rachel Blakely have the means to leave the city— even the country—very easily if they want."

Tom Severson leaped to his feet. "Your Honor, Counsel's recommendation is nothing short of ridiculous. Dr. and Mrs. Blakely are upstanding members of the community, neither of whom have ever been charged with a crime in their lives. They both look forward to diligently defending themselves as soon as possible. Absolutely no flight risk exists here, and the State knows it."

The judge crossed her hands on the bench. "I agree, Counsel. Bond is set at five hundred thousand dollars per defendant. Defendants will be held until bond is posted. Call the next case, please."

Tom directed Nick and me to stand. We were led through padded leather doors to a room behind the courtroom. "That was our best-case scenario," Tom said. "As soon as we can get the money for the bond, we can get you out of here."

"My parents can handle it," Nick said. He gave Tom the cell-phone numbers for his mom and dad.

"How long will it take?" I asked.

"I'll get on it immediately," Tom said. "It really depends on how fast we can get the funds transferred. It could be a couple of hours or a couple of days."

A couple of days. I couldn't take a couple of days in the cage. Then it hit me. If we were convicted, a couple of days would be a fraction of our prison time.

"My dad is a politician," Nick said. "And my mom basically ran all his campaigns. They know how to do things quickly and discreetly."

Right before the guards led us away, Nick said my name. I turned and faced him. We stared at each other. I tried not to cry. Nick tilted his body slowly forward until his forehead came to rest on mine. "We'll get through this," he said.

I inhaled the scent of him. I savored the minuscule touch of his flesh on mine. "I know."

Twenty-nine hours after I was arrested, I was freed on bail.

The county worker put my paperwork on the counter. "That's it," she said. "Good luck."

I had nothing else, and I felt bare without my cell phone, my purse, my credit cards.

"Is there a phone I can use?"

The worker laughed.

"I'm not sure how to get home."

"I'm not sure either."

I suppressed an urge to slap her. "Is there any way I could borrow some change?"

She snorted, then stopped and looked at me. Finally, she reached under the desk and lifted a battered orange purse. She dug through it and slapped some quarters on the counter. "Courtesy of Cook County. And me. Pay phone is over there."

"Thank you. Can I find out if my husband has already been released?"

"Like I said, phone's right there."

I called Tom Severson.

"I'll send a car to take you home," he said. "Nick should be out within the hour." He directed me to stand on the steps of the courthouse.

A minute later, I stepped into the cold afternoon sunlight, blinking like a blind person who has just regained her vision. The jacket the cops had grabbed for me yesterday was insufficient for an early December day, and I immediately began trembling. The steps were filled with people coming and going. Many were attorneys, it seemed, who were in suits and heavy overcoats. They laughed and talked as they entered the courthouse together. The cops were quieter, climbing the stairs in pairs. Then there were my brethren—the other defendants—some, like me, slinking out the doors, others encircled by families.

I strained my neck to see the curb, looking for a black town car. I descended the steps farther and looked both ways. There were cabs and Mercedes and junkers, all passing the courthouse, but no town car.

I waited five minutes, then another, and another. I pulled my jacket around me tighter and fought back the panic. Maybe I could borrow money for a cab. But from whom?

I glanced around and saw a woman about my age ascending the steps with two men. The woman wore a red coat and black high heels. She had a black cashmere scarf around her neck and her sandy-brown hair in a high ponytail. She looked warm and fashionable. I felt like a sloth in comparison. But she looked like someone I might be friends with, and for a second, she and the men paused on the steps. She seemed to be telling a story. Before I could think about it more, I walked toward her.

"I'm telling you," she was saying. "Judge Tower wouldn't know his ass from a—"

She stopped when I reached her side.

She gave me an easy, welcoming grin. "You don't work for Judge Tower, do you?"

"No, I…I'm sorry to interrupt. Look, this is really embarrassing, but I'm waiting for a ride," I said, then felt the need to add, "in a town car." I looked at the street. "But it hasn't come, and I'm not sure how I can get home, and well, I was wondering if I could maybe borrow ten dollars, and I'll send it back to you today." I marveled at how little shame I had in saying this.

The woman looked at the two guys. "See you in there, okay?"

They nodded and walked away.

"I'm so sorry to trouble you," I said.

She shook her head. "No worries. Are you okay? I mean, other than the money? You look a little lost."

"Well, I just got out of…" I looked up at the courthouse, embarrassed to say the words.

Her kind expression never changed. "Sure, I know how it is." She took a twenty out of her purse and handed it to me.

"God, I am so grateful."

She held up a hand. "Seriously, don't worry about it."

"Thank you," I said, my voice suddenly shaking a little.

"Hey, it'll work out."

"Where can I send you the money?"

She reached in her purse again. "Forget about the money. But if you need any help, give me a call."

She handed me an ivory business card embossed with chocolate-brown letters. *Sharon Pate,* the card read, *Attorney-at-law.* At the bottom it said, *Specializing in Criminal Defense.*

"Thanks," I said. "I appreciate you stopping."

"No problem." She looked past me. "Hey, there's a town car."

A black Lincoln pulled to the curb, with a sign in the front window reading Blakely.

"Thank God," I said. I handed her back the twenty.

"Good luck."

In twenty minutes, I was at the apartment. All the lights were on, and the chemical smell of paint punctuated the air. The living-room wall was half cool gray, half warm taupe. The paint roller lay abandoned. And although nothing appeared grossly out of place, I could see the photo album in the living room was turned at an angle that I'd never left it. The books on the shelf had been moved and a few lay on their sides now, when I always left them standing straight up. They'd gone through our place. Why hadn't I realized they would? The thought that our stuff had been pawed through, examined, was creepy. The place felt haunted.

But I could do nothing about it. I went to the kitchen and ate for ten minutes straight, nearly anything I could find—cheddar cheese and crackers, a carton of yogurt, leftover takeout pasta from two days ago. Finally, my stomach was full. I put my hand there, wishing the baby well.

The door opened, and Nick came in. He walked slowly through the apartment, and we stood looking at each other for a long second. Then he walked wearily to me and wrapped his arms around me.

"Are you all right?" he asked. "The baby?"

"Yeah. Fine." My words were muffled by his shoulder.

We stood, embracing, for a long time.

He finally pulled back and looked at me. "Rach, are you ready for a fight?"

I didn't hesitate. "Yes."

We both showered quickly, then called Tom

Severson and got on separate phones. "Tom, we want to play hardball," Nick told him. "What do we do?"

"I've been thinking about it," Tom said. "Their case is circumstantial. Everything hangs on the witness from your apartment building."

"Did you find out his name?" I asked.

"Sawyer Beckman. He used to be a pilot. Now he's a consultant with a company that leases jets. That's all I know so far, but I'm going to find out more. A lot more, hopefully. I've put my investigator on it. If we can discredit him, we'll take a big step forward."

"What else?" Nick asked.

"I'm looking into Alain Trudeau, the French embassy man that Kit dated. There might be something there. And I'm trying to get phone records to show that Kit called you that night, and that you were only calling her back, Rachel."

"That's great," I said. "That sounds perfect. What can we do?"

"Not much right now. Go about your business. I'll let you know when I've got anything."

"Do we have to enter a plea or something like that?" I asked.

"Shortly," Tom said. "I'll give you the date as soon as I know. And I assume I know your plea?"

Nick and I looked at each other.

"Not guilty," we said in unison.

20

Nick's parents, Nora and Peter Blakely, blew into town the day after our bond hearings.

Nora Blakely was a woman who saw everything. She was at once utterly sensible—she had never dyed her black hair when it turned gray, and she wouldn't even consider a facial much less plastic surgery or Botox. And yet Nora was always aware of how she and her husband were perceived. As a wife of a long-standing politician, she was cognizant of appearances and sound bites.

"Rachel, how are you?" she said, giving me a cursory hug and stepping into our apartment. It was 10:00 a.m.

"Okay," I said. "Tired, but okay."

Peter Blakely, with his tanned politician's face and equally coiffed gray hair, followed his wife inside, stopping to give me a kiss on the cheek and a murmur of "Congratulations on your pregnancy."

"Thank you," I said. I was about to ask them for their bags and offer them something to drink, but I'd forgotten how Nora and Peter operated, particularly Nora. They didn't visit, they descended.

"Nick?" Nora called, shedding her gloves on the hall table by Nick's keys. Nick hadn't wanted to take a day off work. He'd wanted to go in as if we hadn't been charged with Kit's murder, but when his mother called the night before, she'd rejected that notion. "Don't do anything until we get there," she'd said, and Nick had relented.

Nora took off her wool coat and walked straight to the hall closet, as if she'd been to the apartment a hundred times. "Nick!" she called again, gesturing for her husband to hand over his coat.

"Mom, Dad!" Nick said, coming into the foyer. He hugged them both tightly, squeezing his eyes shut as he did so, looking like a little boy, relieved to be rescued.

"Let me show you to your room," I said. "I'm sure you want to freshen up."

"Nonsense," Nora said.

I had to admit, they both looked impeccably dressed and perfectly rested, as if they hadn't learned only yesterday that their son and daughter-in-law were accused murderers. They'd arranged for our bail, put their lives and careers in Philadelphia on hold and flown to Chicago in a matter of hours.

In contrast to their spotless appearances, I felt sloppy and exhausted. The future was a yawning, terrifying chasm, and I'd spent most of the night wondering if I might have to give birth in a prison.

"We need to talk," Nora said.

"That's right, son," Peter said, "let's discuss strategy."

Nora led the way into the living room, not bothering to comment on our new home much less even glance around the place. And yet, it was a relief to have them here. After years in Philadelphia politics, the Blakelys had weathered more than one tempest.

But then, they'd never been accused of murder.

"Who knows?" Nora asked.

I looked from Nick back to his mother.

"Who knows about the murder charge?" Nora said impatiently.

"Well, everyone, I expect."

"Don't assume anything."

"Have the papers called?" Peter asked. He sat on the couch and leaned back, one leg crossed casually over another, his hand at an imaginary beard.

"One or two," I answered.

"Well, that means it hasn't hit hard yet," Nora said.

Peter nodded. "We can still control it."

"What should we do?" Nick asked.

"Don't answer the phone," Nora said. "I'll handle that." She turned to face me. "Now, who knows you're pregnant?"

"No one except my doctor. I'm very early." I thought about the past two days. "Well, the cops know, and the detective."

Nora and Peter looked disappointed.

"Don't tell another soul," Nora cautioned. "We'll use it when we need to. The public loves a pregnant woman."

Peter smiled at her. "That's true. Nora became pregnant with Nick during my race for comptroller. I think it's what helped me seal the deal."

"But we're not running for office," I said. "This is different."

A pall crossed Nora's face. She looked at Nick, and for a second, I wondered if she might cry. In the next instant, she straightened up and smoothed her perfect, chin-length gray hair. "It's not at all different," she said. "It's about control. And I know how to control."

Nora set up her "war room" in the kitchen with her laptop, her two cell phones and our phone. On the laptop, she pulled up an extensive media list and did a search for all Chicago media. Then she began making calls. Peter and Nick wandered in and out of the kitchen, leaving the work to Nora, the master of the press.

"Dee Dee, honey!" she said to one of the reporters she called. "It's Nora Blakely." She paused, smiled. "That's right. We're in town to see our son, Nick." She paused again, her face full of concentration. "Yes, it's all a big mix-up." She talked for another minute or so. "That's exactly right. That will happen shortly, and I'll call you back to let you know exactly when."

I was standing at the counter watching her, nursing a cup of herbal tea that tasted like lawn grass. "What will happen shortly?"

"A press conference. As I said, control, control, control." She picked up one of the cell phones and began to scroll through numbers with a look of intense concentration.

I coughed up some of my tea. "A press conference?"

Nick came into the kitchen then and slipped an arm around my shoulder. He put his other hand lightly on my belly. "What's going on, ladies?"

"Your mom wants to have a press conference."

Nick's brow furrowed. "Mom, you think we need that?"

"I *know* you need it," she said, picking up the handset on our landline.

"Whoa, hold on," Nick said.

She sighed and put the phone down.

"I don't think that's the way to go," Nick said. But I noticed tentativeness in his voice.

Nora sat back and folded her hands in her lap, as if she had to keep them tied together to stop them from taking action of their own. "Of course it is. If you don't get your own message out there, and fast, the media will do it for you."

"I don't know," he said. "I don't want Rachel to do anything that might upset her or the baby."

"Well, the murder charge has already taken care of that," I said jokingly. No one laughed. I cleared my throat. "We have to check with our lawyer before we do anything."

"Absolutely not," Nora said. "He'll never let you do it."

"Then we shouldn't do it."

Nora shook her head. "You're not getting the point, Rachel. If you don't command your message, other people will."

"I don't have a message."

Nora's eyes became steely. "I certainly hope that your message is that you did not kill that girl."

That girl.

"I didn't," I said.

"We didn't," Nick said.

"Good," Nora replied. "Then *that* is the message that must get to the media, and soon. Otherwise, it's the police who will front *their* message. And I think we all know what that is, don't we?"

Nick and I said nothing. He squeezed my shoulder, as if in solidarity. Or apology.

"Rachel, believe me," Nora said. "Your lawyer was hired to represent you, and I've heard he's very good. But what lawyers want to do, particularly in a criminal situation, is keep you quiet."

"Right. So you can't screw up."

"That's right. But you will *not* screw up. And Nick will not screw up." She crossed her arms. "We will give a short press conference. I will coach you on exactly what to say, both in a statement and in response to the few questions you will take. Then you will be done. That's all you have to do. And when it's done, and right when we need it most, we'll release the news of your pregnancy, and you will have sympathy all over the city. It will be *your message.*"

None of this feels like mine, I wanted to say. I could barely recognize my marriage, my home, my precarious situation. And yet, Nora's take-charge attitude was a balm. It was a relief to think I could do *something*.

"All right," I said. "I'll do it."

The next morning in a rented hotel conference room, Nora strutted up to the podium with the assurance of someone who belongs in the spotlight and relishes it. The podium top was encrusted with microphones, each festooned with the insignia of the channel it belonged to. From the sheer number of cameras and microphones, it seemed that not only had the local stations shown up, but some of the national networks, as well.

"Good morning." Nora spoke into the microphone with a somber tone. She was wearing a black St. John knit suit with a choker of large pearls.

Earlier that morning, she'd instructed me on a black suit of my own, and had lent me a tiny diamond tennis bracelet. "This bracelet always brought me luck," she'd said, clasping it onto my wrist.

"Thank you." I felt touched by the gesture and strangely soothed by her cool fingers on my wrist.

"I want you to know something, Rachel." She

was still working on the clasp, her eyes down. "I know I can be harsh at times, particularly when I suspect that my husband or one of my boys is in danger. But you're part of the family, too." She looked at me then. "I don't know if you had that affair, and I don't need to know. Whatever you've done, you are family, and we are here for you. I hope you know that I'm only doing what I think is best for you and Nick."

I nodded. "I know."

"And I'm delighted that you're bringing another Blakely into this family. Have I told you that already?"

"No."

"Well, I am. I'm thrilled. I support you and Nick no matter what, okay?"

"Okay. Thank you."

The whole episode had taken less than a minute, but I felt infinitely calmer. Now, as Nora made a few opening remarks, I glanced at Nick next to me. He smiled, but it was a sad, resigned smile. Neither of us had slept last night. I had the baby as a partial excuse. I had to use the bathroom all the time, and I was consumed with a generalized nausea that never left.

I knew that Nick had been thinking how the press conference would look to his medical partners, the board members, our "friends" in the community. But I knew he believed his mom and felt that this way was the only way we could assert our innocence.

I searched the crowd of about thirty media people in the room. There were no familiar faces.

"The Blakely family is here," Nora was saying, "to confront the awful accusations that the Chicago Police Department have made. My son, Dr. Nicholas Blakely, and my daughter-in-law, Rachel Blakely, will make a short statement and answer a few questions, and then we ask that the media respect the privacy of our family during this trying time."

I wondered what my parents thought—my mom with her husband in their big house in Florida; my father with his wife at their second home in Michigan. They'd both offered to come into town, but I'd told them to wait. With the whirlwind of Nora Blakely here, not to mention dealing with the police, I felt it would be too much to handle other guests right now. And although I'd called my mother about my pregnancy, the truth was I'd long ago stopped looking for solace from my parents. Nick and I had turned almost exclusively to each other for that, even when it was one of us who'd hurt the other.

I snapped back to the present when I realized that Nora was introducing Nick and me. "Ready?" Nick whispered, stroking my back.

I looked up at him. I stared at the freckles across the bridge of his nose. Those freckles had always been there—from the first day I met him in that gallery to the early, easy days of our courtship spent in the sun at Cubs games, to the long, gray days of his residency. And now here we were, Nick and me, and Nick still with those youthful freckles that seemed not to know the innocence had long since disappeared.

I nodded. Nick and I walked to the podium.

Nick cleared his throat, and one of the microphones screeched. He pulled his head back, and with his hand still on my back, he spoke. "I'm Dr. Nick Blakely, and this is my wife, Rachel."

Some of the media members shifted. Their expressions remained impassive, some even bored.

"Rachel and I are here today," Nick continued, "to respond to allegations the Chicago Police Department has made against us. We are not frequently in the public eye, nor do we want to be, so you'll have to excuse us if we aren't quite as polished as my dear mother and father." It was a scripted moment, straight from Nora's mouth, and it drew a couple of chuckles from the reporters. "We'll both answer a few questions," Nick said, "but first I have something to say about my wife."

This was not on the script, and I tried to stop my eyes from widening. *What are you doing, Nick? What are you going to say?* He was supposed to greet the crowd, and in a few simple words, introduce me. I was to speak my rehearsed lines, then Nick would speak his. We'd "answer" questions with statements already prepared by Nora, and then we'd leave. What was he doing?

Nick took a breath, as if what he had to say was beyond difficult. *Oh, God,* I thought. *Oh, no.*

"My wife, Rachel Goldin Blakely, has had a very hard time of it lately."

I snuck out my hand and surreptitiously pinched the back of his arm. *What the hell are you doing, Nick?* I could see Peter Blakely, standing at the back of the room, shake his head very slowly from side to side, trying to signal his son to stop.

"But Rachel is a survivor," Nick continued, "and she is persevering. And in doing so, she has amazed me." He shot a glance at me, his eyes kind and loving. "She's amazed me since we started dating, but every year with her, she develops into a more beautiful woman, an even smarter and stronger woman.

She is truly the blood that pumps through my veins, and without her I would be nothing. I just wanted to publicly thank her for that. For being who she is."

I wanted to cry now. I looked down and composed myself. When I looked back up, Nick was watching me. "Thank you," I mouthed.

Nick gestured to the podium and made room for me to speak. Time for my lines.

As I shifted into place, my mind swirled with Nick's words, with that look of love on his face. In a long, odd moment, I thought of how my husband utterly baffled me sometimes. But then maybe that was what marriage was—the states of being alternately confounded and then relieved and comforted by the other person. And certainly marriage had to include forgiveness, and that forgiveness would only make the marriage stronger.

And so I took a deep breath and spoke my first words into the microphones. "Nick and I did not kill Kit Kernaghan."

Nora and Peter flew home after the press conference, promising to return soon. She left us with explicit instructions not to talk to the press, no matter what they printed the next day.

"You were both magnificent," she said to us.

"They were eating you up. It's a pity you can't go into politics."

She didn't have to add, *Now that you've been charged for murder.* It reminded me that no matter what happened—whether I had our baby in a prison or if we somehow managed to escape this mess— we were forever tarnished.

"And remember your sympathy card. Let them know you're pregnant when things get too hot."

She kissed us on the cheek, Peter hugged us, and then they were gone.

Without the whirlwind of activity that Nora and Peter had created, the apartment seemed still and quiet and filled with foreboding.

Half an hour after they'd left, the doorman called up. "You've got a messenger here," he said. "With a letter."

The letter was from Tom Severson. Nick and I stood together in the front hallway to read it.

Dear Dr. Blakely and Mrs. Blakely,
    This correspondence will serve to notify you that I can no longer represent you in the matter of State v. Nicholas Blakely and Rachel Blakely. *It is imperative that counsel be involved in the planning of a defense, as well as any statements made to the press or public. By holding a press conference, you re-*

*moved me from that planning, and I feel you
would be better served with different counsel
who will approach this case in the manner you
desire. Please inform me as soon as possible
of the name and address of the substitute attorney, and I will forward my complete file.*

*I wish you the best of luck in mounting your
defense.*

Sincerely, Tom Severson.

"Shit," Nick said. "Shit!"

"I can't believe this," I said. Although I couldn't
blame him.

"He's friends with Joanne," Nick said under his
breath.

I shot him a death look.

"Sorry," he said. "It's just that—"

I held up my hand. "I truly hope our baby doesn't
inherit your need to please."

Nick blinked at my harsh words.

"Now I'm sorry," I said. "The pregnancy is making me cranky."

At the mention of the pregnancy, Nick bent and
kissed my stomach.

"What are we going to do?" he said when he'd
straightened up.

I fought a wave of panic. We had lost our attorney. We had no one to help us.

I took a deep breath, imagining Nora. What would she do?

"Wait here," I said to Nick.

I went into the bedroom. When I came back, I handed Nick a business card.

"Sharon Pate?" he said, reading it.

"I met her at the courthouse." I told him the story.

"We don't even know if she's any good."

"You're right, and this isn't some small charge." Our eyes met.

"I'll call the attorney who represented me for that deposition a few months ago," Nick said. "I'll see if he knows Sharon Pate or anyone else."

Ten minutes later, Nick came out of the office. "He says she's young but she's great. His exact words were 'she's got balls.'"

"Sounds like exactly what we need."

21

Society Couple Says They Didn't Kill Actress.

Chicago, IL—Rachel Blakely, wife of plastic surgeon Dr. Nicholas Blakely, trembled as she stood at the podium, but in a clear voice, she declared their innocence. "Nick and I did not kill Kit Kernaghan," she said.

Blakely, 35, and her husband, 36, are accused of killing Rachel Blakely's friend, Katherine Kernaghan, 35, after Kernaghan allegedly blackmailed Blakely about an extramarital affair she'd had. Chicago police allege the couple lured Kernaghan to their home and onto the balcony of their twenty-second floor luxury condo on Lake Shore Drive. "They incited a physical fight with Ms. Kernaghan," Detective John Bacco said in a statement. "They pushed her over the railing, causing her to fall to her death."

"The charges against us are ridiculous and

based on nothing but supposition," Rachel Blakely told a crowd of about thirty media personnel. "We will vigorously defend ourselves against these baseless allegations."

Dr. Nicholas Blakely also spoke, calling his wife a "survivor."

The Blakelys were arrested Wednesday morning and charged with first-degree murder. Their case is set for preliminary hearing in two weeks.

"I love it," Sharon Pate said, pointing to the newspaper article about Nick and me.

When we'd called her, she said, "Hell, yes, I'll represent you." She was at our house within the hour, wearing a black-and-white-checked suit and red shoes. Again, her sandy hair was in a swingy ponytail.

She sat at our dining-room table now, suit coat off, taking notes and firing comments. "I mean, I never let my clients talk to the press, but you did it on your own, and it sounds like you did a good job. So we'll work with it."

"Good. Okay," Nick said. I think we were both a little taken aback by Sharon's staccato questions and topic shifts. Tom Severson had been calm and even-keeled. Sharon was a powder keg.

"Now, moving on," Sharon said, "Severson tells me you're pregnant, right?"

"That's right." I couldn't help but give a small smile.

"Congrats!" She clapped and whooped like she was at a basketball game. "This is great. Really great. We're going to drop that bomb right when we need it."

I rubbed my stomach.

"I got the files from Severson," she said, "and I'm firing the investigator he's got."

"Why?" I asked.

She scoffed. "The guy he's got looking into Sawyer Beckman and Alain Trudeau is too nice. Way too nice. I'm putting my guy on it. He'll squeeze out every detail of these guys' lives. If they shoplifted a pack of gum in fifth grade, we'll find out. We'll destroy them."

"I don't think we want to destroy them," I said. "I mean, they're just telling the cops what they know, right? It's not their fault that they've gotten pulled into this."

Sharon looked at me with pity. "Look, in a week or so a grand jury is going to indict you."

"How can you say that for sure?"

"Because the grand jury is a rubber stamp. They

always indict. You won't even get to be there. *I* won't even get to be there. Once that happens, we're going to have to fight these charges. I want to fight them *before* we get to trial. Bacco's case is all circumstantial. I want to discredit his witnesses, shoot holes in his evidence and get you guys out." She pointed at me. "How does that sound?"

"Fine. Great."

"Good. Because this shit is real, and it's not pretty, and we're going after those two guys." She clapped her hands again. "God, I love this stuff."

Her glee was off-putting—this was a job for her, a *fun* job—but her aggression was appreciated

"Sharon, do you need a retainer?" Nick asked.

"Oh, yeah. And it's big." She smiled. "My office manager will call you about that. Now, I want you two to hang low for the next couple of weeks. No press conferences unless I get center stage, all right?"

Nick and I gave weak grins.

"It's business as usual until I contact you. And if Bacco calls you, tell him to fuck off."

Nick took Sharon's advice and threw himself into work. Some of his partners suggested a leave of absence, which he rejected. Some of his patients quietly switched physicians, but Nick said it wouldn't stop him from practicing medicine. "I *have* to work," he said to me. "It's important for our family. I can't just stay home."

Meanwhile, I spent the next week primarily in two activities—eating (a lot) and planning the nursery. I became obsessed with every baby furniture Web site and every baby clothes site. I ordered diapers and wipes and onesies and bibs and soft, tiny socks the size of a thumb. I debated a Victorian spindle bed versus a more contemporary pine one. I labored over descriptions of changing tables and rockers. I acted as if these were the most important concerns in my life. And in a way they were. Nothing should have been more important than the baby.

My ob-gyn, a woman in her sixties with sharp green eyes, recommended genetic testing for Down syndrome and other disorders. The baby passed with flying colors. We wouldn't get our first ultrasound yet, but I could already see her in my mind. And I'd decided it was a girl. I knew this with a certainty that surprised me.

The only times that broke my baby reverie were the calls from Sharon Pate. "Do you ever talk to that doorman, Hector?" she said one morning, without any other greeting.

"Yes, sure, but just hi and hello. The usual stuff."

"Well, it looks like our boy Hector is into some very *unusual* stuff."

"What do you mean?"

"His home computer is clogged with porn."

"Does that matter?"

"Well, not now, but it might lead us to something else. Something that might really slay him."

"Do we need to do that? I mean, all he's going to say is he can't remember Kit, but he probably waved her in."

"He's a piece of the state's puzzle, Rachel. We want to make them all look bad."

"How did you get into his house?"

She laughed. "You don't want to know."

Sharon was right. I didn't want to know anything bad about Hector. I didn't want anyone else to get dragged into a mess that had been made by Nick and me and Kit. But if I'd learned anything from the experience so far, I'd learned that no one's actions ever affect them alone. Every action has a reaction, sometimes very unintended ones and sometimes this impacts very unintended people.

That afternoon, I was on the elevator, holding a package that had just come in—*Baby It's You!* the package read, *Uncommon Clothes for the Unique Baby*—when a hand shot in the door, causing it to slide back open.

I glanced up from the package and smiled blandly at the man who had entered. He was probably a few years older than me, and he had black hair with too much gel in it. It looked shiny in the elevator's lights. He gave me a quick nod and stepped into the far corner.

The doors closed, the elevator started its upward climb. We glanced at each other again. I noticed something familiar about his profile—the way his chin was prominent and the way his nose fell straight from his forehead. I had been thinking of that profile for weeks.

"Sawyer Beckman?" I said.

He gave me a small smile. "You're Rachel Blakely."

We both looked away, then back at each other.

Sawyer tried another smile. His face was tight, as if he didn't smile often. He had lines in the corner of his eyes and lines extending from his nose to his mouth, yet his skin had a polished look, as if he'd just had a facial. "I'm not sure what to say," Sawyer said.

"You don't have to say anything. You're just…"

"I'm telling the truth."

"As you think you saw it."

"Yeah. Exactly."

"That's what you're supposed to do."

"Yep. Look, I had no interest in getting involved in this crap. They came to me."

I felt the need to apologize. I simply nodded instead.

Tell him he's wrong, I thought. *Convince him that he didn't see Nick push Kit.* But then the elevator doors opened up at his floor, and Sawyer Beckman stepped out quickly.

"See ya," he called casually over his shoulder.

I had never run into Sawyer anywhere in our building before. The place was so large, and there were so many residents on so many different schedules that aside from the doorman and a few other folks, there weren't many people I saw on a regular basis. The next time I saw Sawyer Beckman might be on a witness stand.

"Yeah," I said as the elevator doors closed. "See ya."

The grand jury indicted Nick and me for first-degree murder on a Tuesday morning, a week after we'd been arrested. We were not allowed to be there, nor was our lawyer, a detail that seemed very wrong to me. And yet, I'd stopped being so sure about right and wrong. Never had those concepts been so difficult to grasp.

"Now what?" I asked Sharon when she called to give us the news.

"We've got an arraignment date. You guys show up and say two words—'not guilty.' It's scheduled for next week on Thursday. Sound good?" She said this in a casual, upbeat voice, as if she was calling to remind me of a dentist appointment.

"Yes, thank you." I tried not to be insulted by her cheeriness.

"I usually tell the clients to wear a suit, but I know you will," she said with a chuckle. "You and your husband don't need to be told how to dress."

I had no idea how to take that, so I simply thanked her, hung up and sat wondering what suit would still fit. Then I stood and decided to get out of the house for once and buy something new.

I wished I had a friend to call. I thought about phoning Valerie Renworth. Recently, she was the person I had shopped with, the woman with whom I'd had the what-to-wear discussions. I'd told Nick that the Renworths weren't really our friends, but I still hoped I was wrong. She'd acted oddly at her party, but as Nick had said, she was probably surprised to see us. And now I craved female companionship. Someone to try on clothes with, someone who would listen to my talk of sonograms and car seats and strollers.

I stared at the phone for at least a minute before I decided to go for it. I dialed Valerie's number, which was answered by her nanny. "I think she's around here somewhere," the woman said.

Soon a breathless Valerie picked up the phone. "Hello?"

"Valerie, it's Rachel Blakely."

Silence. Complete, full-stop silence. Then finally, "Oh, Rachel, hello." There was no *How are you?* or *How great to hear from you,* and I knew instantly this had been a mistake.

But I had to say something now. "How are things?"

"Oh, you know, the usual. I'm redoing the kids' rooms, and then the board holiday party is taking up so much time."

I didn't remember receiving an invitation to the board holiday party. Not that I cared. I really didn't. That was Nick's pet project. So why did I feel so miserable?

"I'm sure you're going crazy," I said, "but I was just heading out to Bloomie's to look for a new suit, and I wondered if you could join me."

"I'd like to but I can't." This time there was no pause, no hesitation. "Too much going on around here."

"Of course. I understand."

"Thank you for calling, Rachel."

"Sure."

"We'll see you soon," she said.

After I'd hung up, I felt like a little girl left out of games on the playground. I reminded myself that I didn't care about Valerie or any of those people. But the fact remained that I was desperately lonely.

Get out of the house, I told myself.

I put on mascara for the first time in a week, threw on a parka and headed out.

It was snowing lightly outside, the snowflakes complementing the Christmas lights that now adorned every home and business. As I neared Michigan Avenue, I felt my spirits buoy. Christmas carols played from outdoor speakers and the bells of the Salvation Army Santas added a clanging beat. The old Water Tower was aglow with white lights.

By the time I entered Bloomie's, I was glad I'd come. The store carried the scent of cinnamon and cloves, and the crowds bustled, everyone in the holiday mood. I stopped at a makeup counter to look at new lipstick. I had a flash that if I went to prison for Kit's murder, I would probably never shop for makeup again.

I tried on three different shades, which somehow led to the saleswoman talking me into trying foundation, blush and an eyelash curler. I bought them all, the purchase giving me a jolt of everyday consumer happiness.

As I signed my credit-card slip, two women stepped up to the counter and began smelling the bottles of perfume.

"I like this," one said.

The other sniffed. "Oof, that's awful."

They both laughed, and it was infectious. I smiled with them. Then I recognized one of the women, who had blond hair.

"Nicole?" I said. "Nicole Bobbin, right?"

The woman turned. "Yes," she said with a smile.

"I'm Rachel. I met you at the Glitz Ball."

"Rachel," she said, as if searching her mind for the memory of me. And then it clicked. "Rachel *Blakely,* right?"

"Yes."

She motioned to her friend. "Patty, this is Rachel Blakely. She's married to Nick. Nick Blakely, the plastic surgeon? You've probably heard of them."

She said the words with emphasis, as if hinting,

none too subtly, that there was a subtext here, that this was not your average introduction.

"Oh. Oh, right," her friend said, clearly getting the reference. "It's nice to meet you." She didn't offer her hand.

"You, too."

None of us said anything else. The two women stared at me curiously, as if I wasn't standing right in front of them. The clerk came back to the counter and broke the terrible, awkward moment. "Can I show you anything else?" She looked back and forth between us.

"We've got to be going," Nicole said.

"Yeah, we need to take off," Patty said. "See you."

"Yes, see you around."

The two women finally tore their gazes from my face and turned. They linked arms, making their way toward the front revolving doors. Their heads were pushed together, and I could see them whispering.

I handed the credit slip back to the clerk and decided I didn't need a new suit after all.

Society Couple Pleads Not Guilty
Chicago, IL—Dr. Nicholas Blakely and his wife, Rachel Blakely, a former software

*executive, pled not guilty on Thursday to mur-
der charges. After the arraignment, defense
counsel Sharon Pate promised to "fight hard"
against charges stemming from the State's
"overbearing and overreaching investigation" that "is wasting taxpayers' money."*

*"Nick and Rachel Blakely are innocent,
and the truth will come out in court," Pate
said. "We will not plea-bargain. We will es-
tablish their innocence."*

Weeks passed monotonously. Christmas and
New Year's came and went quietly, like any other
days. Nick worked all the time, even weekends, as
if he had to see every single one of his patients in
case he couldn't be there in the future.

At the end of the day, he'd come home and kiss
my belly, then hug me. He'd fall into bed, sleeping
intently until his alarm went off the next morning.

I, on the other hand, couldn't sleep. I'd manage
to nap for an hour or two a day, on the couch in the
living room, staring at the wall that was still half
gray, half taupe. But in bed, in the dark, my mind
raced. I wondered if the guards were nice to pregnant women in prison. I wondered if I would get to
bring the moisturizer I'd used every day since my
sophomore year in high school. I wondered what
would happen after I had my baby daughter. Would

my mother have to raise her? Would I ever get to see her? What kind of food did they serve in prison?

I knew I could ask Sharon Pate some of these questions, but I was terrified to speak them out loud. Instead, I let Sharon talk. She called once a day and asked a million questions. She talked about how the investigation had found nothing additional about Hector. She talked about the height of our balcony railing and how it was low enough that Kit could have stumbled over it. Her fall could easily have been an accident. She talked about Kit's autopsy and how there'd been no physical evidence that could hurt us.

I thought about Nick's fingers on Kit's neck when she said that. Apparently, he hadn't been gripping her that hard. This relieved me. I could almost make myself believe that her fall had been accidental.

Meanwhile, I sleepwalked through my days. After the experience at Bloomie's, I holed up in the apartment that I'd never wanted to live in.

Nick came home early one afternoon after a surgery was canceled. I made us tea, and we sat in the kitchen, silently sipping. There seemed to be little to talk about these days. There was nothing else but the murder charges.

The quiet was broken by the ring of the phone. We both glanced at it, then kept drinking our tea.

The machine clicked on. "Woooo!" someone yelled.

Nick and I frowned, glancing at each other, then back to the phone.

"It's Sharon!" the voice said. "Pick up the damned phone!"

I stood and hurried to the phone.

Sharon was yelling like she was at a Bulls game.

"Hold on, hold on," I said.

Nick and I went into the study and put her on the speaker phone. We could still hear her whooping.

"Sharon?" I said. "What's going on?"

"We got him!"

"Who?"

"Sawyer freaking Beckman! We got him! He's had four convictions for embezzlement and gambling schemes, which is great enough—we could totally discredit him on the stand with that—but then my guy found something even better."

"What?" Nick said.

We looked at each other, our gazes hopeful.

"There are warrants for his arrest in California for domestic assault *and* embezzlement. He took, like, six hundred thousand from his employer, this private jet company. His name isn't even Sawyer Beckman. It's John Tuffano. And get this—he's gone."

"What do you mean?"

"He knew we were on to him, so he took off. His apartment is cleaned out. He's fled the coop. The cops will probably never be able to find him, and they probably won't want to once I tell Bacco about his guy's seedy history."

"So what does this all mean?" I asked.

"This Beckman dude was the linchpin of the State's whole case. He's the one who says he saw Nick push Kit. Without him, the whole thing falls apart. I'm going to file a motion for summary judgment first thing tomorrow morning arguing the State doesn't have enough evidence. And I don't think they're even going to fight it. In fact, I wouldn't even be surprised if they dropped the charges once they see my motion. They don't have a case without Beckman, and they know it."

"So, Sharon," I said, "do you mean that this is…" I trailed off. I couldn't say it.

"I think it might be over," Sharon said. "I should be able to get you guys out."

Nick and I stared at each other, our mouths hanging open. Neither of us could talk.

"Hey, you guys there?" Sharon asked.

"We're here," Nick said. "I think we're both in shock."

"Well, go get hammered or something."

We thanked her, and Nick hung up the phone.

He and I sat and gazed at each other. As we did so, our apartment seemed to come to life for the first time since Kit had died. The clouds outside our windows cleared, and sun filled the living room. The air felt lighter, and infused with something like optimism.

"Do you think it's really over?" I said. "I can't believe it."

"I can." He pulled me into a hug. "The right thing is going to happen."

That night, I slept for twelve hours.

Breaking News— Murder Charges Against Society Couple Dropped
Chicago, IL—Prosecutors have dropped the murder charges against Dr. Nicholas Blakely and Rachel Blakely, saying that a key witness was not a credible source of information.

Dr. Blakely, 36, and his wife, 35, were charged last month with killing their friend, Katherine Kernaghan, by pushing her over the balcony of their apartment in the 1200 block of Lake Shore Drive.

Detective John Bacco apologized to the Blakelys for "this trying time." Defense Counsel Sharon Pate says her clients are thrilled.

Nick was at the office, even though it was a Saturday, and when he called, his voice was giddy. "You heard?"

"Yes, Sharon just called me."

"We have to celebrate. Let me take you to Trotters tonight."

I raised my eyebrows. "My, my. You sure we can afford Trotters after we get Sharon's bill?"

He laughed. "I'm sure we deserve it. Hold on, I'll call the restaurant from my cell." A minute later he was back. "We can't get in until nine."

"Fine with me." I felt that never again would I complain about a late-dinner reservation or the inability to find a cab or any of the other minor annoyances that came with city life. I was grateful for those annoyances now. They were symbolic of freedom.

But now that the case was closed, there was someone I needed to visit before we celebrated. Kit's mom.

I called her, and within the hour, I was pushing the buzzer at her apartment building. I opened the door, stepping into a poorly lit hallway with a brown-carpeted floor. I realized I'd never been there before. After her husband had died, Mrs. Kernaghan moved from the cozy Georgian house the family had owned and into a series of increasingly small, increasingly dingy apartments. From the hallway, this looked like the worst.

At the door to 303, I took a breath and knocked. I waited, staring at the small blue wreath that hung on the door. It was made of fake flowers and had a layer of dust on it. It took Mrs. Kernaghan almost two minutes to open the door. She was leaning heavily on a walker, and it was clearly a struggle for her to simply hold open the door. She wore polyester slacks and a worn, beige cardigan sweater.

"Rachel, it's so good to see you."

I hugged her, relieved that she let me. I had no idea how she felt about Kit's case being dropped or the allegations that had been made against Nick and me.

"Come in," she said. She let the door close, and I followed her down a short hall into a living room that caught a trickle of the day's last light.

"Do you want something to drink?" she asked.

"Oh no, thank you. I just wanted to come by and see how you are, how you're getting along."

She waved at the mustard yellow couch that was

piled high on one side with magazines. "I'm sorry. It's hard for me to clean up."

I sat, and Mrs. Kernaghan took a seat in an old La-Z-Boy that had prescription bottles lined up on one of the arms. On the other arm was a TV remote and a half-full glass of water.

"So how are you doing?" I asked.

She forced a frail smile but looked on the verge of tears. "I miss Kit."

"It must be terrible," I said. Inadvertently, I put a hand on my stomach. How could any parent lose a child? It was unthinkable.

She nodded, a tiny movement, as if any larger motion would cause breakage somewhere inside. "The charges were dropped," she said simply.

"That's right."

She nodded again. "I'm glad."

"You are?"

"I know you wouldn't have hurt Kit."

"You're right. I wouldn't have."

I didn't say anything about Nick, nor did Mrs. Kernaghan.

After a moment, she spoke. "As I said, I'm pleased it's over, but it's awful, too." She looked down at her lap. "It means she's gone."

I shut my eyes. I knew exactly what she meant.

Kit was truly gone now—no court case would display her photos or her name, and the funeral was long over. For better or worse, we would all start the process of forgetting her, and I would forgive her. I would forgive everyone, Nick, too, because it was time for a new chapter.

"Rachel, I'm glad you're here," Mrs. Kernaghan said, "because I want to give you a few things."

"Oh?"

"Yes, the first is something Kit borrowed from you, or maybe she took it from you. I don't know. Kit was…well, she was acting different before she died. She wasn't exactly herself, you know?"

"Yes, I know."

"She kept talking about how she wanted to be like you. She wanted to live your life."

I said nothing.

Mrs. Kernaghan continued, shaking her head. "I didn't pay enough attention to my kids after my husband died. Kit was so gregarious, though. I'd thought she'd always be fine. But then she…well, she became someone else."

I nodded. "I saw that, too."

"She was angry that she wasn't getting what she wanted out of life. I told her that life plays dirty cards. I told her the deal is never fair. But she said she deserved more. She said she was going to get it all." Mrs. Kernaghan made a small sigh. "Her anger turned bad somewhere. It twisted her up inside and changed her." She looked at me. "But I know she loved you, Rachel."

Again, I said nothing.

"And I know she'd want you to have the painting back."

I sat straighter. "The painting?"

"Yes, it's in her room. It's small, red…"

"Yes, I know it."

"If you could go get it." She pointed to the hallway. "It's the second door on the left. I don't feel well if I move around too much."

I stood reluctantly. I didn't want that painting. I didn't want to go into Kit's room. But Mrs. Kernaghan sat with a pained look on her face, and I couldn't add to her discomfort.

I walked down the dark hallway. At the door to Kit's room, I flipped on the light. It was a young woman's room, probably decorated years ago with a purple velvet bedspread and deep purple walls.

On the bed was Roberto's painting, next to piles of books and clothes, probably things Mrs. Kernaghan was going to give away. I moved to the bed and gingerly lifted the painting. There was the woman I'd once thought looked like me. There was Roberto's signature at the bottom right.

I didn't shy away from the thought of that night with him. I didn't have to, because it was no longer anyone's secret. I let the memories flood into my mind.

I tucked the painting under my arm and glanced around the room. There was a cork bulletin board on a far wall, and tacked to it was a familiar picture. I walked toward it.

The photo was of Nick, Kit and me, and it was taken during our wedding reception. Nick stood between Kit and me, looking gorgeous in a black suit and ivory tie. His arms hung around us both—Kit in her bridesmaid dress on one side, me in my ivory chiffon gown on the other. When I looked closer, though, I saw there was a tear in the picture. I peered at it, and saw that actually it was a straight cut, made with scissors from the top to the middle of the photo. That cut separated me from Nick. It was as if Kit had started cutting me out of the picture, leaving herself and Nick, then thought better of it.

I stood back from the photo, spooked. I heard Mrs. Kernaghan call my name in a weak voice.

I left the room gratefully and took a seat across

from her again. "Thank you," I said, "for the painting."

"Of course. The other thing I wanted to give you was the money that you…well, that you gave Kit. It would be wrong of me to keep it."

"Don't be silly, Mrs. Kernaghan. I wanted to help you. I still do. I know your treatments are very expensive."

"Well, I can afford it now."

"That's great. Has your insurance started covering your costs again?"

She shook her head. She turned and with painstaking slowness picked up a stack of papers from the floor. "I just received this. It's records from a bank account Kit had in Los Angeles. It was still open, but she never got statements from it. I guess because she hadn't used the account in over a year. But there's money there, and now it goes to me. She must have forgotten about it."

I frowned. Kit? Forget about money? Somehow I doubted it.

"That's wonderful," I said. "Is it enough to help you for a while?"

She nodded. "Oh, yes, it is. I just can't figure out where Kit got all this money."

My immediate thought was, *She probably black-mailed someone else.*

"I've been going through it," Mrs. Kernaghan said, "but it doesn't make any sense to me. There are deposits and money transferred from here or there. Maybe the money was from jobs she got, you know, acting jobs."

"Maybe."

"She did have that one big commercial in Napa Valley."

"Is that right?" I said, but with only minimal interest. Mrs. Kernaghan was fine. I was relieved. I wanted to leave the apartment.

"I think the commercial was for a car company," Mrs. Kernaghan said. "She was there for at least a week." She smiled. "Kit was so happy after that for a while. She'd met a man there, and she thought everything was going to change for her. He was a doctor, like your Nick."

I felt a strange foreboding seep into the room. "I don't remember hearing Kit was in Napa."

"It was spring. Over a year ago now."

My throat felt parched, and I swallowed hard, wishing I'd taken her up on the offer of something to drink.

"But maybe things did get better for Kit," she continued. "She had all this money transferred to her." Mrs. Kernaghan flipped through a few sheets and pointed to the top of one. "Like this one here."

I moved and crouched next to her chair. The paper was a typical monthly bank statement from roughly a year and a few months ago, and it listed deposits and withdrawals. The transfer that Mrs. Kernaghan was pointing to was for the amount of fifty thousand dollars.

"And this one," she said. She flipped to the next page and pointed to a transfer into Kit's account for twenty thousand, then another for thirty thousand.

"Can I see that a moment?" I asked.

She handed me the statement.

I stood and studied the three transfers she'd shown me. I flipped to the next month's statement, then the one previous and saw two other similar transfers. And then I read the finer print—they had all come from an account at Lincoln Park Savings & Loan. *She'd met a man there…a doctor, like your Nick.*

I felt a quick turning, as if my world had spun on its axis, but then the feeling was gone.

I blinked and scanned the statement for the

dates of the transfers, then looked for others. The transfers had been made in May, June and July of the previous year. Right after Nick's affair in Napa.

22

Lincoln Park Savings & Loan. Lincoln Park Savings & Loan. I couldn't stop seeing the name of the bank stamped on Kit's accounts.

Driving home from Mrs. Kernaghan's, I had to constantly remind myself to pay attention to the road. I reminded myself that there were other customers besides Nick and me at that bank. But it was a small community operation, and who from Chicago would be sending Kit such big sums of money. A better question—why?

Was Kit the goddess who'd slept with my husband? *Kit?* Had Nick betrayed me with the person I considered my best friend? It didn't seem possible. But maybe I was still naive, despite all that had happened. Or had Kit's death and the arrest rendered me paranoid and detached from reality? Was I affected more than I thought?

I thought of Kit calling me *Golden Child* in that scornful voice. She believed I had everything, and she had nothing. Was it possible she'd slept with Nick as a way to take some of that from me? To get it for herself? Had she blackmailed him, too? I tasted bile, felt a grip of nausea that was more than morning sickness.

A blaring horn startled me. I blinked and saw a trucker yelling at me, shaking a fist. I had drifted over into his lane.

Focus, I told myself. *Focus.* I had to be safe for the baby's sake. I blinked again and again and made myself watch the road. I tried to clear my head, but it was impossible. *Just wait,* I told myself then. You might be wrong. You might be jumping to conclusions. Find Nick and find out.

I made my way downtown and parked in the garage.

The apartment was empty. I stood in the kitchen and called Nick's cell phone. It eventually went to voice mail, but it rang first, which told me he wasn't in some emergency surgery. I thought of the office, but it was closed for the weekend. I tried his cell again. Another message.

There was a voice screaming in my head—a scream of alarm. I wanted to join that scream. I even opened my mouth. But again, I thought of the baby, the stress. Instead, I took a breath and swallowed my panic. Then I was glad Nick wasn't answering. I knew how to learn what I needed to know.

I hurried down the hallway to the study. The room was truly Nick's, with an L-shaped desk made of maple and sleek black lamps on either end. Nick was meticulous about our bills and bank statements. I opened the bottom left drawer, and there they were—all filed with perfect precision. I flipped past our electrical and phone bills, averting my eyes, thinking that even a look at our old address on Bloomingdale might make me give in to the shrieks that still wanted to leap from my mouth. My fingers moved through file folders labeled *Joint Account* and *Life Insurance* and *Investments*. Finally, at the back, I found what I was looking for—*Personal Account*. Nick had his own account at Lincoln Park Savings & Loan, just as I did. He had at least six years of records in the office, and as I sifted through them, coming closer to the spring and summer of the previous year, my heart pounded, each beat reverberating through my entire body.

I found the statement for February of that year. Then March and April. Then suddenly, Nick's perfectly organized statements jumped to August. Nick always arranged everything precisely by date. He would never have three months out of place. My body wilted. I felt weepy now. I gulped and made myself page through them again, one by one, but the statements were missing—the statements for the same months that Kit's account had received large transfers, all from Lincoln Park Savings & Loan.

My hands began moving fast, flipping through the statements again and again, some minuscule portion of my brain holding on to the scant chance that I was wrong. If I could just find those statements. *Where are they? Where the hell are they? Nick, what did you do?*

Yet I knew the answer to all these questions. I knew with a certainty that resided somewhere deep inside me but was rising—looming—to the surface.

A horde of different thoughts came to me. Pieces of evidence, Sharon Pate might have called them, pieces of a puzzle I'd never thought to put together.

I thought of how Nick had told me he'd met the woman at a restaurant in Napa. I'd assumed she had worked there, and he'd let me think that.

I thought of how there was a strange period of three or four months that spring and summer, after Nick went to Napa, when Kit didn't return my calls.

I thought of how Kit encouraged me to forgive

Nick. She'd been the only one who seemed unsurprised and unrattled by his infidelity.

I thought of Nick's reluctance to see me travel with Kit.

I thought of the way she averted her eyes from him when we returned from Rome.

I thought of the night on the balcony and how Nick went into a rage at the word *blackmail*. "You're blackmailing *her?*" he had said incredulously. Then he'd lunged.

I thought of Nick's quick forgiveness of me—too quick and easy for a man whose wife has strayed, even if that man had previously strayed himself.

Unless he had strayed with her best friend.

I did start to cry now. I couldn't hold back any longer. The tears flowed and I whimpered like a wounded animal.

I began scattering pages of the bank statement on the floor. I yanked out the file for the next year and searched those, but my eyes blurred with tears and my fingers could no longer perform small movements. I threw the file across the room. I grabbed a stack of bills and scattered them around the office. The screaming in my head returned—a woman's shrill, constant scream, maybe my own. I continued to paper the room with white, crying, until the whole office was covered.

When I looked up, Nick was standing in the doorway. And in that moment, something clicked into place—a conclusion I'd been holding at bay, a truth I'd twisted and shoved aside.

"You killed her," I said.

Nick looked at the papers scattered around the office, then back at my face. "What's going on?" he said, ignoring my statement.

I leaped from the chair and attacked him, the same way he'd done to Kit that night. I threw myself onto him, my fingers tight around his neck.

"Rachel, stop it!" He pried my fingers away and pushed me aside.

"Be careful of the baby!" I shouted, suddenly remembering.

"Well, Jesus Christ, you were choking me." Nick's face was red.

I wrapped my arms around my waist. "You slept with her." I felt a surge of disgust and a sense of everything falling around me. "You slept with Kit. Oh, my God, I can't believe you did this."

He said nothing.

"And then you killed her."

Nick squeezed his eyes shut. He stayed silent.

When I started whimpering and retreated to his

desk chair, he opened his eyes and came to me. He knelt in front of me, tears streaming down his cheeks.

"Rachel, I am so sorry. I never wanted you to find out about Kit. It was the dumbest mistake of my life. I called her when I got to Napa. I thought I'd just say hi."

"Why were you calling *my* friend?"

He shrugged. "I don't know. I was in California, so was she, I was just calling to say hello."

"You always thought she was gorgeous."

He shook his head. "Maybe, but I wasn't calling her for anything like that. At least that's what I told myself. And then it turned out she was going to be in Napa, too. She was shooting this car commercial, so we decided to meet for drinks and…"

"And you slept with her. With my best friend." I laughed and then choked. I started crying again.

Nick wrapped his arms around my legs, like a man holding on to a life buoy. "Rach, listen to me. It was one week. A couple nights, really. I don't know why I did it. I've beat myself up forever about this, and well, you know we've talked about this."

I glared at him. "Yeah, let me see if I can remember this from therapy. You were getting a little bored, right?"

He said nothing.

"You thought you needed some excitement, wasn't that it?"

Again, no response, just a pained expression, one of anguish, on his face. Normally, seeing Nick upset melted me, even if he deserved it. Now I was glad to see it.

I pulled my legs away from him. "You got your excitement, didn't you? Hey, you got to fuck your wife's friend, you got to pay her for it and then you got to kill her."

"God, Rachel. Like I said, it was the biggest mistake of my life. She did blackmail me. I did give her some money. And then I got sick of it. I told her to screw herself, and I told you what I'd done."

"You told me you had an affair! You failed to mention that it was with my best friend!"

"I know. And I am sorry." His voice nearly broke. He cleared his throat. "I love you so much, Rach. I didn't want to lose you. I knew you would leave me if you knew it was Kit, and I couldn't stand that."

I thought of how I'd used exactly the same rationalization when I'd come back from Rome—I loved Nick too much, and our marriage couldn't take my infidelity on top of his, so I hadn't told him. When it finally came out, that night Kit came to the apartment, he was forgiving, because he still had his own secret.

"That night," I said. "You pushed her."

His face hardened. "I'm not sorry she's gone."

"You *killed* her, Nick." I had known this of course; I'd been on the balcony that night. But I'd chosen to believe Nick's story of self-defense. I'd created an alternative reality that better suited my world.

Nick didn't flinch at my words. He met my stare, and I thought I saw a hint of pride in his eyes.

Then his head sagged a little. "I didn't know she was going to be here. It's not like I lured her here."

"So it was just a good opportunity?" I said incredulously.

"Look, I was shocked as hell when I heard she'd been blackmailing you, too. I was so goddamned pissed off. I just flew into this rage. I couldn't see anything else. I felt like we had our life where we wanted it, and Kit was destroying it."

"We made our mistakes. Kit just excelled at taking advantage of them."

"Rach…" He paused and took one of my hands. "You are the love of my life. And I am so sorry I was with Kit. I'm sorry I didn't tell you. But it is really and truly over now. All of it. Kit is gone, and we have no secrets, and I love you so damned much. I know you love me, too."

I stared at the desktop. "What does that matter?"

He reached up, turning my face to his. "We're going to have a baby, Rach. We're creating a family, and with the love we have for each other, it's going to be a great family. There've been a lot of mistakes, but the worst is over, and we can choose to go forward. For our child."

"No."

"Please. Think about this. What are you going to do? Are you going to go live with your mom and get another sales job? Are you going to be a single mom?"

"Maybe."

"We're a family." He said this simply, in a strong voice. "Don't break that up. Give me a chance to show you how much I love you. How strong we can be."

I shook my head.

"Please." He clasped his hands around both of mine, squeezing them tight. "Please, Rach. Be my wife. Be the mother of my children. I will make you happy every day of your life. Just give me a chance."

"How am I supposed to just go on like I don't

know about you and Kit? Like I don't know that you pushed her?"

"I didn't plan it."

"Semantics!" I screamed in a short burst. Then I lost my steam and said quietly, "That's just semantics."

"No, it's not. It's the truth."

That word again.

"Just stay," he said. "Let's go through this pregnancy together, let's see if we can make it all right."

"How will it *ever* be right?"

"I'll show you. I'll show you every day. Just say you won't leave. Give me a few weeks to show you we can get back on track. Please."

I pulled my hand from Nick's and put it on my stomach. *The poor baby, with us for parents.*

I had once thought I was a great friend, a good wife, a strong person. All these things had turned out not to be true. Certainly, I wasn't strong, because I actually considered Nick's offer. I did want the baby to have two parents and live in a wonderful house and go to the right schools and have the ability to be happy, even if her parents weren't. At that moment, I could see only two things—hope that we might make a decent world for our daughter and intense dislike for myself. The combination flattened me. I felt like I was frozen in ice. I couldn't move, couldn't find safety.

Nick covered his hand with mine.

I pulled it away again, and the movement exhausted me.

"A few weeks," I said. "That's all I can promise."

23

Nick told me that the first time we met, he noticed me long before I saw him. I was standing in front of a painting at an artist's studio in Bucktown. The painting showed a deep blue night sky, with a black tree taking up the foreground. Nick watched me holding my champagne, thoughtfully studying the painting, while, according to him, the rest of the partygoers glanced at the artwork as they danced and laughed loudly and drank heavily. Nick said he was struck by how I wasn't afraid to be alone in such a crowd; how I was so entranced by the art rather than caught up in the scene.

A week after I learned about Nick and Kit, I stood alone, again, in front of another painting at another party. In my hand, I had a glass of sparkling cider that looked exactly like champagne. But I was not entranced by the artwork—splashes of yellow on a large brown canvas—and Nick was not standing somewhere watching me with a little smile. Instead, he was holding court amid a throng of well-wishers. He beamed at them, enthralled with his—or should I say *our*—new status as local celebrities.

Over the past week, we had been raw and miserable. I swung rapidly between blinding rage and overwhelming, paralyzing depression. When Valerie Renworth called to remind us about a black tie gallery party—acting as if she would have always made such a phone call, even before we were cleared of murder charges—I told Nick I would go, but only because I needed something to do, something that didn't involve staring at the half-painted wall, and wondering what to do with our future.

That night was our first time in public since the charges had been dropped, but we needn't have been anxious. With the clearing of our names came a clearing of a path in the Chicago social scene. We'd been in the papers and on the news so many times everyone felt as if they knew us. Those we'd already met before Kit's death loved the association with someone famous for the next fifteen minutes.

I turned slightly from the painting and watched Nick making the rounds. He shook hands like the politician he might have been; he kissed the powdered cheeks of rail-thin women dressed in glittering jewels and shiny gowns. His face bore relief and something else. Triumph.

But I could not forget the reason for our celebrity—the death of Kit Kernaghan, who used to be my friend, who slept with my husband, who was killed by my husband. None of those people had any clue.

Or maybe they did. Maybe they had their doubts, but they knew that the Blakelys weren't serial killers. They knew they were not in danger themselves. It was so much more interesting to celebrate us and to know us than to shun us.

I was wearing a russet-red gown that reminded me of Kit's hair. It was strapless, the bodice corsetted in order to hold it up. It strained across my growing belly. It felt as if it was slowly constricting, becoming tighter and tighter around my lungs, so that I was having trouble taking deep breaths. My makeup felt heavy, a mask I didn't know if I could ever remove.

I watched Nick get pulled into a group of men, all in the exact same tasteful tux. They clapped him on the back; they guffawed.

I tried to drink my cider, but the opening of the

champagne glass seemed inordinately small, forcing me to bend back slightly in my too tight dress to sip it. The room seemed to tighten, too. I saw a woman in a blue gown, holding the arm of a tall, gray-haired man. They approached me from across the room, the woman waving an arm, a happy smile on her face. I didn't know them, and yet I could already hear the woman telling her friends, *I met that couple last night, the ones who supposedly murdered that girl. You know, the balcony thing?*

I turned and took another tight sip of the cider. A vision came to me as my lips touched the glass, an abrupt, vibrant knowledge of the life Nick and I would lead from then on—the endless parties, the curious stares of the partygoers, the bold introductions, the quiet, pained nights at the condo, both of us knowing what really happened and unable to confide in anyone outside our tiny circle of two. Nick and I were bonded by our terrible secrets. We were prison confidants, holders of a reality no one else knew.

The couple reached me, but I skirted around them, muttering, "Hello. Excuse me." The woman let out a short, disbelieving laugh.

I crossed the room and touched Nick on the elbow. "I need to see you."

He took hold of my wrist without looking at me, his fingers and thumb encircling it, reminding me of handcuffs.

He was finishing a story about his residency that I'd heard at many parties. "...so I just told the old guy that he could use his bed pan or his bed, but no one was going to change the bed."

The men in the crowd guffawed again, although I seriously doubted they found the story amusing.

"Nick," I said with more insistence.

He looked at me. "Hey, hon." Then to the men, "Do you guys know my wife, Rachel?"

They nodded and stared at me with interest.

Nick started another story about his residency—something about a guy who turned a staple gun the wrong way.

"Nick," I said, interrupting him, "I need to talk to you."

"One second, hon." He launched into the story again.

"Nick," I said louder, and the men shot looks between Nick and me.

His fingers around my wrist grew tighter. I imagined them cutting off the blood to my hand. "One second, Rachel," he said, enunciating his words.

I looked down at his hand around my wrist. I

thought of how Nick prioritized his convenience above everyone else's. Doctor or no, he put his life first, even if it meant taking away someone else's. *I* could become expendable to him at some point. Or our child.

"Now," I said forcefully, ignoring the looks from the men. "I need to talk to you right now."

He gave the men a fake jovial smile. "Excuse us a second."

I led him to a far wall, where an exhibit of small etchings on wood had been ignored by the partygoers.

"I can't do this," I told him. "We can't do this."

He stared at me. He knew what I meant.

His expression slid into something sad. "We're going to be *fine*, Rachel." He kissed my forehead, then bent down so he was looking at me square in the eyes. He smelled like clean laundry and shampoo. "They love us. It's okay."

"It's not."

"Let it go."

"How can I? How can you?"

He righted himself. He sighed, then kissed my forehead again. "It's all over. Finally. Done. Do you get it?" Then he repeated, "We're *fine*."

I said nothing. I noticed two women heading our way. "Rachel! Nick!" they called.

I turned and greeted them by name. I felt Nick relax as he watched me talk to them about the cuisine tonight and the auction starting up in a few minutes. They didn't say anything about the fact that they'd been wondering if we were murderers. I didn't say that I had been wondering the same thing all this time and now I knew for certain.

As Nick answered the women's questions about the board, I felt a stab of pain low in my belly, and I had to stop myself from doubling over. It happened again and again. One of the women shot me a look. Nick seemed not to notice. Then the pain was gone. I sucked in air. Water. I had to drink some water. I felt the need to splash my face, which felt slick with sweat.

I excused myself and made my way to the bathroom, noticing people pointing at me, smiling curiously.

When I was six feet from the women's restroom door, I felt a rush of warmth where the pain had been before, and then the warmth was between my legs. I stopped for a moment and tried to work out what was happening.

"Rachel!" I heard. It was one of the women I'd met at Joanne Weatherby's dinner party. "I hear you've been through such an ordeal."

"Yes." I put my hand on my belly. I knew that something awful was happening, but I couldn't figure out what to do.

"It's just terrible what the police will do to innocent people," she said. She halted briefly, as if waiting for me to respond to the word *innocent*.

The warmth between my legs intensified. "Excuse me."

I moved around the woman and into the bathroom. In the stall, I pulled my dress up and my panties down. And all I saw was red.

I lost my baby.

Spontaneous abortion, the E.R. doctor told Nick and me. *Happens in about fifteen to twenty percent of all pregnancies. And don't worry because the chances of a successful pregnancy after a spontaneous miscarriage are very good.*

Nick nodded. He knew such words. He understood and did not fight against the unfairness and inequities of science.

"Why?" I asked the doctor. "Why did it happen?"

The doctor, an East Indian man who looked about twenty but who had the resigned air of someone who has seen too much, shrugged. "The fetus couldn't survive for whatever reason."

I looked at Nick. I knew a reason.

The doctor discharged me, telling us I would keep bleeding and that I would "simply miscarry" at home. The word *simply* enraged me.

All night, I moved back and forth from our bed to the bathroom. Pain cramped my stomach. It made me see odd colors in front of my eyes and feel weak to the point of fainting. Nick was by my side through it all. He spoon-fed me chicken broth. We said little. When the cramping subsided, I slept an hour here or there. I dreamed fever dreams of babies and Kit and the yellow gold of a Roman morning.

Now it is two in the afternoon. I lie on the sheets, damp from hours of my sweat, and I think of how only one week ago, before my visit to Mrs. Kernaghan, I was pregnant, I was happy, I was ready for Nick and me to move forward, together.

Nick comes into the bedroom. "Do you want me to open the drapes?"

"Yes, please."

It's gray again outside. A light snow spits on our windows.

"Can I make you something solid to eat?" Nick asks.

"No, thank you."

He pauses, and I feel a sense of nervousness

from him. Meanwhile, I am sated with an eerie calm. "You should go to work," I say.

"No. No way. I'm staying with you."

"You should go."

Nick tells me he's not leaving. He says this over and over, and he seems to be talking about more than just leaving the apartment and walking to his office.

I turn my head to look at his worried expression, his pained eyes. "You've taken too much time from the office as it is," I say. "I'm fine. It's over now."

Nick shakes his head.

"Please, Nick. Go see a few patients, talk to your medical partners, return some calls."

"Do you feel like being alone?"

His question reverberates in my mind. It is truly the question I have to ask.

"Yes."

More silence.

Nick moves to the bed, and gently kisses my forehead, as if afraid to hurt me any more. "I'll be back in a few hours."

When he is gone, I sit up shakily and make my way to the kitchen. I gulp orange juice straight from the carton. I make a bowl of instant oatmeal and eat it fast, surprised at how my body seems to grab at the food.

When I am full, I go to Nick's study. I pull a sheet of white paper out of the printer and begin writing. I tell all of it, everything. I seal the letter in an envelope and address it to "Detective John Bacco."

I turn on the computer and dial up our bank's Web site. I find the page displaying our accounts. With a few clicks, I transfer precisely half the money in our joint account to my own individual one.

I leave the study and walk from room to room, scrutinizing each one. I look at the blue vase Nick and I bought in Mexico. I pick up a wedding photo of the two of us and tuck it into the crook of my arm. I walk down the hall to the nursery. I stare at the unfinished border—mint-green with yellow chicks and white bunnies. I run my hand over the pine crib. When I leave, I close the door.

When I have been through every room in the apartment, I take a small suitcase from the hall closet. I put it on our bed and pack the wedding photo and Roberto's painting. Some things are meant to be remembered. On top of these items, I put in my passport, a small kit of paints and brushes, a few pairs of jeans and shorts, a couple of T-shirts and sweaters, a pair of pajamas, a bathing suit and my toiletries. I take a fast shower and then dress in khakis, a turtleneck and leather shoes that are flat and good for walking.

I turn off the lights as I pull the suitcase through the condo. At the front hall closet, I put on my black wool coat. I button it up tight and wind a pink scarf around my neck.

I look around the condo one last time. My eyes stop at the living-room balcony, and I feel a surge of emotion through the calm. I gulp it down. I turn off the hall light, and I leave.

Outside the building, I cross the street and walk a block and a half to the mailbox. I open it and am about to drop in the letter to Detective Bacco. But I don't. I stand motionless for an instant. Then longer. I wonder whether this is the right thing to do. I am no longer tapped in to obvious rights and wrongs. I breathe in deeply, pull away the hand holding the letter and let the lid of the box bang shut with an empty boom.

I turn and hail a cab. Inside, it smells spicy and foreign. "O'Hare, please," I say to the cabbie.

He turns on the meter and pulls away from the curb. "Which terminal?"

"International."

"Which airline?"

"I'm not sure yet."

The cabbie scoffs, but falls silent.

Outside O'Hare, it is brisk but sunny. A skycap smiles as I step from the cab. "Checking luggage today?"

"No, thank you."

I walk into the terminal and study my options. *Aer Lingus. Air France. Air Jamaica. Alitalia.* I stop there for a moment, then shake my head no. My destination is somewhere completely new. I know this much.

I let my eyes continue to roam over my choices. *British Airways. Cayman Airways. Korean Air. Mexicana. Royal Jordanian. Turkish Airlines.*

Then I think of something I should do before I decide where I'm going. Before I will be able to decide. I cross the terminal to an information booth manned by an elderly woman.

"Do you know where I can buy an envelope and stamps?"

She points. "Take this hallway down and to the right. There's a little store."

I find the store and purchase a white envelope and one stamp. I take the other envelope from my purse, the one addressed to Detective Bacco, and fold it into a thin strip. I place it in the new envelope and address that to Nick, to the Lake Shore Drive address.

Before I seal it, I find an old business card of mine in my wallet. On the back I write,

Nick, This letter contains what I know to be true. I won't tell, but I won't forget. Just let me go.
I hope you find everything you want. Rachel.

I slip the card in the envelope. I seal it, stamp it and walk across the hall to a mailbox. This time I don't hesitate. I drop it inside. Immediately, I feel almost weightless, as if that letter, and the truth, had been a heavy, dense mass I'd been carrying forever.

I walk back to the ticket counters, my gait quicker, lighter. I search the names of the airlines once more. Behind a row of ticket agents is a board listing flights to various, exotic-sounding places. One is at 4:50 p.m. I look at my watch. It is four o'clock.

I wait for an available agent.

"Can I help you?" she says. Her smile is uncomplicated, her blue eyes wide and bright.

"Are there seats available on the four-fifty flight?"

She taps at her computer. "Quite a few, yes."

"I'm looking for a one-way ticket."

She mentions a price. It is entirely too high, and I don't care.

"One, please," I say.

"Coming right up."

She taps away again, humming under her breath as she does so.

I look around the terminal. The mood seems buoyant and full of possibility. Some travelers wear shorts, despite the chill outside, with sunglasses pushed high on their heads. I grin at the sight. I feel a shot of hope, a burst of excitement.

I turn back to the agent. "Make it first class."

New York Times bestselling author

KAREN HARPER

Julie Minton thought nothing of her fourteen-year-old daughter, Randi, leaving home earlier that morning to go Jet Ski riding with Thad Brockman. But now Randi and Thad are missing—and the hurricane that hours ago was just another routine warning has turned toward shore.

With the help of Zack Brockman, Thad's father, Julie begins a race against time to find their children—but first, they must battle not only Mother Nature, but an enemy willing to use the danger and devastation of the storm for their own evil end.

HURRICANE

"Harper has a fantastic flair for creating and sustaining suspense."
—*Publishers Weekly* on *The Falls*

Available the first week of June 2006 wherever paperbacks are sold!

MIRA®

MKH2307R

If you enjoyed what you just read,
then we've got an offer you can't resist!

Take 2 novels FREE!
Plus get a FREE surprise gift!

Clip this page and mail it to The Reader Service

IN U.S.A.
3010 Walden Ave.
P.O. Box 1867
Buffalo, N.Y. 14240-1867

IN CANADA
P.O. Box 609
Fort Erie, Ontario
L2A 5X3

YES! Please send me 2 free novels from the Romance/Suspense Collection and my free surprise gift. After receiving them, if I don't wish to receive any more, I can return the shipping statement marked "cancel". If I don't cancel, I will receive 4 brand-new novels every month, before they're available in stores! In the U.S.A., bill me at the bargain price of $5.24 plus 25¢ shipping and handling per book and applicable sales tax, if any*. In Canada, bill me at the bargain price of $5.74 plus 25¢ shipping and handling per book and applicable taxes**. That's the complete price and a savings of over 10% off the cover prices—what a great deal! I understand that accepting the 2 free books and gift places me under no obligation ever to buy any books. I can always return a shipment and cancel at any time. Even if I never buy another book, the 2 free books and gift are mine to keep forever.

185 MDN EFVD
385 MDN EFVP

Name	(PLEASE PRINT)	
Address	Apt.#	
City	State/Prov.	Zip/Postal Code

Not valid to current subscribers of the Romance Collection, the Suspense Collection or the Romance/Suspense Collection.

Want to try two free books from another series?
Call 1-800-873-8635 or visit www.morefreebooks.com.

* Terms and prices subject to change without notice. Sales tax applicable in N.Y.
** Canadian residents will be charged applicable provincial taxes and GST.

All orders subject to approval. Offer limited to one per household. Credit or debit balances in a customer's account(s) may be offset by any other outstanding balance owed by or to the customer. Please allow 4 to 6 weeks for delivery.
® and ™ are trademarks owned and used by the trademark owner and/or its licensee.

BOB06R

© 2004 Harlequin Enterprises Limited

Laura Caldwell

32183 LOOK CLOSELY	___ $6.99 U.S.	___ $8.50 CAN.

(limited quantities available)

TOTAL AMOUNT	$ _____
POSTAGE & HANDLING	$ _____
($1.00 for 1 book, 50¢ for each additional)	
APPLICABLE TAXES*	$ _____
TOTAL PAYABLE	$ _____

(check or money order—please do not send cash)

To order, complete this form and send it, along with a check or money order for the total above, payable to MIRA Books, to: **In the U.S.:** 3010 Walden Avenue, P.O. Box 9077, Buffalo, NY 14269-9077; **In Canada:** P.O. Box 636, Fort Erie, Ontario, L2A 5X3.

Name: _____
Address: _____ City: _____
State/Prov.: _____ Zip/Postal Code: _____
Account Number (if applicable): _____

075 CSAS

*New York residents remit applicable sales taxes.
*Canadian residents remit applicable GST and provincial taxes.

MIRA®

www.MIRABooks.com

MLC0606BL